Morgan & Archer
Jonathan & Amy
Mary Fran & Matthew

Grace Burrowes

 sourcebooks
casablanca

Published by Sourcebooks Casablanca, an imprint of Sourcebooks, Inc.
P.O. Box 4410, Naperville, Illinois 60567-4410
(630) 961-3900
Fax: (630) 961-2168
www.sourcebooks.com

Morgan and Archer originally published individually in ebook format in 2013 by Sourcebooks Casablanca.

Jonathan and Amy originally published individually in ebook format in 2014 by Sourcebooks Casablanca.

Mary Fran and Matthew originally published individually in ebook format in 2013 by Sourcebooks Casablanca.

Printed and bound in the United States of America.
RRD 10 9 8 7 6 5 4 3 2 1

Contents

MORGAN & ARCHER

One

In a sea of chatter and movement, silence and stillness caught Archer Portmaine's attention.

The ladies at the front of the shadowed box might have been any pretty pair enjoying a night at the orchestra, the elder exhibiting the fashionable attire of a young matron of means.

The younger woman held Archer's focus when he ought to have been scanning the other boxes for his quarry. She did this not by craning her neck or leaning over the railing, but rather by unhurried and quiet inspection of the glittering, laughing, bejeweled throng.

Archer had the niggling sense he'd seen her before, in a different setting. He might forget the occasional face, but he did not forget the graceful turn of a woman's bare shoulders, or a chin that shaded toward determined but stopped short of stubborn.

Her profile was classic, her brown hair tidily coiled at her nape, her cream dress the very next thing to plain. She was quietly lovely, and yet, everything about her begged to be passed over at a glance, everything except for her stillness and the way she held her own counsel in a venue where talking—loudly and cleverly—was more a part of the program than the music.

If the lady could chatter a bit while she perused the audience, or send the occasional flirtatious glance to a random, lucky swain below, she might make a passable spy.

Which notion would insult any proper lady mightily.

Archer left off watching the quiet young woman, lest even lurking at the back of this box he'd be spotted by those whose paths he'd rather not cross.

He shrank closer to the velvet curtains, glad for whatever breeze had doused the lights of the nearest chandelier. A man in pursuit ought always to be alert for pursuers and avoid even so fascinating a distraction as a pretty young woman's silence.

⋙⋘

"Did you know Valentine dedicated the final work on the program to you?"

Amid the hum and bustle of the orchestra tuning up and the audience gossiping and greeting one another, Morgan James was barely able to discern her sister's soft words.

"What young lady wouldn't want the Windham musical genius dedicating a work to her?" Especially a young lady who owed the recovery of her hearing to the selfsame musician?

Anna, Countess of Westhaven, studied her program by the limited light of the theatre's chandeliers. "You are *over* Valentine, aren't you? Please say you are."

"I am." Morgan felt a curious relief to say the words honestly, a weight winging aloft like the ascending scale of a flute warming up. "Valentine Windham was the first gentleman I met who behaved like a gentleman, and he was such a wonderful contrast to our late brother." Why had she not realized these things before?

"He is obsessed with his music though, enthralled with it," Morgan went on, "and Ellen understands this about him. I was alone in my own silent world for so long, I cannot fathom seeking an isolated existence on purpose, regardless of how much beautiful sound I could fill it with."

"You are very sensible, Sister. Westhaven said I was fretting for nothing." Anna's husband often made confident pronouncements about his family, and he was right an aggravating percentage of the time.

"I consider Valentine a dear friend," Morgan said, "and I'm certain he holds me in the same regard. The last piece is a piano sonata. I look forward to hearing it."

She would also look forward to having the evening over, to being alone in the commodious chambers Westhaven's family provided her, where—oddly enough—she'd begun to enjoy the silence and solitude.

Anna rose gracefully. "I'll fetch Westhaven from the corridor. He gets caught up by his father's cronies from the Lords and is too polite to leave them talking to themselves, which is their proper fate on what ought to be a social outing."

The pretty, dark-haired countess bustled out of the box, off to rescue some old curmudgeon from Lord Westhaven's endless fascination with what he called economics, leaving Morgan to wonder at her own proper fate.

Spinsterhood loomed close at hand, and likely a return of deafness not long after that. The physician had warned her, after all.

A shadow along the back wall of the box moved, distracting Morgan from her dismal thoughts. She caught the scents of rain on wool, laced with cedar. Cool scents, masculine and beguilingly pleasant.

And yet, those scents belonged to someone who had no business in that dark corner. People chatted and strolled in the corridor only a few yards away, so Morgan couldn't be alarmed, but neither was she pleased at the intrusion.

"Make yourself known, sir, and explain why you lurk in the Windham family's private box."

As her eyes adjusted to the gloom, Morgan made out a few more details: height, blond hair, broad shoulders. Westhaven's plummy baritone came drifting in from the passage, followed by Anna's quieter tones, something about not leaving Morgan alone.

The intruder pressed a finger to his lips, a signal for silence, then winked and blew Morgan a kiss. His teeth gleamed in a smile, audacious behavior indeed for a trespasser.

Anna sailed into the box, followed by her husband at a more decorous pace.

"My love, I was not lecturing old Quimbey, I was engaged in Socratic dialogue such as men of reason and intellect often enjoy with one another." Westhaven did not sound as if he were defending himself, but Morgan knew her sister's husband well.

Next, he'd start in with the nuzzling and cozening, and sure enough, as he assisted Anna into her seat at the front of the box, he leaned down closer than the situation warranted. "You were about to take him on yourself, weren't you, dearest Wife? You're as inclined to rational discourse as any member of either House. Morgan will support me in this observation."

The earl was subtle about it, but managed to land his lips on Anna's neck right there in the theatre box with a stranger looking on. Morgan turned and rose, intending to take the stranger to task again… only to find he no longer lurked in the shadows.

The smiling, kiss-blowing, silent man who bore the scent of fresh night air and northern forests had simply vanished.

⁂

Valentine Windham crossed the green room and possessed himself of Morgan James's hand. "My dear, you are looking delectable, as usual." He bowed low but did not presume to kiss her knuckles. "Panford, allow me to appropriate the lady's company for a moment. I cannot take my leave without hearing her opinion of the night's performance."

Val kept his tone jovial, though he'd spoken nothing less than the truth.

Panford was a talented, handsome cellist—also quite married and the sole support of a wife and several small children. Val tucked Morgan's hand around his arm and waited just long enough for Panford to stammer his parting.

"The performance was delightful," Morgan said. "The Sixth is a lovely piece, cheerful and lively."

Val walked her in the direction of the refreshment table. "And the piano sonata?"

Morgan had a sense of reserve Val had taken some while to puzzle out. A person deprived of sound for ten years learned a quality of focus that the hearing population never acquired. Despite the restoration of her hearing, Morgan yet had that stillness, an utter calm that was unusual in a woman with only a few Seasons to her name.

"In the first two movements, you were trying to create silence with sound," she said. "That is quite a challenge."

He'd been trying to re-create her world, her calm. "Did I succeed?"

She smiled up at him, a winsome flash of teeth and benevolence. "Oh, yes, Valentine. You succeeded, and the robust, romping final movement was a pure delight. I do thank you."

Her smile allowed something inside him to unknot, to come to a restful cadence, for Morgan's discernment regarding music was as keen as it was honest. He'd tried thinking of her as a sister, but she wasn't quite, and yet, as young as she was, he'd never considered pursuing her with marriage in mind.

"Morgan, would you thank me for introducing you to that blond fellow by the mirror?" He'd spoken softly, as if they flirted or exchanged confidences—or as if Val might have been willing for her to ignore his question.

"Who is he?"

Val suffered a small pang of chagrin that she didn't dismiss the man altogether, though the fellow had been studying her for some minutes in repeated, all too casual *passing* glances. "I thought you preferred the tall, dark-haired, handsome types."

"With green eyes and bottomless musical talent? Those fellows are fine to have as friends, they are *wonderful* to have as friends, in fact, but whoever he is, he's a credit to his tailor."

The blighter was good-looking enough, if a woman's tastes ran to golden hair, aristocratic features on the skinny, aesthetic side, and eyes of an infantile blue all wrapped up in conservative evening attire. Women, in their well-intended generosity, might call those eyes captivating.

"He is Archer Portmaine, a cousin to my sister Maggie's husband. He was Hazelton's business partner, also his heir until the baby showed up. You might have been introduced to him at Ben and Maggie's wedding." Though if Morgan had been introduced to Portmaine, she'd forgotten the encounter—cheering thought.

Curiosity lit in Morgan's eyes at the mention of Portmaine's role in the business. "He's an investigator?"

"Keep your voice down, if you please. I haven't any idea what the man's prospects are. Portmaine might still be employed in such a capacity, but Hazelton himself no longer snoops."

Val hoped. As a man with a wife, a mother, and five sisters taking an interest in his welfare, Val hardly needed one of those sisters marrying a professional investigator.

"Introduce us, please." Morgan sounded very certain.

Valentine tended to the civilities, keeping Morgan's hand on his arm the entire time. Portmaine was not as tall as Val—not much over six feet—which was some consolation. The smile he beamed at Morgan made Val want to break the man's perfect white teeth.

"And Lord Valentine." Portmaine turned that smile on Val. "My compliments on a lovely interpretation of the Sixth. F major has a reputation as a restful, sanguine key, though I'd be interested to hear an accomplished musician's opinion on the matter."

Val said some damned thing about well-tempered tuning and concert hall acoustics, but in truth he would have preferred if Archer Portmaine, of the charming smile and guileless blue eyes, were cursed with a bit of tone deafness.

◆

Charm was a discreet investigator's best weapon. This was the first lesson Archer had learned when he began nosing into the shadier dealings of Polite Society. As he smiled and bowed over Morgan James's hand, he found himself in the unusual position of having that weapon turned on himself.

"Mr. Portmaine."

She didn't have to say anything save his name, and Archer wished every other person in the room—most especially the glowering Lord Valentine—to Jericho.

Her smile held a warmth, a benevolence that suggested she'd been waiting all evening to find him and bestow that very smile upon him alone. Her voice was low for a woman, but even in the simple utterance of his name, he could *hear* that smile.

"Miss James, a very great pleasure."

When he held her hand the requisite moment-too-long, she didn't simper or blush. She instead kept *his* hand in *her* grasp for an instant when he went to pull away.

Maybe Windham caught something of that opening salvo, because he shifted closer to Miss James. "Morgan, perhaps you'd like some refreshment? My darling wife has been swept into the ducal clutches, and I am quite without worthy company."

Windham's tone was possessive, and his insult to Archer blatant, which was exactly the kind of complication Archer did not need—particularly when years in the music room had apparently given his lordship the muscles of a stevedore.

"I'll excuse myself, then, my lord. Again, a lovely performance. Miss James, a pleasure." Archer launched a slow, obsequious bow—even bowing could require a touch of art—when Miss James laid a hand on his arm.

"Mr. Portmaine can escort me to the refreshments, Lord Valentine. Your baroness is by the window, encircled by adoring swains. I believe His Grace has abandoned your wife to go in search of your mother."

Something flickered in Windham's eyes before he bowed and withdrew, and Archer revised his assessment: Windham wasn't possessive of the lovely Miss James. He was protective. Regarding his wife, however, he was possessive *and* protective.

"Miss James, did you just manipulate that poor man into leaving you in the care of a stranger?"

She turned placid eyes on him. "Some punch is in order, and perhaps a bite of cake."

As they made their way through the crowd, Archer silently congratulated her on having self-possession sufficient to ignore a question he really should not have asked. "May I fix you a plate, Miss James?"

She left off her study of the offerings on the buffet. "I beg your pardon?"

"May I fix you a plate?" He'd leaned closer, as if the hubbub of the crowd made such a thing necessary. A scent hit him, one emanating from her person. His nose filled with the fragrance of roses laced with spices—a touch of nutmeg, maybe clove or cinnamon. He was at risk of *sniffing* her when a second realization came barreling into his awareness.

Morgan James was watching his mouth. Her gaze was fixed on his lips, staring at the part of him that was willing to steal and bestow kisses, sometimes even in the line of duty.

"A plate is a fine idea," she said. "Some sustenance would be appreciated."

They moved down the buffet line, with Archer taking every opportunity to keep close to her. He told himself he was trying to parse out her scent—his cousin Benjamin had an extraordinarily acute sense of smell—but he was also admiring the curve of her nape and the way she made her choices easily and decisively.

In the same manner, she led him to a back terrace off the green room. Other couples were at the railing, and the place was adequately lit by torches, but Miss James took a bench in a quiet corner near the building.

"Please sit," she said, setting down her cup of punch and reaching for the plate. "And before you start with the small talk, you will explain why you were lurking in Westhaven's box. Your cousin Benjamin has married Maggie Windham, which means you're nearly family to the Windhams. Skulking about on your part makes no sense at all."

Archer sat, felled by the very same combination of charm and boldness he often used in the line of duty. Lest his explanation tumble forth without any planning whatsoever, he took a sip of the punch, realizing too late, he'd brought the lady's own cup to his lips.

⊙≪⊙

The terrace was blissfully, blessedly quiet, which improved the chances Morgan would comprehend anything her escort said—and she very much wanted to understand what came out of his handsome mouth.

He set the cup of punch down after only the barest sip, for he'd likely been expecting something other than tepid orgeat.

"My usual approach with pretty ladies is to apply great quantities of flirtation and flummery to the encounter." Portmaine moved the cup so it sat on the flagstones a foot away from his left boot, where any passing servant would know to gather it up and take it away. "I suspect flummery isn't going to work."

Neither would flirtation, Morgan hoped. "If you mean flummery isn't going to distract me from interrogating you, you are quite correct, though I won't mind if you try."

"Very obliging of you." He'd muttered this, but Morgan had been watching his mouth, so she caught the sense of his words.

"Are you in danger, Mr. Portmaine?"

He peered at the toes of his boots, his expression bashful and maybe a tad surprised. "I'm in danger of losing my heart to a woman who doesn't find direct speech an unconscionable rudeness."

Perhaps he was giving flirtation a try after all. She passed him a quarter of a pear. "I am duly charmed, but you didn't answer the question. If your situation is perilous, the Windhams are here en masse, and they will rally to your defense out of family loyalty."

"My situation is not perilous in the sense you mean it, else I would not be sitting here with you."

Morgan said nothing—a woman's company might be all the shield he needed if the danger to him was from a source bent on remaining hidden. She took a bite of her pear and indulged for a moment in the pleasure of a texture both creamy and slightly grainy, and a taste both sweet and spicy.

The Windhams did not skimp on hospitality, not ever.

"Here is my dilemma, Mr. Portmaine: if you mean mischief of any kind toward the Windhams, or more specifically toward my sister or her husband, I will do all in my power to stop you. I will be watching you the way you watched me for the first thirty minutes of this reception, and should you mis-step, I will alert my in-laws."

She munched on the rest of her slice of pear, detecting a tensing in the man beside her. He would not threaten her here, and he needed to know that loyalty was not exclusively a Windham characteristic.

"Miss James, I am going to violate every tenet of my personal philosophy, flirt with a deviation from the dictates of honor, and without doubt commit rudeness."

"All that? Would you like some more pear while you misbehave so prodigiously?"

"Please."

Their fingers brushed, though she couldn't think it was deliberate on his part, because the contact appeared to fluster him. The lapse was slight—a firming of his mouth, a double-blink—but Morgan excelled at reading faces, and even short acquaintance told her Archer Portmaine normally enjoyed great self-possession.

Normally, so did she. "You were saying, Mr. Portmaine?"

"I was in Westhaven's box to elude the notice of a woman."

Plausible, but she did not believe him—not entirely. "A married woman?"

Another blink. "Well, yes, but it isn't what you think."

Morgan finished with her pear and began to lick her fingers one by one, then caught her companion watching her. So far, he wasn't gaining many points for originality. "Not what I think?"

"She is *not* a former inamorata."

He passed her a handkerchief, tucking it into Morgan's hand. While she made use of the monogrammed cream silk—his middle name apparently also began with an *A*—Morgan concluded the conversation had not yet achieved her goal.

"I know you are an investigator, Mr. Portmaine, and that you are involved with keeping scandal from befalling the best families in the realm." Had he been involved in averting scandal for the Windhams?

The look he shot her was barren of charm and even friendliness. "The lady was among those I've investigated. I do not think she could recognize me, but one doesn't want to take chances."

"So you were eluding embarrassment."

"I was, and being found in Westhaven's box 'by accident' might have had to serve, though I'd rather nobody knew I was there, even momentarily."

He was still at least partly lying. "And yet, the lady is not a former inamorata."

He studied Morgan for a moment more, which allowed her to examine him in return by the torchlight. He was an exponent of Classic English Good Looks—blond, blue-eyed, and rangy, but imbued with a little Celtic ferocity too, in the slight hook to his nose and the angle of his jaw.

"And now I shall be inexcusably crude," he said, "which will likely earn me a sound drubbing from your musical knight. The lady, Miss James, prefers women. If I avoided her notice, it was as much to spare her as anything else."

Morgan stopped wiping at her fingers with his handkerchief. "Prefers *women*?"

Several long, lonely years of practice allowed Morgan to impersonate a young lady of good family enjoying a musical evening and the company of a near-relation. Mr. Portmaine's disclosure suggested he could see beneath that artifice, and grasp some of the past Morgan struggled to keep from Society's sight.

For she knew exactly what he meant, and in the next instant, figured out exactly why he was back to staring at his boots. "How mortifying—for you."

When she thought Mr. Portmaine would bid her a curt good night and stomp away, he instead turned a self-deprecating smile on her. "This revelation was rather a blow to her husband, whose grand schemes were utterly thwarted. Point to the lady, I say."

"Oh, you poor man. I hope you were paid for your troubles."

The words were out, blunt and only half-teasing, but they revealed gaps in Morgan's gentility that she suspected were part of the reason she'd had no serious offers.

And as for the other part…

"I was compensated, not only for my troubles, but I suspect to hold my silence as well. Now that's enough inexcusable crudeness for one conversation, even from me. Are you going to eat those strawberries?"

Morgan had the first inkling she might be in difficulties when she realized she rather liked the fellow when he was inexcusably crude—and since when did honesty become crudeness?

"Unless you stop me, I will eat every morsel on this plate," Morgan said, holding the plate out to him. "So you must join me. Keeping one's silence can be a strenuous undertaking." Particularly when that silence lasted for years.

The moment passed, the strawberries, cheese, ham, and lemon cake disappeared, and when Mr. Portmaine offered to escort Morgan back inside, she paused before allowing him to assist her to her feet.

"I will keep my silence on this matter too, Mr. Portmaine. You haven't been completely honest with me, but my guess is you've been as honest as you could be. You were not in Westhaven's box with any mischievous intent toward my sister's in-laws."

"I was not." He said this quietly, but Morgan heard him, and heard the truth of his words. It was enough.

"Then let us part on friendly terms, and I will wish you a pleasant evening."

When she rose, he put her hand over his arm, and without saying a word, he smiled down at her. It wasn't a flummery-and-flirtation smile, not in the sense he'd used the phrase, as if referring to flummery and flirtation as a set of matched pistols from Mr. Manton.

His smile was warm, genuine, and honest. She smiled back and let him return her to the noisy, crowded, uncomfortable confines of the green room proper.

⁓

"It's damnably frustrating, Your Grace." Archer did not need to pretty things up for the Duke of Moreland. "All we know is this plot is aimed at the Crown itself, and the French are as puzzled as we are."

The duke nodded genially at some whiskered old fellow across the card room and raised his wineglass a few inches in salutation. "It's a sorry day when we must rely on the Frogs for our intelligence, Portmaine. When do you think you'll have more information?"

That was the only question that mattered, and trust Moreland to pounce on it.

"I'm circulating as much as I dare, Your Grace. All we know is people in high places are in support of whatever's afoot. I drowse in mine host's library of an evening, chat up the wallflowers and companions all over Mayfair, lose at cards with more skill than anybody would credit, and I've yet to hear even a juicy innuendo."

"Then you keep listening, Portmaine. The Crown is worried. Very worried. Shall we put it about I'm backing you for a pocket borough?"

Shrewd blue eyes regarded Archer levelly enough that the question might be sincere, and not asked merely in the interests of justifying tête-à-têtes like this one.

"I believe, Your Grace, that the fewer political aspirations I show, the more likely somebody is to let something slip in my presence."

"Best be flirting and courting, then." This time, His Grace raised his glass and aimed a smile at a turbaned older woman sitting several yards away at the loo table. "Nose about this year's herd of young beauties, turn them down the room as if you're in contemplation of marriage."

"That can be a perilous ruse, Your Grace."

"Only if you're careless. It can be a lot of fun if you're not."

Moreland winked at Archer, clapped him on the shoulder, and strode off in the direction of the men's punch bowl.

Leaving Archer to take a swallow of gaggingly sweet ratafia and wonder how great a sacrifice a man was supposed to make for King and Country. He was pondering the same dismal notion as he sorted through the contents of Lord Braithwaite's escritoire thirty minutes later.

"Nothing. Not an obscene snuffbox, not a lurid novel. Not a single indication of manly imagination, much less treason. No wonder Lady B. terrorizes the university boys." Archer addressed his remarks to the room, then spotted a painting of foxhunters immortalized at that moment when the pack had set upon Reynard and tossed him bodily into the air. Several fellows on horseback in their pinks were pointing jovially at the carnage; another gestured with his hat while his horse shied at the commotion.

The painting was abominable, also ever so slightly askew.

"*Voila.*" Archer had no more than swung the thing forward on its hinges to reveal the safe behind it when the door to the adjacent sitting room opened. In the time it took to silently concoct a foul oath, he replaced the painting and took a seat on a sofa along the wall.

"Pardon me, sir! I was not expecting anyone to be in our private apartments."

Lady Braithwaite paused in the doorway and studied Archer with more curiosity than indignation. She was on the tall side, buxom, and approaching the age when she'd be described as matronly rather than well endowed.

"My lady." Archer rose slowly and showed only welcome in his eyes as he approached her. "I beg *your* pardon. I presumed, because I was certain these were the chambers of the house most certain to afford privacy. I'll just…" He heaved a sigh and glanced around the room, wall by wall, his gaze lingering on the hapless fox. "I'll just be going."

"You're Portmaine, aren't you?" She perused Archer more closely than he'd inspected the room. "Were you waiting for a young lady, Mr. Portmaine?"

Did every member of the titled set think people had nothing better to do than swive each other and flirt?

"I am a gentleman, my lady." Archer allowed a hint of a knowing smile into his expression. "A gentleman would not admit his good fortune were he in anticipation of an assignation."

She approached, and observing her walk, Archer felt a sinking sensation in his middle. He was doomed, *doomed*, to kiss women he didn't desire, and to bid a fond farewell to the ones he did.

"My husband would not like to find us here." She stopped a mere foot away, scrutinizing Archer's chest and shoulders with the same pursed lips and cocked head displayed by the fellows who looked over the equine offerings at Tatt's. "To be alone like this is completely improper."

"As I said, I'll just be going."

She proffered her hand on cue, and he grasped it in his own. If he was lucky, she'd content herself with a racy—

Over Lady Braithwaite's shoulder, Archer watched in horror as the sitting-room door swung open to reveal Morgan James standing in the entrance. She stopped abruptly, her eyes going wide, her gloved hand covering her mouth.

Very possibly, the damned woman was hiding a smirk.

Two

ARCHER LET HIS SMILE DEGENERATE INTO A LEER AND USED LADY BRAITHWAITE'S hand to tug her against his body. "I'll leave as soon as I've stolen at least a kiss."

Bother. A bit of wretched melodrama was the best he could think of, and when he'd followed through on his declaration, he saw Miss James was standing as if she'd sprouted roots, watching every moment of the performance through dancing eyes. While Lady Braithwaite's tongue imitated an auger, boring against Archer's lips, Archer pointed directly toward the corridor, and—to the extent a man could while enduring an oral assault—he glowered at the intruder.

Miss James withdrew, smirk and all, while Lady Braithwaite plastered herself against Archer from north to south and at every point in between. She was a substantial woman and determined on her objective.

Archer had nearly resigned himself to at least pleasuring the woman, when a bad situation threatened to become worse.

"Oh, my Lord Braithwaite! I am pathetically relieved to see you!" Morgan James sounded near tears right outside the sitting-room door. "I am completely turned about, the women's retiring room is nowhere in sight, and my need for it is becoming *urgent*."

Lady Braithwaite retracted herself as if bitten. "He mustn't find me here. My pin money, my allowance for the modiste, my little habit at the whist tables—"

She twisted about, eyes huge, while Archer stifled the urge to clap a hand over her mouth.

"They're leaving," he whispered. "He's escorting the young lady down the hall. Listen to the footsteps."

Relief replaced panic in Lady Braithwaite's gaze, followed by an air of wounded dignity assumed with astounding rapidity. "I must be going, Mr. Portmaine. Steal your kisses from somebody else."

With pleasure. "My apologies, Lady Braithwaite. I should not have presumed." He bowed low, the better to encourage her departure. If she ran true to Archer's experience, her first stop upon returning to the ballroom would be her husband's side. She'd fuss and coo and spend at least ten minutes making sure all and sundry observed their marital accord.

Which gave Archer about fourteen minutes to open the safe, review its contents, and return to the ballroom without being seen.

Seen *again*.

⟡

Morgan checked the clock above the mantel in the card room. Mr. Portmaine had needed approximately sixteen minutes to make his way back to the ballroom. She did not believe those minutes had been necessary to cool a passion on his part for Lady Braithwaite, but that left the question of what, exactly, he'd been about.

"You, sir, have a knack of appearing somewhere, as if you've been lounging in that very spot all evening." *When I know you haven't.*

"Miss James." Mr. Portmaine's smile was cool, his expression giving away nothing. "A pleasure to see you *again*." He bowed over her hand correctly, and Morgan did not bother playing the game of keeping his hand in hers. "Might I inquire as to whether you're engaged for the supper waltz?"

Oh, damn. "You're not supposed to be this bold when confronted, Mr. Portmaine."

"You're confronting me? This confrontation is by far more charming than others in recent memory. Will you dance with me, Miss James?"

What was he trying to say? What was he trying to *do*? Couples positioned themselves in the middle of the ballroom, where Morgan would be able to interrogate him for at least the duration of a dance. "It would be my pleasure."

He looked not pleased, but relieved, the scoundrel. She placed her gloved fingers over the knuckles of his proffered hand and let him escort her to the dance floor. They observed the protocol for beginning the dance, and then the orchestra swung into a lilting triple meter.

Because the Braithwaites hadn't hired a mere quartet or trio, but an orchestra, and because that ensemble boasted a piano and a proficient double bass rather than a mere harpsichord, Morgan could *feel* the music.

Or perhaps her pleasure in this particular waltz had to do with her partner. "You are light on your feet, Mr. Portmaine."

He turned her through a corner and momentarily brought her a hair closer in his arms than propriety allowed. "The better for sneaking about? You are a graceful dancer as well, Miss James."

"I like waltzing." With the buzz of the surrounding crowd, and the good efforts of the orchestra, Morgan would not catch Mr. Portmaine's every word. She would, however, be able to see his face while he spoke, which helped tremendously.

"Is the appeal of the waltz its scandalous nature, Miss James?"

"Scandalous? When Wellington himself enjoys it? Hardly. I like it because of the downbeat."

She hadn't meant to say that.

His smile suggested he knew she hadn't meant to say it, too. "Explain yourself, Miss James."

"I can feel the rhythm, particularly if there's a piano, even better if there's tympani. *One*-two-three, *one*-two-three…" From the puzzlement on his face, Morgan realized she was in the arms of one person who hadn't heard of her "unfortunate history."

She regretted her disclosure for half the length of the room, then caught Mr. Portmaine regarding her closely. He was tall, but not so tall as to make her feel like an adolescent. At her come out, she'd danced with Valentine Windham…

Who was too tall for her. *That*, she realized between one violin trill and the next, was what had been off about every dance they'd shared—that and her besottedness with him.

"You are distracted, Miss James. Or perhaps you're simply enjoying yourself?"

"I am planning your interrogation, sir."

"I will answer your questions as honestly as I can."

His reply wasn't what she'd expected, but it allowed her to enjoy the balance of the dance and move through the buffet line beside him without further conversation. He left the choice of seating to her, so she decided on a small table far down the gallery.

"A good location for interrogation and torture, if one is allergic to roses," he remarked. "What would you like to know?"

She wanted to know if he'd enjoyed kissing Lady Braithwaite and where he'd learned to dance so well. She wanted to know if he was in trouble, and she wanted to know what his kisses were like.

Morgan waited until they were seated, a single plate between them, before she put her first question to him.

"Why did His Grace tell you the Crown is very worried?"

❧

The trouble was, Archer *liked* Morgan James. He'd bungled the search of Braithwaite's chamber badly, and Miss James had saved him from exposure. He liked practical women, women who could deal with life's vagaries without making a fuss.

He liked pretty women as well as the next fellow did.

He also, however, liked smart women, which was unfortunate indeed when his line of work meant how he spent his time ought to remain undiscussed, or better yet, unnoticed.

"You were not in the card room when I had a conversation with His Grace which might have included those words." Those exact words.

"I was a few feet outside the doorway." She tugged off her gloves, exposing hands that sported short, unpainted nails, and a sturdy, practical quality at variance with her graceful evening attire. "Care for a strawberry?"

"I would rather hear how you were privy to a discussion taking place twelve, even fifteen feet away from you. The card room was buzzing, the orchestra sawing away, and you could not have heard us."

"I didn't hear you. Eat something, Mr. Portmaine, or people will suspect we're quarreling." She served up a section of orange, along with a saucy, naughty smile.

He whipped off his gloves and set them down next to hers. "Thank you." His mind raced over dire possibilities as he took a bite of the orange. Nobody had overheard them—nobody. He'd been sure of it.

"I do not hear well," Miss James said.

He paused mid-chew. "I beg your pardon?"

"I do not hear well." She looked right at him and spoke slowly, as if *he* didn't hear well.

"I'm sorry to—" *Hear* that. He accepted another section of orange from her. "That's too bad, though given what goes on in the typical Mayfair ballroom, you might consider yourself lucky."

"You're an idiot if you think deafness is a blessing." Her voice was a low hiss, making it plain the subject was sensitive. Archer liked that the momentum of the conversation was in his hands; he did not at all like that she was upset.

"Tell me."

She passed him some ham rolled up around a nibble of pineapple, suggesting the lady shared Archer's penchant for fresh fruit. "Tell you what?"

"Tell me what it's like when your hearing troubles you."

She hadn't expected that question—her expression was positively flummoxed. He chewed the tidbit and realized on the two occasions when he'd had substantial conversations with her, she'd chosen quiet locations.

"Hearing trouble is a constant frustration," she said, holding up another bite of ham. "If you're blind, people will help you. They can close their eyes and get a taste of what you deal with. It scares them, but they know it isn't catching. If you're deaf…"

She trailed off, staring at the food in her fingers. Archer plucked it from her grasp and held it to her lips. "Eat, Miss James. If you're to interrogate me properly, you must keep up your strength. You were telling me what it's like to be deaf."

She nibbled the food from his fingers, a delectable, delicate sensation with erotic overtones Archer suspected Miss James was oblivious to.

"If you are deaf," she said slowly, "people think you're stupid. They shout at you—you can *see* when a voice is raised at you—they use little words and use them loudly. They give up trying to speak with you, and don't think to write down their words instead. You let them give up, because the shouting causes others to stare, and the pity is worse even than the disgust."

Archer had an image of an intelligent young woman bombarded with shouting she couldn't hear, and jeering glances she couldn't avoid. "I'm sorry,

Miss James." To underscore the sincerity of his sentiment, he reached across the table and wrapped her bare fingers in his own. "I'm sorry it hurt."

"Everybody has hurts and burdens." She said this wearily, like an aphorism passed down from exhausted, burdened mother to exhausted, burdened daughter.

"We do. Lady Braithwaite was my burden for a few moments. My thanks for waving off his lordship."

Miss James brightened. "I considered letting him have at you, then I recalled His Grace's comments."

Drat the damned luck. Morgan James's interest in a very private conversation could well be that of a woman plotting mischief against the Crown.

"How and why were you privy to that comment?" Archer still grasped her wrist, and she made no move to withdraw. Either she had the steady composure and regular pulse of a practiced spy, or she had nothing about which to be anxious.

"I saw what His Grace said. He is well known to me, so I can make out most of his words. I could not follow you as easily."

"You *saw* what he said?"

"Watch my mouth." She sat back and slipped her hand from his grasp. "*How are you, Mr. Portmaine?*" She did not speak audibly, and yet he knew what words she'd formed.

"I'm well enough for a man who must consider his every private word has not been private at all. The ramifications are… daunting."

Worse than daunting, considering the safety of the Crown was at stake.

She patted his knuckles. "You needn't worry. The ability to read lips is hard won and rare, also an imperfect skill. Every person I've known who had the ability was deaf. In my case, I manage much better with people I know, like His Grace."

"What did you see him say?" Archer held out a slender hope that the lady might be able to see others' speech, but that her recall would be significantly imperfect.

She knit her brows. "He mentioned relying on the Frogs for intelligence, said the Crown was worried—very worried. He offered to support you in a bid for a pocket borough and suggested you resort to flirting and courting. I could not see the entire exchange, because he raised his glass twice and obscured my view of his mouth."

"And what of my words, Miss James?"

"Your back was to me for much of the conversation. I saw the word perilous though, and when Lady Braithwaite followed you from the room, I thought I'd best go along in case you needed assistance."

"You went along to *protect* me?" The notion offended his dignity almost as much as it warmed his heart.

Her chin came up half an inch. "And was successful in this regard."

"You were. My thanks." He fed her more ham, mostly to keep her quiet while he tried not to dwell on what might have occurred if Miss James hadn't come along. When much of the food had been consumed, Archer sat back and indulged in a curiosity lively enough to get him into trouble.

"Tell me more about being deaf."

Miss James's mouth quirked, and not with humor. "Deafness isn't something one often discusses."

"So you have a rare opportunity to enlighten a curious mind. Was it lonely?"

Her gaze shuttered. She put back the strawberry she'd just picked up.

"Forgive me, Miss James. I did not mean to presume. The line of work I'm in frequently isolates one, particularly when one no longer has a partner." While she considered her strawberry, he forged on. "I hadn't made that realization until this very moment. Carrying secrets makes one into a type of mute, I suppose, though nothing like... I'm babbling."

The smile that rose in her eyes was breathtaking. "You're also quite correct. I expect any disability leaves one lonely, deafness especially, because it's so hard to connect your mind and heart to another's when you dwell in silence."

She was an emotionally fearless young lady, and perhaps deafness had bequeathed that to her as well. "You are not deaf now."

The smile died, and Archer grieved its passing.

"A little, I still am, particularly when violent weather changes are in the offing. My physician has warned me my hearing might get worse with age."

This possibility haunted her. Archer perceived as much by the way she popped the strawberry in her mouth and chewed it to bits. "We all lose ground as we age, and you are far from old, Miss James. May I escort you back to the ballroom?"

"You may not—yet. What were you and His Grace discussing?"

She deserved an answer, but he tried yet again to avoid giving one. "Will you desist with this inquiry if I tell it had to do with the security of the realm?"

The lady managed to contain her amusement, though Archer suspected it was a near thing. "And that interlude with Lady Braithwaite was a matter of delicate diplomacy?"

"That was an occupational hazard." One he increasingly resented.

"You liken yourself to a chambermaid? Accosted in the course of your duties through no fault of your own?"

She was finding her balance with this exchange, so Archer rose to the spirit of mild antagonism. "What would you know about the vicissitudes of being a chambermaid? You hobnob with dukes and turn down the ballroom with their sons—when you aren't spying on the Regent's loyal minion."

"I was not spying on you, Mr. Portmaine, and for your information, I was a chambermaid for three years. I know a great deal more about presuming footmen, unscrupulous gentlemen, and having to defend my virtue on the back stairs than you could possibly comprehend."

Miss Morgan James, favorite of the Windhams, friend to their virtuoso, and potential disaster to Archer's objectives, blinked and looked around her as if someone else had spoken.

"I beg your pardon, Mr. Portmaine. That is a disclosure I've not made in Polite circles since before my come-out."

Every woman who'd ever captured Archer's heart had been in service. This explained his attraction to her, or explained part of it, and put to rest any notion he had of disentangling himself from this extraordinary lady in the next half hour.

"You will explain yourself nonetheless, and—if I might presume on both your good nature and a family connection—I would be most pleased if you called me Archer when you did."

᠅

"You should expect a visit from me at your town house tomorrow, Your Grace."

Moreland paused on the steps of a gentlemen's club to which he'd probably belonged since adolescence, one Archer was unlikely to ever see the inside of. To appearances, they were striking up a casual conversation between passing acquaintances, nothing more.

"Is that wise, Portmaine? To fraternize openly when such delicate matters are in train? It's one thing to cross paths in the social crush, but a morning call to my home?"

"I will not be fraternizing with you, Your Grace. I heeded your advice the other night and undertook some flirting."

Except it hadn't been flirting. Talking with Morgan James had been… delightful.

"Flirting? With one of my ladies?" The old fellow looked torn between curiosity and surprise.

"I would not reach so far above myself, not that your daughters aren't lovely women."

Moreland tipped his hat to a trio of dowagers waving from a passing landau. "My daughters are lovely handfuls, every one of 'em."

"And you are as proud of this as if it were exclusively the result of your paternity." Which it well might be.

Moreland positively preened. "Before all save my duchess, I maintain that the girls take after their papa. Her Grace can take credit for the boys, but the girls are my treasures. If you're not calling on me, and you're not calling on an unmarried daughter of the house, then what business have you bestowing your presence on us?"

"I'll be taking Miss Morgan James driving, weather permitting."

His Grace gave the pink rose on Archer's lapel a nudge. "Morgan's brother was an earl, and her sister is married to my heir, Portmaine. Some would say Morgan is entitled to be called lady, the same as my girls are."

Morgan apparently was not so inclined. "Are you warning me off, Your Grace?"

"Perhaps I am."

The reply hurt a bit, but it did not surprise—nor did it deter Archer in the least. "I did not take Your Grace for a snob."

"I am an aristocrat, though others will consider me a snob." Rather than proceed into the building, His Grace gestured toward the fenced square across the street. "My duchess requires certain standards of me, and I am her slave in all things. Let's enjoy a pretty day a while longer, shall we?"

In other words, there was more to be said, provided they had privacy.

Archer crossed the street with His Grace, and when they'd passed through the wrought iron fence encircling the wooded square, he waited for the older man to explain himself.

"Morgan is a pretty little thing," His Grace observed mildly.

"What has that to do with anything?"

"In the opinion of some men, a great deal."

Archer felt an urge to kick something—something resembling a duke. "Beautiful women are a deal of work, Your Grace, in the typical case. My tastes run to ladies with backbone, a good sense of humor, and a lively mind." A lusty nature was an asset Archer was not about to mention to an "aristocratic" duke.

"Pragmatic of you. Many thought my duchess was plain, though none regarded her as such by our wedding day."

The duke was a canny old veteran of more parliamentary plots and skirmishes than Archer could count, and he was circling around to something now. Rather than try to draw the old boy out, Archer ambled along in silence.

"Morgan is dear to my family, Portmaine. Very dear. The boys would fight duels for her, the girls gather for hours over the teapot when she's with us. She is an aunt to my oldest grandson."

Archer understood that in His Grace's order of precedence, an aunt to his grandson stood only slightly lower than the angels and well above any pettifogging old archbishops.

"Your Grace, I mean no disrespect when I say, for all your family dotes on her, Miss James is lonely. She has few friends outside of your family circle and regards the young men slobbering at her heels as so many nuisances. The social Season is a trial for her, and if you had any understanding of her at all, you'd realize a noisy, dimly lit ballroom is torture for her."

His Grace used his walking stick to whisk a cluster of dead leaves from their path. "Why is a ballroom, of all places, torture?"

"She can't *hear*, Your Grace. With all the background noise, the chatter, the orchestra, the stomping of the dancers' feet, she can't hear well at all. In the dim lighting, she has a hard time reading people's lips, and so she must always have vague, pretty replies on hand, though she knows half the time they aren't spot on."

His Grace's expression turned thoughtful. "If she is so uncomfortable, then why does she attend?"

"She attends because she doesn't want anyone to think she's ungrateful, and please don't ask me any more questions, because I've come as close as I dare to betraying her confidences."

Which was perhaps understandable, when a man had more practice dealing in secrets than confidences.

His Grace paused to spear Archer with a glower. "You also come close to being insubordinate, young man, though if you're going to risk such a thing, the interests of a young lady are as good a justification as any."

While they resumed walking, Archer decided he'd just been scolded—and forgiven—in short order.

"Take Morgan driving, then, but keep a sharp eye out."

"I *always* keep a sharp eye out."

"No, my dear young man, you do not. Sometimes you sit for almost two hours among the ferns and portraits with a pretty young lady who is known to avoid lengthy conversations, and you do it in such a location that anybody might remark upon it."

"What is Your Grace implying?" And who else had seen Archer whiling away an evening with Miss James?

"Your line of work has become dangerous, Portmaine. You need not fear much from the wives whose husbands hire you to catch the ladies at their folly, but you've been drawn into a game where you will make enemies. Your present task is to do nothing less than save the Regent's life. The caliber of foe you're facing is commensurate with that task, and so is the danger."

His Grace sounded more like a general now than a duke, a general with a lot of battlefield experience. "You are saying any lady with whom I'm seen to associate might be in danger as well?"

"I'm suggesting it. Morgan is well dowered, attached to a prominent family, and well known in Polite Society. She'd make a fine victim of a kidnapping, wouldn't she?"

His Grace paused to sniff an odd, blooming spray of honeysuckle, such was his sangfroid when discussing plots on the sovereign's life.

One didn't argue with dukes, though one might ask a question. "And absconding with Miss James would threaten the Regent's life, how?"

The duke spoke gently. "Kidnapping Morgan James would sure as hell distract the only person close to discovering the details of this damned plot, wouldn't it?"

His Grace wasn't wrong. The duke's fear was far-fetched to the point of paranoia, but it wasn't completely wrong.

"Take her driving," His Grace said, resuming their walk. "Just don't favor her. Flirt with every debutante the hostesses let you get near, leer down a few of the matrons' bodices. Take some other young lady out for the church parade this weekend. You know how the game is played."

"I do." Goddamn it all to hell, Archer did know how the game was played.

The duke departed, strolling briskly across the green and leaving Archer to address the surrounding maples. "I know how the damned game is played, and I'm getting bloody sick of playing it."

❧

"By now, I should know better than to get involved in such a stupid game." Morgan stroked her hand over an enormous, smoky-gray, long-haired cat, more to quiet her nerves than to please the beast. "I felt like an idiot. It's one thing to be unable to hear or speak, but that dratted man treated me as if I were invisible."

Aquinas began to rumble with contentment on her lap.

"He expects me to call him Archer, and then he flirts with every girl, lady, and woman—he was smiling at the governesses and dairymaids, too—in the park. I do not understand it, Aquinas. He's no better than you."

"For a moment there, I thought I had a genuine rival."

Shock and pleasure coursed through Morgan—quickly followed by pique—at the sound of the male voice behind her. Here in the privacy of her bedroom, it seemed as if...

"Greetings, Miss James, from the scoundrel who made such a poor showing in the park earlier today."

She picked up the cat and rose to see Archer Portmaine standing just inside her balcony doors—wet, unsmiling, and as starkly handsome as ever.

"You will please leave, Mr. Portmaine." She could pitch the cat at him if she had to, and that would feel good, though such an impulse would likely put Aquinas out of charity with her permanently.

"I owe you an explanation, and if you don't mind, I'd prefer not to shout it up to you from the garden." Gone was the flirting idiot who'd taken her driving, and in his place was a grim, damp, unhappy man.

"Stand on the hearthstones. You're dripping on my carpet."

He did not immediately obey. Instead he went through the awkward maneuver of tugging off his boots while standing. The boots he put right outside the balcony door. Next, he shrugged out of his coat and hung it on the back of the chair at Morgan's vanity, then placed the chair several feet from the fire.

"Leaving your balcony door open is not wise, Morgan James."

"Trapping Aquinas in the house isn't either, particularly when he longs to go courting."

Letting Archer Portmaine remain in her bedchamber was a great deal more foolish though, especially when he started unbuttoning his waistcoat.

"Where is your cravat?"

"For this type of call, I don't usually wear one."

"That's why your shirt is black, isn't it. The better to lurk and skulk on moonless nights. A white cravat would give away your location."

He pulled his damp shirt over his head and stared at it as it hung in his grasp. "A full moon hangs above the clouds, though we can't see it for the infernal rain." He draped his shirt somewhere—Morgan neither knew nor cared where, for she was too busy studying the breathtaking muscular geometry of Archer Portmaine's half-naked body.

"Are you quite comfortable, Mr. Portmaine?" For Morgan was finding it difficult to breathe evenly.

"I'm quite chilled, also exhausted, neither of which is your fault." He sank onto the raised hearthstones, and the scent of steaming wool reached Morgan's nose.

He was weary; she could see it in the lines of his body, sense it in the bleakness of his gaze. He was weary and alone, and she knew what that felt like.

She pulled an afghan off the back of her fainting couch and draped it around his shoulders. When she would have moved away, he wrapped an arm around her leg and rested his forehead against her thigh. "I really am sorry, Morgan."

This afternoon, he'd gone back to Miss James-ing her, and she'd hated that as much as she'd hated his leering and flirting. She gave in to the temptation to run a hand through his damp hair. "We'll talk."

But first she'd pour him a cup of hot tea from the pot under the towel on her night tray. She brought it to him and held it out. With him sitting on the hearth, the moment reminded her of a knight reaching to take a chalice from a lady's hand.

"Sit," he said, moving a few inches to the left. "Or perhaps you should lock the door."

She sat, but the hearth was not wide, and as she lowered herself to the stones, he opened the blanket so it enveloped her too. "The door is locked, though you're being sufficiently familiar that I must question the wisdom of informing you of this."

Morgan did not scold him further, nor did she move away. Her guest said nothing, just sat at her side, the tea in one hand, the other hand resting on her shoulder. A shudder passed through him, making the tea tremble in the shallow cup.

"You really are cold."

"I'll warm up."

"And you'll tell me why you were acting so oddly this afternoon?"

"Why I was acting like an absolute ass?"

She did not correct him.

He drained the teacup and set it aside, then tucked the blanket more closely around them. "When we were at the Braithwaite's ball, you did not question me too closely about my activities in our host and hostess's private chambers."

"It is not my business." Then too, she'd been far too enthralled with their conversation, a discussion where she'd been invited to talk about things most people regarded as unfortunate, if not downright shameful.

"It is not your business," he concurred, "and I don't want it to become your business."

Under the scent of wet wool, she caught a whiff of something lovely and woodsy—from him. "What you're doing is dangerous, isn't it?"

Because they were side by side, because his arm was around her shoulders, Morgan felt him come to a decision before he spoke, a momentary weighing conducted more quickly than thought.

"My present task likely is dangerous. I was supposed to meet a man tonight at the docks. Somebody met him before I did, or possibly he decided it was too dangerous to keep our appointment."

Dear God. "Was he a friend?"

"An acquaintance of long standing. I knew him years ago... in France."

She was not going to ask what Archer Portmaine had been doing in a nation with which England had been at war for most of twenty years. Instead, she slipped her arm around his bare, cool back, feeling the last of her irritation with him shift into worry. "I'm sorry, Archer. This is more than a missing necklace or a straying wife, isn't it?"

He heaved out a sigh then closed his arms around her so she was enveloped in his embrace inside the blanket. "We were followed today in the park."

He was cool to the touch and bearing bad news, and yet his embrace was a wonderful comfort. "That's why you took every turning and side path you could, isn't it? Why you made sure to be seen by all and sundry—even the dairymaids?"

"That's part of it. His Grace warned me that I must not become entangled with you, at least not until this present difficulty is resolved. I was trying to earn your disdain, if I might be honest."

"You should have been honest much earlier. Did you think I would not comprehend such a tactic, Archer? And as for His Grace, he meddles only in the lives of people he cares for."

"He cares for you, Morgan. The entire family cares for you."

He sounded so tired, so bleak and burdened—who cared for him?

She felt more than sympathy for this man. Her deafness had taught her what it was to carry an entire world of communication around in silence—reactions, questions, joys, observations, all of it stored up in the airless vault of one isolated heart.

And yet, when he'd slain the present dragon, another would rise up to take its place, and his silence would expand to accommodate that one too.

"Some men need danger, they need excitement and risk. It's how they're built." She tried not to make it an accusation or a lament, merely a statement of fact.

"I'm not built that way."

"You sound sure of this." And Morgan was also sure he was speaking with his mouth pressed against her temple, a talking kiss.

"I am damned sure of it. I thought I was going to take over the investigations from my cousin, step right into his shoes, but as a solo operation, things
don't run as well. It takes longer to sort through information, longer to gather
it. I have no one with whom to parse ideas or air my brilliant and invariably
erroneous theories."

He fell silent, while behind them a log shifted on the andirons. Morgan cast
around for something to ask him, something that would let her again feel both
the way his mouth shaped words against her temple and the way those words
vibrated through his body.

"I should be going."

No, he should not. "You've barely stopped shivering, and you haven't told
me why we were followed."

"I wish I knew why."

A non-answer from a man too distracted, tired, or upset to effectively pre-
varicate. She tightened her hold on him, as if she'd prevent him bodily from
leaving. "Don't speak in riddles, Archer Portmaine. You have some idea."

This time when she felt him assay risks and reasons, the process took longer.
Maybe fatigue was making his brain sluggish, or maybe he wasn't as indifferent
to sharing a blanket with her as he seemed.

"We believe a plot is brewing against the Crown."

He spoke slowly, each word no doubt dragged forth against the dictates of
both training and habit—though he made no move to pull away.

"And the Regent has many detractors."

"We don't know if this plot is against Prinny himself—the target might be
a high-ranking minister, though I'm damned if I can figure out which one."

"What about the royal dukes? Aren't they the next logical target?"

He shifted away enough to frown at her. "How do you reach that
conclusion?"

"Prinny is not in good health, and his wife is past childbearing, even if
they could tolerate each other. With Princess Charlotte's death in childbirth,
Prinny's brothers must assure the succession, but they are not young men. A
blow against one of the dukes could have grave consequences for the stability
of the government."

He'd been a handsome, convincing buffoon earlier in the day. Now his
expression was deadly serious—and even more attractive. "Your reasoning is
sound. Your reasoning is damned sound. Kent's only daughter is but a few
weeks old, and Clarence's daughter didn't live a single day."

"His duchess is rumored to be carrying again."

She'd surprised him. His reaction wasn't visible on his face so much as it
registered in a lack of expression. "How could you know such a thing?"

"I don't hear well, but I do listen, Archer Portmaine, and I trundle about
with Anna and Her Grace, making endless morning calls where there's nothing
to do but listen."

A smile started to turn the corners of his mouth up, then his expression shuttered again. "I really must be going."

"Damn you, Archer Portmaine, you just had an idea. You may leave if you like, but not until you tell me what you were thinking."

While his brows drew down, and he no doubt cast around for some plausible dodge to placate her, *Morgan* had an *idea*. Her idea was wicked, wanton, and everything she'd dreamed of for years in the dim silence of a lonely young lady's heart. Before she could reason herself out of it—it was a wicked, wanton, *wonderful* idea—she seized the moment and kissed him.

Three

THE EVENING HAD REACHED ITS MIDDLE HOURS, NEITHER EARLY NOR LATE. THE beau monde swilled champagne and arranged adulterous assignations to the strains of the waltz, while the shopkeepers slept snug in their beds, and the whores trolled for custom on the street corners of Covent Garden.

In a club more respectable than prestigious—the address was technically Soho rather than Mayfair—a man sat alone behind the day's copy of *The Times*. He was a surpassingly unremarkable man, his age somewhere north of five-and-thirty, though south of five-and-fifty. His hair was medium brown, his eyes medium blue, his height simply medium.

He dressed well but not ostentatiously. A careful observer might have said he looked like a diplomat, and that would have pleased him, for a diplomat he was—among other things. He was fluent in nine languages and competent in six more. His native tongue was French, though in English, his public school accent was flawless, despite the fact that the only academy he'd attended had been run by thugs and strumpets on the docks of Calais.

The young ladies of Polite Society considered him safe; the older women thought of him as a well-mannered fellow, and that would have pleased him too.

He was, at all times, in all languages, well mannered.

He assured himself yet again that every shade was down on each of the room's four windows. At quarter past the hour precisely, the door to the reading room opened, and a young man of pale countenance and wheat-gold hair admitted himself to the diplomat's company. The younger fellow was dressed in natty evening attire, to all appearances a scion of the *beau monde* enjoying an evening on the town.

The diplomat rose with a gracious smile. "You are punctual. Such an undervalued quality in a gentleman these days. May I pour you some brandy?"

"Please." The young man did not quite stutter, but as he reached for his drink, his hand shook.

"How is your wife?"

"Fine, thank you. Quite in the pink."

"And your son?"

The young man's smile was sickly. "Thriving, thriving."

And well the little shoat might be, for the wife's propensity for lactation would be the envy of His Majesty's pet milch cow. This had been verified by a reliable informant on more than one occasion. "Glad to hear it. Shall we sit?"

The younger fellow gave a jerky nod and appropriated a chair with its back to the window. An amateur's mistake, but tonight was not the time to point that out.

"I gather things did not go well earlier this evening. Perhaps we should discuss it?" The diplomat let the question hang delicately while the young man downed the rest of his drink.

"Things went terribly. The Frenchman showed up, but he wasn't at all inclined to parlay peaceably."

"More brandy?"

Another quick nod, so the diplomat brought the bottle over to the small table near the other fellow's chair.

"I am here to help, you know. Not every assignment will go smoothly, and the people whose interests we benefit will never be able to aid us or acknowledge our contributions. We must rely on each other."

"I cut him. That fellow, the Frenchie, he pulled a knife, and I was afraid he'd call the watch, and it was awful."

That the young man was rattled was to his credit. He was a reluctant traitor, after all, so the diplomat adopted his most avuncular tones. "I was proud of you."

Wary surprise greeted this observation, probably accompanied by the young man's first inkling that being a spy meant being spied upon. "You were there?"

"I was not about to let you handle this without some support, and under the circumstances, your mistake was understandable."

"A man is injured, possibly dead, a man who never meant me or mine any harm, and you call it a *mistake*?"

Scruples were such touching, dreary inconveniences. "He meant you harm. You didn't imagine that knife, and if you hadn't thought to come armed yourself, he might well have brought down the authorities. That is the last thing we need."

"And if he'd cut me? How would I explain that to Lucia?" He scrubbed a hand over his clean-shaven features while the diplomat filled the brandy glass for a third time.

"Your efforts were not in vain, you know. The evening yielded some interesting information."

The traitor looked up from his drink. "Not from the Frenchie. He hared off without saying more than *bon soir*. I've never known a man to fight so quietly."

Because schoolboy rows were mostly noise, while the professionals battled in silence.

"And then you demonstrated yet more sound reasoning and took yourself off, to be seen bowing over some hostess's hand in a far better neighborhood." To begin drinking the memory of spilled blood and injured scruples into oblivion. "I, however, remained on the scene."

"What did you find?"

"Not a what, but a whom. Archer Portmaine came along, stealthy as a cat."

The young man studied his glass rather than drain it. "Portmaine is the pandering idiot I followed in the park."

Followed with all the stealth of a drunken gorilla. That too was a discussion for another night. "Not such an idiot. I have reason to think he knew the Frenchman."

"What reason?"

"Merely a hunch." A hunch resulting from the way Portmaine had sauntered around the block, not once, but three times in the pouring rain. And though the fellow had lingered under the windows of a boarding house for young females, the diplomat had his doubts. "Nothing more than a hunch, one we'll follow up on."

"I'd rather not be the one following up, if you don't mind. You never said anything about this business being deadly. You said I was to attend the usual parties, frequent the clubs, listen in a few card rooms, and await instructions."

"And tonight, you followed instructions. You were to cozy up to the Frenchman, and he was not cooperative. I can assure you that in the general case, violence and killing, in particular, are frowned upon among those engaged in pursuits similar to ours. It's messy and can bring down the authorities and the press. Nobody wants that, so killing is understood by all players to be a very, very last resort."

"*Messy?*" The poor boy put his head in his hands. "I wish I'd never set foot in that damned hell."

Such melodrama. The kindest thing to do was deliver a figurative slap to the fellow's common sense.

"Ah, but you did. Not once, but many times, and each time, your debts grew. If you want a new start on the Continent, my friend, if you want to be on hand to see your newborn son grow to manhood, then the course you've adopted is the only reasonable one."

"I've changed my mind."

Oh, they always changed their minds, or tried to. The diplomat did not laugh, did not even smile. "I beg your pardon?"

"I want to go to America. When this is done, I'll take my wife and son and go to America. The Continent is too close, and I'm bound to be recognized by some dandy making the tour."

America, of all the barbaric notions… "If that's your choice, I can only accommodate it." Provided the journey to America for the young man and his little family started by way of the Low Countries.

Archer pulled his mouth away from the houri threatening to make a hash of his wits. "Morgan, for God's sake, this isn't—"

She silenced him by virtue of a hand anchored on the back of his head and her mouth sealed to his. He could not get away; he did not *want* to get away.

His fuse was so short as to be nonexistent, and before his common sense or scruples or some damned inconvenient thing could stop him, Archer scooped Morgan up and carried her to the bed. He settled her on the mattress and blanketed her with his half-naked, damp self.

"Send me away again," he rasped against her neck. "Scream, threaten me with something dire, Morgan." He didn't want her to see this side of him, the side that could take, that could need blindly and selfishly.

"I'm not as innocent as you think, Archer Portmaine, and not nearly done kissing you." She emphasized her point by spreading her legs and lifting her hips, a maneuver so bold it cut through some of the urgency fogging Archer's brain.

"Do that again."

She undulated more slowly this time, and much of the frustration eating at him ebbed away. "Again."

He curled down to her shoulder, feeling a different arousal awaken and stretch through his veins as she indulged in a voluptuous rhythm. His wanting shifted from the wanting of a man in despair for a possibly deceased friend lost in pursuit of a hopeless goal—a wanting for oblivion—to the wanting of a man for the particular woman in his arms.

"I need to leave."

"You *need* to stay. I was in service, Archer. A deaf girl can't remain in service without learning much no decent female ought to know."

He nuzzled her temple when he should have been vaulting off the bed. Her rose-and-spice fragrance was soothing, even as it muddled his tired, unhappy brain further. "What are you saying?"

She kissed his jaw. "Who is a better victim for the randy footmen than a girl who can't say a word against them, a girl who barely knows the terms for the liberties they're taking? Anna was as vigilant as a mother hen, but she couldn't go everywhere with me."

"God." He started to climb off of her, but she wrapped both her arms and her legs around him.

"I want you to stay, Archer." She sounded very, very certain.

"But if you were forced…" The notion was horrific enough to dampen his lust. He lifted up onto his elbows. "I'm leaving."

He didn't move, didn't shift away from the scent and softness of her, though he could have broken her hold easily.

She buried her nose against his neck. "I was not forced."

"You could not give your consent in the King's English. You were not of age to consent to marry. You were hardly—"

She kissed him again, lingeringly, as if to remind him without words that even a woman incapable of speech or hearing could communicate some things quite well.

When Archer stopped bracing himself against her hold, Morgan let out a sigh.

"He was a running footman, more a boy than a man," she said, her tone indicating any disclosure was a grudging concession. "I was fascinated with him because he spoke very little English, only French, and while I could read French, thanks to Anna's diligence, I'd never seen French spoken consistently before. He noticed me."

"How could any man with eyes in his head not notice you?"

"Not like that. He was deaf and mute in English, just as I was, you see? The difference was he could overcome the lack while I could not, but for a time…"

She opened her mouth on his shoulder and set her teeth against the muscle. She wasn't biting him; it felt more like an exploration of his person with the part of her that had spent years unable to express her thoughts.

"For a time you did not feel so alone," Archer concluded.

She nodded, the top of her head grazing his chin.

The wanting inside him shifted again, to a desire he'd felt frequently before—the desire to pleasure the woman in his arms—and something more, too: the desire to ease her aloneness, and even more surprisingly, to allow her to ease his.

He yearned to tell her this. Instead, he touched his mouth to hers, a slow, tender echo of her previous kiss. He would give to her, and in allowing it, she would give to him.

When he shifted slightly to the side, she tightened her arms around him. "Don't go, Archer. Please."

"Hush. I'm not going." He could not go, though he should not stay.

Her grip slackened as he arranged himself along her side. "You are such a beautiful man."

Her touch on his face was beautiful. Her skin where he untied the bows of her dressing gown and chemise was luminous. Her scent was rosy and female at the same time, and her taste when he took her nipple in his mouth was luscious.

This intimacy did not cause her to tense beneath him, as it might if she'd never felt such a thing before. She relaxed into it, tangling her fingers in his hair and sighing against his temple.

"I have longed…"

She had longed in silence, possibly for years. "Tell me." He whispered the words against her breast then lifted his face so she might see his mouth when he spoke. "Tell me what you longed for."

Without warning, she skimmed her hand down Archer's belly to shape him through his falls. He was hard and aching, and her touch brought both torment and relief.

"Archer, please."

She whispered the words against his chest, nigh cindering Archer's reason. He was already moving to unfasten his breeches when something caught his eye, a glow from the night table, or rather, two glows.

The damned cat sat there, staring at the figures on the bed. Firelight reflected against the beast's eyes, giving its mother-of-pearl gaze a flat, otherworldly quality. Morgan's fingers applied a slight, lovely pressure to Archer's cock, but the moment had shifted yet again.

The cat's eyes held reproach and a call to reason. Archer stared back for one annoyed instant before the beast silently took itself off. In that instant, Archer's conscience regained its voice.

Morgan was not a lusty serving maid trying to find a moment of pleasure in an otherwise exhausting and lonely existence. She was aunt to the Moreland heir, much loved by her sister and her in-laws alike, no matter her life was still likely exhausting and lonely.

She deserved far more than a furtive tumble that could leave her ruined or, perhaps worse, hastily married to a man from whom she'd sought only passing comfort.

A man who owed his first allegiance, and quite possibly his life, to the Crown.

❦

"Lie back." Archer peeled Morgan's grip from his cock—she knew only footmen's words for that lovely part of his body—and kissed her fingers. "Close your eyes and trust me."

The picture he made propped on his elbow beside her in the bed was both beautiful and erotic, despite the fact that he was still wearing his infernal breeches.

Beautiful, erotic, stern, and yet somehow beseeching too. She closed her eyes and felt him shifting on the mattress.

"Spread your legs, Morgan." As he spoke, he shifted himself and her limbs too, so Morgan's spread legs were draped over his thighs, giving her the impression he sat facing the headboard.

"I cannot touch you like this." Worse, she was intimately exposed to him, vulnerable even though the dying fire would not illuminate much.

"Which arrangement works to your advantage if I'm to acquit myself properly, believe me." He ran a hand down her midline, a slow, warm sweep of male palm against female midriff.

"How is it to my advantage?"

"I would lose my mind were you free to touch me." He tugged gently on first one nipple, then the other, and Morgan's ability to reason skipped off a few yards from where she lay.

"Again, please."

She did not have to be more specific. With his two hands, and her two breasts, he explored all manner of touches and pleasures with her. He used his mouth as well, creating backfires and crosscurrents of sensation as overwhelming as they were novel. When he paused and rested his hand very low on her belly, Morgan opened her eyes.

"This is… different." *Intimate* was what she meant, and *precious*, but she would not say either word with him looking at her so solemnly, lest she bring up what it was different from.

Furtive gropings in the stillroom, a stolen kiss or two between wet sheets flapping in a cold spring breeze, and such disappointment, no words had been necessary to convey it.

"*You* are different, Miss Morgan James."

She wanted to ask him what those intriguing words meant, what they meant to him, and what they meant to him in this context, but he brushed his thumb lower, over her curls, then lower still.

For all the kissing and fondling and cuddling she'd done with Bertrand, Morgan had never felt a man's bare fingers on her sex.

"That is…" not merely different. She cast around for a word to describe the impulse his touch raised, the impulse to move her hips, to grasp the spindles of the headboard above her pillow and to let soft, needy sounds come from her throat. "That is *marvelous*."

He smiled, the sternness ebbing from his features, leaving an expression breathtaking in both its intensity and its tenderness.

And then things progressed to something far better than marvelous. Morgan was soon hanging onto the headboard for dear life, her hips thrashing beneath Archer's hand. What happened next became unbelievably, wonderfully, *miraculously* better and better and better.

Then better still.

Long moments later, when Morgan could breathe again, when she could again join action and will, she reached for Archer and hauled him up over her body. "Archer Portmaine, you must hold me. Hold me tightly." She gripped him hard, shamelessly clinging to his solid warmth and locking her ankles at the small of his back.

He worked an arm under her neck and embraced her, his hold secure and sheltering, while Morgan tried to blink away tears.

"Go ahead and cry." His hand cradled the back of her head; his voice soothed her heart. "I'll hold you as long as you like, as long as you need me to."

This kindness, coupled with the feel of his lips brushing against her temple, turned a trickle into a deluge, until Morgan had to cease crying if only to assure herself she could.

"This has to be bad form, to take on so." She spoke steadily enough, but she didn't feel steady. She felt as if his weight was the only thing holding her body and soul together. He hadn't given her exactly what she'd wanted, but he'd given her something she'd needed desperately instead, and she ached from having been the recipient of such generosity.

"When two people choose to share with each other like this, there is no such thing as bad form." He sounded quite certain and damnably steady.

"Is that a royal decree?"

"If not, it should be. It's certainly an eternal verity with me. Would you like a handkerchief?" He nuzzled her eyebrows, as if asking the question with his nose.

"I don't want to move."

"I account my exertions a success." He stretched up without leaving her embrace entirely, and procured a handkerchief from the night table.

"I hate that you can form sentences and pronounce eternal verities, Archer. I cannot think…" She fell silent while he gently blotted the tears from her temple and cheeks. She tolerated it until he finished, then pitched into his chest. "I am undone."

"Is this the sort of undone that requires discussion?" His question was amused, rather than the wary inquiry another man might have made.

"And if it does require discussion?"

"Than a different arrangement is in order." He shifted off of her to stretch out on his back, and then it was Morgan who was hauled up over his chest to straddle him. He patted her bottom in a gesture that felt… friendly.

"Get cozy, Miss James, and talk to me."

This was worse than when they'd shared supper at the Braithwaite's ball. The words flowed from her in a steady stream, all about Bertrand, about the footmen who'd attempted to take more than Morgan was inclined to give, about missing the sound of human voices and church organs and even the sound of horses' hooves on cobbled streets.

He held her and he listened, until Morgan was fighting sleep to snatch another moment of nearness with him, until she went silent for longer and longer periods.

He held her until she was silent altogether, until she *was* asleep, and still, he held her.

❧

"I've told him all of it, Ellen." Morgan hadn't intended this disclosure, and certainly not to the woman sitting beside her on the Windham's garden swing.

Ellen readjusted the baby in her arms, while strains of lilting piano drifted out over the Windham back gardens—for Valentine visited not only his family, but also their pianos.

"All of it? You are not much past twenty, Morgan, and you've had but three Seasons. What *all* could there be to tell?"

The baby fussed in her mother's arms, making noises that communicated discontent for all they weren't very loud.

"I told Mr. Portmaine that when Anna and I fled Yorkshire we went into service. I told him I'd scrubbed my hands raw in the scullery and turned my fingernails black cleaning andirons." She'd also told him she'd emptied chamber pots, which was an appalling—and amazing—disclosure in itself. And as lovely as the physical intimacies were, this talking, sharing her life in words with Archer Portmaine for the past several nights, was to Morgan even more precious.

For the first time in years, Morgan looked forward to social events, knowing she'd spend at least part of her evening in a secluded corner with Archer.

Ellen set the swing rocking with her foot, and the baby went quiet. "I've washed many dishes, and so has much of the female half of England, I'll warrant. How did Mr. Portmaine receive your confidences?"

To compose an answer required forethought, because his reaction hadn't been anything Morgan might have anticipated.

"After I told him these things, when he bid me good night, he kissed my fingers as he handed me up into the coach. Really kissed them, and yet it wasn't indecent." None of what had passed between Morgan and Archer Portmaine had felt indecent, whether they were chatting in the corner of a ballroom or curled up in Morgan's bed.

Ellen rubbed her cheek over the baby's fuzzy crown. "Mr. Portmaine sounds like a good dinner companion."

"He's more than that." They'd not made love completely yet, though Morgan was sure they would, and soon. For now, it seemed more important to hold each other and to learn one another in words. "I've never spent so much time in conversation with a man and had it be so little work."

"Do you mean so little effort to hear him and follow the words, or so little effort to find things to talk about?"

An excellent question. "Both."

"This child is finally falling asleep. Let's stroll while we can." Ellen settled the baby into a basket thickly padded with blankets and linked an arm through Morgan's. "I'd like to check on His Grace's roses. It's still early, but the scent of even one bud is worth a trip into Town."

Maybe this was why Morgan enjoyed Ellen's company, for all that friendship with the woman's husband might have made such a thing awkward. "You are the only person I know who is as fascinated with scents as I am."

"Or maybe I'm just fascinated with moving among the flowers. When that child is truly fussy, it seems like days go by without my being able to turn loose of her. Valentine says all Windhams excel at cuddling, and—" Ellen fell silent as they moved down the graveled path, then she bent to untangle two stems of daisies. "If I recall Mr. Portmaine aright, he's quite good-looking."

"It's all right, Ellen. I know Valentine is an affectionate man—and a devoted husband. I could not respect him otherwise."

Ellen rose and smiled down at the daisies. "He treasures you, you know. At first I was jealous."

"You were jealous? *Of me?*"

"A wife becomes familiar, but I think in Valentine's mind, you will always be a little unknowable. He greatly admires how you coped with being deaf. He said it gave him courage when he faced difficulties of his own, and reassured him that if you, who were deaf for years, could still treasure music, his joy would never be entirely lost to him. I do not doubt he thinks of you as his muse."

Archer Portmaine had gone much further: he had admired her for how she'd coped with being deaf *and in service*, and yet, Morgan appreciated the trust Ellen placed in her as well.

"Men are easily impressed. The roses closest to blooming are down this way, behind that hedge."

They progressed a few steps in companionable silence before Ellen stopped short and cocked her head.

"She's awake. I knew it was too early for her nap." Ellen turned and headed back the way they'd just come, while Morgan held completely still and tried to hear the baby.

But try as she might, no matter how long she stood straining to hear, no matter how badly she wanted to detect the smallest sound from the crying child, Morgan heard nothing. Not the distant piano, not the fretful child. Not one sound.

⤫

"It's bad timing." Benjamin, the Earl of Hazelton, offered this observation along with a frown. Archer knew his cousin well enough to sense pity in that frown rather than judgment.

"It's bloody awful timing, but then I have never been known to fix my affections on the logical woman at the logical time." Archer continued his progress around the office Hazelton shared with his countess, and shook his head when Benjamin gestured with a decanter.

"You have no leads in the case?"

"We have nothing but leads, and each one takes us to some filthy rat hole in the stews, when my every instinct tells me that's the wrong direction to look. Such people can't get close to the royal family, and if we were looking at a simple assassination attempt, why all the whispers and hints?"

"Sit, Archer. Your perambulations are making me dizzy." Benjamin toed off his boots and set them neatly at the corner of the rug, then sank onto a long leather sofa. "I can ring for tea, if that will help, but I sense that as frustrated as you are with your current assignment, you're even more confused by your interest in Miss James."

Confused. A prosaic word for the ongoing riot that characterized Archer's feelings for Morgan James.

"She's…" Archer dropped onto the sofa beside his cousin. "She's different."

"Different how?"

Archer had not come around to his cousin's town house to solicit Benjamin's perspective on the baffling situation with Miss James. Surely a plot on the Regent's life ought to be of greater interest to both himself and his cousin—if in fact a plot on the Regent's life was afoot.

"Part of the difference is that she talks to me," Archer admitted. "She has the prettiest voice, low and musical, as if there's some Welsh in it, when I know it's just that North Country lilt. And the things she says…"

"All the ladies talk to you. It's part of what makes you such a good investigator." Ben sounded amused, a shot he could take from the safety of his recently acquired marital bliss.

"Don't be an ass. Your countess talks to you, and I'm certain you talk to her too. You tell her things you don't tell anybody, about your boyhood, your daily frustrations and hopes, your body's undignified little aches and betrayals. You tell her the fears and insecurities you used to not even admit to yourself."

Benjamin slouched down against the cushions and crossed his feet at the ankles, a sure sign some philosophical profundity was to follow. "How can you have these tête-à-têtes with Miss James, Archer, when any woman you're seen with might arguably become mixed up with this other business? The Crown's enemies aren't playing for farthing points."

"We're discreet." They were scandalous too.

Ben gave him a long, measuring look from beneath dark brows, but Archer wasn't about to admit he'd taken to a nightly climb into Morgan's rooms.

Much less into her bed.

"Of course you're discreet, but your interest in the woman is still a distraction you can't afford."

And there it was, probably the real reason Archer had sought his cousin's counsel: spending time with Morgan, any time at all, took hours away from a critical investigation and increased the likelihood she'd somehow become tangled up in a very dirty business.

"I know how to keep my focus, Benjamin." To emphasize his point, Archer appropriated a sip of Ben's cognac and set the glass out of Ben's reach.

"Like hell you can. Not this time." Benjamin was exercising a friend and family member's prerogative of simultaneously dispensing honesty and kindness when Archer needed both.

Though Archer wanted to do violence to his cousin's person anyway. "What makes you think I'm distracted?"

"It's only midnight, Archer, and you bear the scent of roses and spices. You've already been with her tonight. Your coat and hat were soaking wet, suggesting you'd not been lurking in a hackney, but rather, traipsing about Mayfair. Your shoes are a trifle muddy, and the mud is also streaked, as if you made an effort to wipe it off in the grass. My guess is you gained access to the ducal mansion through Moreland's prized rose gardens, spent time with the lady, then took yourself here so I might deliver a birching to your conscience and your common sense."

"This is your idea of a birching?"

"You have an alternative, you know."

"To quit the case?" Archer rose from the sofa, as if he'd get away from the idea itself, and stood staring at the rain dribbling down the window overlooking the dark garden. "If I quit, then when Prinny's laid out in state, I'll have myself to thank for the poor fellow never being king. What a legacy that makes."

"Archer, a woman who wanted to see Prinny dead would not have protected the Crown's investigator from exposure, as Miss James did at the Braithwaite ball."

Benjamin's words landed like soft lashes to Archer's frazzled nerves. "I should not have told you about that."

Without making a sound, Ben appeared at Archer's elbow. "She knows you're an investigator; she knows you were skulking about Braithwaite's personal domain for some reason other than theft. If she were a stupid woman, you would not be breaking and entering in the dead of night to gain access to her."

Stupidity on the part of the lady was not the problem. "I've told her enough to explain what I was about."

"Then you have two choices: you either bring her up-to-date on the investigation, so she knows enough to protect herself, or you cut her loose for the duration."

Archer stood staring at the window, watching the raindrops on the glass trickling down, down, always down into the dark of night. "Not quite, though you're close. The Frenchman has gone missing. We're assuming the worst."

"What does that mean?"

"It means my only option at this point is to lay enough of the situation at Miss James's pretty feet that she'll be safe, and *then* stay the hell away from her."

The pity in Benjamin's gaze was not veiled now. "Be careful. Be damned careful."

Archer grabbed his hat and coat and slipped out into the cold, dark, rainy night.

Four

"You and Mr. Portmaine make a lovely couple. Have you saved him a dance this evening?"

Ellen Windham's question held no guile, of that Morgan was certain. Morgan stood beside Ellen at the edge of the Winterthur ballroom, watching as Archer turned Maggie Windham, now Maggie Portmaine, Countess of Hazelton, down the room.

"He's a good dancer." A good dancer and an excellent listener.

"Are you considering his prospects, Morgan? I suspect he could keep you well enough."

Longing shot through Morgan, followed by a sharp pang of regret. "He's a gentleman without family to speak of, other than Hazelton. I doubt he's all that well set up." Not that his lack of wealth would matter.

Ellen turned to regard Morgan with a look that, oddly enough, reminded Morgan of Valentine Windham in the mood to Get to the Bottom of Something. "You should talk to Maggie about her cousin-in-law, or better still, talk to Hazelton about his cousin. I have no doubt Mayfair's best families pay dearly to have their little troubles dealt with quietly."

They probably did, and Archer was always turned out perfectly, complete with jeweled cravat pins and gold shirt studs and cuff links. He even smelled of excellent, expensive tastes.

"His prospects are not the problem." The music came to a close, and Archer bowed gracefully over Maggie's hand. "I am not inclined to marry, and no, lest you even think it for a moment, I am not pining for your husband."

"I know you are not."

"You do?"

Ellen was smiling, and not unkindly. "Valentine has been over in the corner for the entire set, letting Lady Winterthur pester him about taking a turn at the piano for her guests, and you haven't looked his way once."

"The hostesses always pester him. I think he half enjoys it."

"I quite agree, but the point is, you haven't taken your eyes off Mr. Portmaine."

Morgan took her eyes off Archer long enough to stare at Ellen. "I'm not looking at him now, am I?"

"Why not encourage his suit, Morgan? He's comely, a gentleman despite his investigations, and connected with the Windham family. Moreover, I think he's smitten with you. You could do much worse."

Sometimes, it was a mercy to be able to pretend not to hear well. "Shall we get some punch? It's quite warm in here."

They made their way toward the refreshments, and just as Morgan was about to accept a cup of sangria from a Winterthur footman, she caught a whiff of cedar and spices.

"Good evening, my lady, Miss James." Archer bowed very correctly, beaming what Morgan termed his Ballroom Bachelor Smile at her and Ellen both. "If your next dance is not spoken for, Miss James, would you do me the honor of a turn on the terrace? My need for fresh air grows pressing."

"Do, Morgan. I have it on good authority you spend too much time in stuffy, noisy ballrooms." Ellen took the cup of sangria when Morgan might have reached for it.

"From whom do you hear such things, Ellen?" Morgan asked.

"His Grace, among others. Take her outside, Mr. Portmaine, before the next sets form."

Ellen smiled at them both as if she were particularly pleased with herself, then strolled off in the direction of the minstrel's gallery.

"The Windham menfolk have the knack of marrying ladies who are as pretty as they are dear." Archer winged his arm at Morgan. "Would you rather be dancing, Miss James?"

The question was rhetorical when Morgan had already confessed that the background noise in a ballroom made it one of the most difficult environments she dealt with.

"I will enjoy a respite out-of-doors." She couldn't quite dredge up her own Company Smile, not even when they were seated on a low bench amid the fragrant abundance of the bouquets gracing the Winterthur terrace.

"Are we far enough from the noise for you?" Archer asked.

"Not nearly, but we're as far as we can get without causing gossip. You look tired."

"I am tired. My days and nights are getting mixed up, and I miss you."

Morgan had wondered. After five nights of spending hours in each other's arms, Archer had been absent for the past two nights. When he hadn't come gliding into her boudoir on moonlight and shadows, Morgan told herself that was for the best. If Archer did not maintain his distance, before too much longer, she would be begging him to make love to her, properly and completely.

Improperly.

And then begging him to leave.

Archer sat close enough that they touched from knee to shoulder, though

Morgan wished they might risk holding hands. "Will you tell me the truth about something, Mr. Portmaine?"

"Something in particular?

The comment was meant to be teasing, but she'd also felt him tense up along her side. "Yes, something in particular. The first night we met, after the concert, were you working on the same project that consumes you now?"

"I've been working on it for weeks."

More of a yes than a no, and a yes with an edge of frustration to it. "Would you make more progress on that project if you were getting more rest?"

He did not answer immediately, which meant he understood her oblique question. "Perhaps *you* are in need of more rest, Miss James? You do look a trifle fatigued."

His tone remained solicitous while his expression became guarded. Were she stronger, she'd smile at him and agree cheerily that too many late-night diversions were not good for a lady's health or peace of mind. He'd agree with equal good cheer, and whatever it was that grew between them in the small hours of the morning would be allowed to die an unremarked, civil death.

As it must—though not quite yet.

She was not strong enough for that, so she did not close the door between them. "I will likely turn in early tonight. My dreams lately have been very sweet."

He studied her by the torchlight. "Mine as well. I'll be guided by your example and also take my leave of the Winterthurs before supper."

They rose shortly thereafter and wandered back into the ballroom, just another couple exchanging pleasantries in the soft evening air. They left the establishment within eight minutes of each other, careful not to share even a single glance as they climbed into separate coaches.

◈

What in the bloody *hell* had Morgan been asking him?

Archer used the privacy of his coach to change into a black shirt and waistcoat, worn black riding breeches, and black boots. His hands discarded clothing, did up buttons, and effected the change of wardrobe without him having to concentrate, and that was fortunate.

When a man was screwing up his resolve to talk a lady into remaining a safe distance from him, he did not expect the lady to drum him out of her boudoir on her own initiative.

Morgan was up to something. Perhaps she was ready to move on; perhaps she had tired of their intimacies. Archer certainly had not—he did not think he ever would.

He was surprised to no little degree to realize that by intimacies, he had not referred exclusively to erotic pleasures, but rather to the sense of closeness that characterized all of their dealings. In some way, the closeness was part and parcel of Morgan's poor hearing, though he could not fathom exactly how.

For a long time, Archer stood in the Moreland gardens, planning what he'd say to her.

We fear the game has turned deadly.

Somebody follows me at least half the time, and I don't want him following me to your bedroom.

This should all be wrapped up in a matter of weeks...

Except he had no guarantee of that, and after this threat had been thwarted, there would be others.

He shoved that miserable conclusion aside and started up the tree that rose along Morgan's balcony. As always, her door was slightly ajar, and the coals from her hearth burned low, giving her bedroom a cozy, comfortable warmth.

"You change in your coach, don't you?"

Morgan remained on her chaise as Archer advanced into the room. The picture of feminine serenity, she folded a book closed on her lap and watched as he tugged off his boots. Usually, she embraced him before he'd taken three steps.

"I change in my coach and in other places as well. I keep all manner of disguises in convenient locations."

The trade secrets tumbled out around her, another reason to put some distance between them—for now. A lady had no business learning the ins and outs of investigating.

"I won't keep you long." She got to her feet, the sight of her in a sheer silk nightgown nearly knocking Archer on his backside. The garment wasn't even a decent summer length, but left her ankles, calves, and even her knees exposed to the firelight.

"I'm not in *any* hurry to leave, Miss James. Come here and greet me properly, or I'll tackle you where you stand."

Her lips quirked as she bundled into his embrace, the warmth and sweetness of her bringing a peculiar sort of relief.

"Are you in anticipation of the female complaint? Your mood is off, my dear."

She buried her nose against his chest. "You are as bad as the footmen in Westhaven's house. They had all manner of vulgar terms for a lady's indisposition."

"It deserves vulgar terms. You're dodging the question."

He propped his chin on her crown—she was the perfect height for it—and prepared to jolly her out of whatever megrim she'd fallen into. For the hundredth time, he told himself that difficult discussions could be put off just a little while longer.

"I am not indisposed, not the way you mean. When will you make love with me, Archer? Really make love?"

❧

Esther, Duchess of Moreland, turned to greet her husband as he joined her on their private balcony. "Percival, good evening. I thought you'd be up late drafting that infernal bill."

"It's late enough." Moreland came closer and slipped his arms around her waist from behind. "You are pretty at any hour, my love, but moonlight particularly becomes you."

She leaned back against him, loving the solid, lean strength of him. "You are shameless."

"In my preference for your company? Absolutely. What draws you out-of-doors at this hour, Esther?"

She had decided to tell him. They were in each other's confidence and had been for more than thirty years—and he probably knew already anyway. "We have a housebreaker, Percy."

Percival snuggled her closer. "What is the world coming to? Must I snatch up a stout poker and start beating the intruder about the head in the family tradition?"

"This housebreaker seems inclined to plunder only the treasures in Morgan's rooms, and the one time I saw him leaving, he was empty-handed."

Percival chuckled, for which Esther loved him dearly. "Young Portmaine is calling at unfashionable hours?"

Esther turned in his arms to regard him by moonlight. "How did you know it was he?"

"I gave him a subtle, backhanded nudge, and he rather took off at a gallop in Morgan's direction. Do you think they'd suit?"

Percival's idea of a nudge often bore a close resemblance to the kick of a sturdy mule. And yet, Portmaine struck Esther as a man who neither trifled with young innocents nor accepted suggestions merely because they'd been made by a meddling—if well-meaning—duke.

"Whether they suit might be a moot question if Morgan's common sense is not asserting itself."

"They're young," Percival whispered against Esther's neck. "It's the loveliest time of year, and they're lonely. I'm lonely too, though a bit old to have such a pretty wife."

"Shameless and ridiculous." His lips grazed the spot on her nape that made Esther positively melt, even after all these years. "So you won't intervene?"

"I thought I already had."

"I suppose you have at that. Shall we retire, Your Grace?"

"Soon." He turned her by the shoulders, bringing her against his body. "If you aren't averse to the notion, I'd like to enjoy a little more of the moonlight with my beloved duchess."

Such romance in a young man had been enough to sweep Esther off her feet. In a man of mature years, it kept her lingering on the shadowed balcony in Percival's arms much longer than she'd intended.

❧

"What do you call lovemaking, if climbing into your bed and sharing all manner of intimate pleasure with you doesn't qualify?"

Though Archer knew what Morgan meant. They'd not indulged in actual coitus. Rogering. Intercourse. Swiving. The King's English included a ribald horde of terms for the *marital* act.

"Not the tame sort of lovemaking," she said against his throat. "The kind a lady prepares for with vinegar and sponges."

"I see." In his mind's eye, Archer *saw* himself, freed for once of every stitch of clothing, even his breeches. He saw the lithe, naked beauty of Morgan James entwined with him on the sheets.

He saw his future, and a world of trouble preventing him from reaching for it.

"We have to talk." He eased his arms from Morgan's waist and led her to the bed.

They undressed each other, a ritual they'd fallen into before the third night of their clandestine trysting had passed. He untied the bows of her nightgown; she unbuttoned his shirt and took his cuff links and watch—both finished in matte black—to put on the night table.

"I'm not much interested in talking," Morgan said. When Archer sat on the bed in only his breeches, she knelt between his legs. "Not yet."

While he tried to muster some restraint, she undid his falls and rearranged his clothing until she could draw his cock into her hands. He gritted his teeth and endured her generosity, though it tested him sorely. She was good with her hands, knowing to linger on that spot under the tip, but not too long. She caressed his stones with just the right pressure, and she leaned close enough that Archer could feel her breath on his thighs.

He envisioned her having to learn this skill to preserve herself from intimacies of a more forced nature, and the thought brought a lurching pause to his arousal. "You should not be giving me these attentions if they're something the footmen required of you."

She paused, her mouth about two inches from his cock, Archer's sanity about two inches from expiring. "Nobody *required* anything of me. It's something I'm learning with you, Archer. I've a mind to learn a few more things, too."

She dipped her head and licked him, a long, wet swipe of her tongue up his shaft and then—God in heaven—a flourish around the tip.

"Let me get out of my breeches." He was half-strangled with equal parts anticipation and self-restraint, but he managed to peel himself out of the last of his clothing and drag her over him onto the bed. "I *must* kiss you."

Some desperate part of his brain tried to argue that what he *must* do was talk to her, explain to her that their clandestine trysting, and even their public waltzes, were going to have to stop for a time.

Only for a time.

She kissed him, kissed him as if in the next hour they were going away to separate wars. Without letting their mouths part, Archer got her nightgown off and anchored both hands on her hips.

Morgan straddled him, which was a fine, fine inspiration, but when her hand glided down between their bodies, Archer realized her intent. He caught her fingers before she could bring his engorged arousal into her body.

"Morgan, wait."

"I have been waiting. I have waited night after night. I don't want to wait." She sounded not determined so much as... upset.

She'd used the vinegar and sponges, he was *almost* confident of that. He and she were going to have to separate for a time—he knew that too. With equal certainty, he knew he was naked in bed with the woman he intended to marry.

The woman he loved. The knowledge landed in the dark expanse of his thoughts like a sunbeam, gentle, inexorable, and sweet.

"Slowly, then. As slowly as we can." He shifted his grip to stroke his fingers over her breasts. "I want to savor this, to wallow in the beauty of it. I want it to echo in my memory... forever."

She closed her eyes, taking from him the only hints he could gather as to the desperation driving her, but she did not take him in her hand again.

"Morgan, shall I?" He flexed his hips, brushing his cock over her sex to complete the question. She nodded once and curled forward to brace herself over his chest on her hands.

"Kiss me, Morgan."

Archer had always thought lust should be a merry thing, mostly pleasure and affection, generously shared and happily recalled. With Morgan, joining his body to hers became a *reverent* undertaking, the tenderness of it nearly eclipsing the arousal.

He leaned up to capture her mouth in a soft kiss, even as he used his hand to stroke the head of his cock along the damp crease of her sex. "Kiss me, Morgan James, and let me kiss you and love you in return."

She touched her lips to his, her mouth open, and Archer began a gentle invasion of her every sense. Morgan smiled while he traced her lips with his tongue and her sex with his cock. By languorous degrees, he effected penetration above, then began to advance toward the same goal below.

Morgan lifted her mouth from his and went still, as if listening with her very body. Archer stopped teasing them both, stopped flirting with heaven, and let himself flex minutely into her heat.

He retreated and drove forward again, letting her body glove him by excruciating, ecstatic degrees. She was snug and hot, and so lovely, so unutterably lovely.

"Tell me this is what you want, Morgan. Tell me I am who you want." The growling creature who'd spoken was a man at the limit of his control, and yet Archer forced himself to keep still as he posed the question.

She brushed a hand over his heart. "I want this, with *you*, Archer Portmaine. Now, *please*..." She curled down to his chest, and he wrapped his arms around her.

In the instant before desire wrested the reins from his discipline, Archer tried to name what he'd seen in her eyes. Tenderness and desperation, certainly, but not the sort of knowing arousal he might have expected.

Morgan shifted on him, anchored her body more snugly to his, and anything resembling cerebration flew from Archer's grasp. Carefully, he pushed himself the smallest, most maddening increment into her body then retreated.

In the same careful manner, Morgan accepted him. Progress was slow at first, but after several moments, Archer was hilted inside her, his cock throbbing and his stones aching with urgency.

"Move, Morgan. I'm not going to last, and I want you—"

She shifted her hips, a slow, voluptuous sweep of pleasure and lust. Archer held still while she developed a rhythm, then moved in counterpoint to her when her breathing picked up. He managed to get a hand on her breast, and she lifted up enough that he could tease her nipple while their tempo gradually increased.

"Archer…" She was pleading, and then she was crying, and then she was coming hard, her body fisting around his cock while he drove himself into her in tight, sharp thrusts.

His own satisfaction was an afterthought, a blossoming of sensation when Morgan was again moving on him slowly, the occasional aftershock shuddering through her. He felt completion approaching but did not allow himself to return to the more emphatic passion of moments earlier. Instead, he kissed her, hilted himself in her body, and let the end come on a slow, unstoppable rush of pleasure that became more intense than if he'd been thrashing and pounding his way through it.

They would marry. They would marry and learn how to manage this great passion, learn how to be together like this and lose their souls to each other every night.

Hell, every night, most mornings, and even some afternoons.

All he had to do first was thwart a few enemies of the Crown, explain the situation to various Windham males who might think themselves Morgan's protectors, and then convince the lady herself she belonged with him forever.

A short list, the last task being far more important than the other two.

"Archer?"

"My love?" He cradled her closer and stroked a hand over her hair, wondering if they'd still make love like this when their children were grown.

"I want you to leave, and I never want you to come back."

As her words penetrated the fog of pleasure and sweetness in Archer's brain, he realized what he'd seen in her eyes as he'd joined his body with hers: despair. Where there should have been passion and joy, what he'd seen in Morgan's eyes had been despair.

❧

"If my children have taught me nothing else, it's that unsolicited advice is wasted air, at best, and bad will in the making, more often." The roses were past their prime, but His Grace paused and feigned an interest in the surrounding flowers—while making sure Portmaine *was* listening. "Nonetheless, I feel compelled to warn you, Portmaine: You can't go on like this."

The younger man turned glacially blue eyes on the duke. "The royal family is the target, we're sure of it. Higgins intercepted a note intended, we think, for somebody in the Foreign Office. I'm not about to let up now."

His tone was as hard as the marble bench they occupied among the duchess's flowers.

"Oh, the Foreign Office, as if that den of intrigue *wouldn't* have something to do with this." Moreland sat back and waited, having learned patience from his children as well.

"We're close, Your Grace, and if I have to haunt every social function every night for the rest of the Season, and follow every damned lord to his mistress's house, or every lady to her milliner's shop, then I'll do it."

Something had shifted in Portmaine's demeanor in recent days. He'd gone from dependable to dedicated, from careful to calculating. The transition was not pretty, like the blooming roses turning to bracken and thorns were not pretty.

"And how long do you think you can work at this pace without your opponents finding you in a weak moment? How long do you think to serve your Regent with exhaustion and carelessness?"

Portmaine's head came up, a battle light in his eyes. "Carelessness, Your Grace?"

"Sooner or later, somebody will catch you falling asleep at keyholes, young man, or worse."

Exhaustion was indeed taking a toll, because Portmaine's gaze traveled over the gardens and up to a certain balcony, a silent admission if ever His Grace had seen one. "Somebody already has, Your Grace."

Portmaine scrubbed a hand over handsome, drawn features and hunched forward, bracing his elbows on his spread knees. His posture was rife with weariness, perhaps even defeat.

"I have investigated you, Your Grace."

The Papists had a name for this "Oh-my-God, I-am-heartily-sorry..." business. "Of course, you have. I have investigated you, too. Precautionary measures are what pass for the civilities in the dark business you're engaged in now."

Gratifying, to see he'd surprised such a clever young man. A bee went lazily inventorying the few flowers not yet budded out.

"I have been in your home without your leave, after dark, and I'm hoping others will think I was simply nosing about in your affairs."

A chill slithered down the ducal spine. "Portmaine, explain yourself."

"I have come and gone from your domicile by dark of night on more than few occasions, Your Grace. I am not proud to admit this."

"You are not ashamed either, I daresay. Was your investigation so very thorough, then, Portmaine?"

"It was, but that took only a single visit. The rest of the time..."

Young people were given to dramatics, but Portmaine wasn't being dramatic. Beneath his cool demeanor, something dark and desperate lurked.

"Her Grace saw you, my boy. She and I trusted to your honor and Morgan's good sense. You are no longer committing felonies on my property, I hope."

"I am not, Morgan's *good sense* having carried the day, but I fear it's too late."

Too late didn't bode well at all. "Spell it out, man."

"Somebody followed me the last time I visited Miss James, Your Grace. From the depth of the tracks left in the mud under the tree, I'm guessing they waited a good long time, until I left, then followed me home as well. I was distracted, exhausted, as you say, and careless. I hope I have not endangered you, or worse, endangered Miss James, with my folly."

This was not good, but it explained Portmaine's absence of a late night— also his desperation. A dozen plots might blossom against a monarch, and it was nothing more than a challenge for a good investigator, but a smitten swain could not abide danger stalking his lady.

"I would offer to thrash you, Portmaine, but your conscience has no doubt flagellated you ceaselessly. If you fear you've lead the enemy to my doorstep, then what in God's name brought you here in the broad light of day? Nothing else would confirm my hand in this investigation as clearly as the conference we're having right now."

Something approaching a smile touched Portmaine's lips, though it wasn't a friendly sort of something. "I hope you're wrong, Your Grace. I hope I can turn recent events into a way to solve the case, and sooner rather than later."

"You have my undivided attention."

❦

To sit among the Moreland roses without staring at Morgan's balcony, to make awkward confessions to His Grace, and to convince the duke to comply with an outlandish scheme had taken the last ounce of Archer's resolve.

He was beyond tired, beyond exhausted, and into that state soldiers knew well, of curiously detached, deliberate functioning. He was no longer a man, he was a mechanical toy in human form, and he liked it that way.

Mechanical toys did not have broken hearts—they had no hearts at all.

As Moreland sauntered off toward the mews, Archer permitted himself one more glance at Morgan's balcony. He saw her there as she'd been last week, her nightgown a pale splash against the moonlight when Archer had taken his leave.

She'd been crying silently and trying to ignore her own tears. Even in his anger at her rejection, he'd hurt for her.

Her explanation had been baffling: she could not marry him, and she could not trust herself to behave decorously around him in the future. She was sorry for having used him shamelessly, but further dealings would only put off an inevitable parting.

She had begged him to leave, and thus had begun a week of flitting from ball to musicale to wherever Morgan James was not. Archer listened at keyholes, drowsed in smoking rooms, lurked in gardens, and followed up every hint of a wisp of a ghost of a possible lead.

Until two things became clear to him.

First, he needed to dispatch the threat to the Crown.

Second, he had better execute that task with all possible haste, for if longing for Morgan didn't kill him, his enemies well might.

Five

"IF YOU CALL ME POPPET, I SHALL KILL YOU." MORGAN SURPRISED HERSELF WITH both the sincerity of her threat and the fact that she'd made it to the man she'd once believed herself fated to love for all time—and in his own father's library.

Valentine Windham lowered himself to a rocking chair at right angles to Morgan's perch on the sofa. "I haven't called you poppet for three years, but it's generally considered a term of endearment. What are you reading?"

She didn't know. She glanced at the book she'd been holding. "Byron, the silly twit."

"Naughty twit, in any case. I might set his poetry to music one day."

Which was relevant to the price of tea in China, how?

"I suspect you think of music at times most people can't hold a coherent thought in their heads." She hadn't meant to glower at him, but really, how did Ellen stand him? When Archer Portmaine kissed a woman, he wasn't humming some theme under his breath as Morgan suspected Valentine did. When Archer watched Morgan, his fingers weren't twitching with a melody known only to him as Valentine's had on many occasions.

"Your mood is off, my dear."

The very words Archer had used. Morgan got up and shoved the book onto a random shelf.

Valentine's dark eyebrow arched in a gesture that put Morgan in mind of His Grace, and he remained seated, the picture of calm, which was also a ploy favored by His Grace. "Are you in a taking because of Archer Portmaine's absence from your dance card?"

She threatened murder, and her dearest friend said she was *in a taking.* "Mr. Portmaine is a very amiable fellow. I'm sure the other ladies are enjoying his attentions."

Though given the stricken expression Morgan had seen on Archer's face in her bedroom a week ago, she doubted Archer had mustered his Ballroom Bachelor Smile yet. His ability to dissemble was good, but not good enough to hide the terrible hurt Morgan had dealt him.

"Morgan, what's wrong?"

Morgan whirled around to find Valentine Windham had silently crossed the room and stood staring down at her, his expression not the least distracted. "Nothing is wrong, except certain men think they can drop in of a weekday afternoon and pry into my affairs at will."

"Shall I call him out for you?" Valentine spoke softly, his green eyes lit with unholy determination. "Westhaven makes a decent second, though Hazelton might not approve. If Portmaine has offended you, Morgan, cast the slightest aspersion—"

Morgan stopped him with a hand over his fool mouth. "Nothing like that. Desist, Valentine, please. I sent him away in every sense."

Morgan endured a long, silent scrutiny, and then another quiet question.

"From what or whom do you think you're protecting him? You care for that handsome, skinny bastard, I know you do, and in some confounded, convoluted way, you think to set him from you for his own good. I suspect he's mixed up in one of His Grace's intrigues, which has nothing to say to anything. If he cares for you, you simply forbid his skulking about, and the man will come panting to your heels… Oh, for God's sake."

Morgan blinked furiously as Valentine dangled a monogrammed handkerchief before her eyes.

"It isn't his fault, Valentine. He's a good man, a dear man, and I thought—"

Damn and blast. She snatched the handkerchief from him, then let him lead her to the sofa.

"Archer Portmaine lurks about Mayfair, collecting secrets," Val said from the sideboard. "He then darts in and out of the slums and stews to collect more. He is not dear, he is dangerous. If he broke your heart, he is also dead, or as good as."

Morgan blotted her tears, the urge to scream now replaced by the urge to break something heavy over Valentine's head—though a smack to his fingers would likely get his attention more effectively.

He passed her a glass with an inch of liquid in the bottom. "Drink this, and don't argue. If you're not going to let me draw Portmaine's cork, then you will at least tell me what's amiss."

Morgan took a sip of aromatic brandy, the fruity, apple-rich fire of it easing something inside her. "No wonder your sisters are so formidable. They've had to contend with four more brothers in addition to you. You take after your father, you know."

"Flattery, Miss James, will not spare you my interrogation."

She turned a glower on him as he stood by the sofa, fists on his lean hips, a depth of concern in his eyes she had not anticipated. "I'm fine. I will be fine."

He settled beside her when she'd intended that he take himself off. "Sometimes even when we're fine, we could use a friend to help us sort out our difficulties. This is your good side, correct?"

The side she could hear better on. She took another sip of brandy and wondered if Her Grace, having raised nine more children like Valentine, cultivated a taste for spirits.

"I don't have a good side. I have a less-bad side. Lord Fairly told me to think of it as having a good side and a better side, but the truth is I have a bad side and a worse side."

She made this confession to her drink, while beside her, Valentine tossed pillows to the rug. "Are you losing your hearing again? Is that what this is about? You don't want to saddle Portmaine with a deaf wife?"

Morgan set the drink down and tried to push some words past her lips. Damn Valentine for being so perceptive when he ought by rights to be off somewhere composing a sonata Morgan might never hear. Damn him for putting an arm around her shoulders, and damn him most of all for being her friend.

She wanted to curse at him, to curse at him roundly, as His Grace could do when the idiots in the Lords fiddled while Rome burned. She wanted to rant and bellow and carry on—to sound out her misery for all to hear—but instead, she pitched hard into her friend's chest and silently cried into his handkerchief.

⌘

"Miss James, a pleasure." Archer bowed over Morgan's hand and held it in his when she tried to snatch it away. Under the guise of imparting some tidbit of gossip, he leaned closer. "Unless you want to spend the rest of the evening without one of your gloves, you will dance with me."

She nodded, which was fortunate. Even holding her gloved hand had Archer's vitals in an uproar. He winged his arm at her and led her to the middle of the dance floor.

He bowed. "You do not look rested, Miss James."

She sank into a perfect curtsy and came up with a glorious smile. "You look exhausted, Mr. Portmaine, and as if you're off your feed. Perhaps this is why you're ignoring my request that you not approach me under any circumstance."

They swayed into the rhythms of the waltz. "I've missed you, Morgan." He made sure to look directly at her as he spoke, because the ballroom was noisy and they were turning down the side nearest the minstrel's gallery.

She tramped on his foot, which didn't hurt so much as it disturbed his rhythm.

"I cannot say the same, Mr. Portmaine. I am perfectly content without you bothering me at all hours." Her usually steady alto bore a hint of tension and was pitched higher than normal.

Archer turned her through the first corner, and it seemed to him she might have clung to him a bit for balance.

Or something.

"You are going to marry me," he said quietly, clearly, and very near her ear. "Though first, I have to get other matters tidied up."

"I cannot marry you, no matter how many other matters you tidy up. Stop being absurd, or I'll leave you here in the middle of the dance floor."

"That would actually help matters, but before you stomp off in a rush, please be aware that things might get sticky before this night is through, and I want you well away from here."

"You're sending me home?"

She might have tried for indignation, but Archer heard worry in her voice. He leaned a bit closer, gathering the scent of roses and spices. "I am asking you to leave early, or if you must be stubborn, then at least do not believe what you see, Morgan. We'll have His Grace home by dawn, even if the Home Office indulges in unnecessary dramatics."

"But what—?"

He gave her the same slow wink he'd offered the first time she'd laid eyes on him, and then fell silent. As the music moved them along, he could see her mental mill wheel turning.

"Archer, are you in danger?"

Ah, to see the concern in her eyes and hear his name on her lips. "You would care if I were?"

Her eyes narrowed, and the worry vanished. "Of course, I would care."

"One wondered. Not for very long, but one did wonder."

"Whatever that means."

If he said one more word, he'd be down on his knees before her, proposing publicly, and tonight of all nights he needed to focus on the task at hand rather than the woman in his arms. All too soon, the music drew to a close, and Morgan asked him to return her to Ellen's side.

Except Lady Ellen was nowhere to be seen, which meant Archer would part with the woman he loved most in the whole world under the sternly watchful eye of Valentine Windham.

Archer hung about and chatted inanely until Ellen came swanning along from the card room and collected Morgan to make a fourth at whist.

"I need to talk to you." Lord Valentine fairly spat the words.

"I most assuredly do not need to talk to you, my lord." *Not tonight, most especially not now, possibly not ever.*

"Yes, you do." Windham aimed a glower at the ladies' retreating backs. "You're going to marry Morgan James if I have to kick your sorry arse up the aisle at St. George's."

"That might suffice to motivate me and bruise your toes to a significant degree, but how do you propose to gain the young lady's cooperation?"

Windham's brows drew down, but before he said a word, the Duke of Moreland's voice rang out over the din of dozens of conversations.

"You want to question *me*? You want His *Grace*, the Duke of Moreland, to voluntarily present him*self* at the Home Office? You, sir, are impertinent and a damned fool if you think a peer of the realm is going to submit to the tomfoolery that passes for state business at the Home Office. The secretary himself shall hear about this."

"What in God's name?" Windham started off in the direction of His Grace so quickly Archer barely managed to lay a hand on the taller man's arm.

"Let it play out. His Grace's liberty is not at risk."

"Not at risk? You heard that imbecile," Windham whispered furiously.

"You interfere now, and His Grace will not thank you." Something of the truth of that sentiment must have penetrated Windham's thick skull, because he turned an emerald glare on Archer.

"Mind you be right, Portmaine, or there won't be enough of you left for Miss James to marry."

Musicians were reported to be a flighty lot.

Windham fell silent as His Grace proceeded to dress down the Home Office functionary who'd been so foolish as to confront the Duke of Moreland in a public setting. Before His Grace concluded, the entire ballroom was listening to the exchange.

"…mine hostess will surely forgive me if I take premature leave of a gathering where such as yourself are permitted access to their betters." His Grace turned to survey the ballroom with a gimlet gaze. "My lords, my ladies, I bid you good night." He swept away from the dance floor, pausing only long enough to deliver a magnificent scowl and an audible sniff in Archer's direction.

"Threat to the realm, indeed."

Moreland brushed past both Archer and Lord Valentine, collected the duchess, and bellowed for his coach, while the ballroom erupted into a roar of conversations.

Windham shot Archer a look worthy of the duke himself, then stalked off in the direction of the card room. Pausing only long enough to be sure Lady Braithwaite was being watched by other eyes, Archer followed after Windham, not caring who saw or what they thought of his unseemly haste.

⌘

"Some commotion has interrupted the dancing." Ellen craned her neck to look, but didn't put down her cards. "The orchestra has fallen silent."

Morgan couldn't have heard much of the music at this distance, but she could see people crowding into the doorway to gawk in the direction of the dance floor.

"My dears, you'll excuse us." The two dowagers who had no doubt been cheating their way to a victory at whist hustled away, turbans huddled together in anticipation of some wonderful gossip.

"That's His Grace," Ellen said, putting her cards down. "He's in a taking about something. Oh, I must find Valentine this instant. Will you be all right?"

Morgan waved her away with one hand and started collecting the abandoned cards. "I'll find you."

If being deaf spared one ballroom dramas, maybe losing her hearing again would not be such a terrible thing. What did gossip ever contribute to one's life after all? Morgan stacked the deck tidily and caught sight of the only other people in the room who were not pressed in the doorway or trying to push through the crowd into the ballroom.

One was Lord Braithwaite, whose demeanor Morgan would have characterized as benign and avuncular. The other fellow would have been altogether nondescript—sandy hair, medium height, unremarkable evening attire—but for the grip he had on Lord Braithwaite's arm and the fire in his eyes.

"It *must* be tonight!" Morgan did not hear the words, so much as she saw them forming on the man's lips. "Now is the perfect opportunity, when suspicion has fallen on no less than the Duke of Moreland himself."

Lord Braithwaite's words were harder to discern, because he was in profile to Morgan, but his posture and the shake of his head suggested he was not agreeing with the other man's importuning.

"My lord, we must act tonight. We could wait months for another chance like this. Suspicion will follow Moreland and his family, and the thing will be done. His Royal Highness will reward our quick thinking, mark me."

Braithwaite's indecision crumbled, as evidenced by the nod of his head and what might have been an admission that, "Now is the time."

His Royal Highness would reward them? The Regent was styled His Royal Highness, but what could George have to do with any underhanded business? While Morgan mentally sorted through the various monarchs and dignitaries who might be suborning treachery on English soil, the nondescript man spoke again, but try as she might, Morgan could not discern every word.

"…small… Vichy… wet… coast."

Lord Braithwaite nodded again while Morgan tried to divide her attention between shuffling the deck of cards and watching what was said in the dimly lit corner.

Her mistake was the result of nerves. She'd learned to play cards only after she'd lost her hearing. Until her hearing had been restored, she hadn't known that cards shuffled between two hands made a loud, slapping sound, then a softer riffling noise as they were manipulated back into a single stack.

At the louder sound, the shorter man glanced up sharply. "Who the devil is that, and why isn't she out gawking at the debacle in the ballroom?"

☙

Archer found Morgan in the card room several minutes after His Grace had made such a stirring exit. She sat off in a corner at a little lacquered escritoire, scribbling furiously with a pencil on some foolscap.

"Miss James? Have you taken a sudden notion to catch up on your correspondence?"

She apparently hadn't heard him, because she kept writing. Archer went down on his haunches, determined not to let her ignore him. "Miss James, is aught amiss?"

Her expression was not the vaguely irritated mask Archer had expected. Her eyes held panic, for all her features were calm and intensely focused on the paper.

"I'm almost done. Give me a moment." She wrote a few more words then sat back. "I must speak with you privately, Mr. Portmaine. Now, if you please."

"I thought you never wanted to see me again?"

"Archer, *please*. This is urgent."

So was finding Lord Braithwaite, who had last been seen in the card room. Archer studied Morgan's features. So pretty, *and so worried*.

"Come." He rose, held out a hand, and assisted her to her feet. The only hope of quiet was out-of-doors, so he led her through French doors to a side terrace. "Now what is this urgent matter?"

"I heard Lord Braithwaite and another man speaking a few moments ago."

"What did they say?" And where the *hell* had Braithwaite gotten off to?

"I'm not sure. I was watching them speak, you understand. I could not hear much, I could only see, and I can't be sure what they said, but I'm sure that I must tell you."

While Morgan recited what she'd caught of the conversation, Archer paced before her, four strides this way, turn, four strides that way. "And they said *tonight*? You're sure they said tonight?"

"Several times. I could hear somewhat, but mostly I saw."

"And Vichy?" What had a spa town in central France to do with anything?

"I'm almost certain that's what he said, but again, watching people speak is not an exact business. Is this important?"

"None of the royal dukes are planning a progress through Auvergne, are they?"

Morgan nibbled a thumbnail. "I don't know. They're of an age to do that, but I doubt the Duke of Kent would leave his duchess so soon after her confinement."

"Vichy..."

Something was struggling to emerge from the back of Archer's tired brain. Something important, something that would get this infernal business taken care of.

"Not necessarily Vichy," Morgan said, her gaze following him as he paced. "It might have been victory without much emphasis on the *o*, or Vickery, or Vicky, or—"

"Vickery? I doubt Lord Vickery is plotting against the Crown."

"Archer..." Morgan brought him to a halt by virtue of grabbing both of his hands. "I don't know if this means anything, but Kent's new daughter, Alexandrina Victoire, is called *Vicky* by her doting family. Her Grace went to see the baby not two weeks ago and said Princess *Vicky* was such a dear, darling little thing one could hardly see her as an addition to the royal succession."

God in heaven. "She might never rule. There could be other possibilities." Please, God, let there be some other possibilities.

Except this had the feel of a brilliant insight, the feel of something that put all the puzzle pieces into a single, coherent picture of mischief and mayhem in high places. "His Royal Highness might refer to Leopold of Saxe-Coburg. If he's grieving the loss of Princess Charlotte and their son badly enough, such a scheme might appeal to him."

"Archer, Princess Vicky is a tiny baby. A tiny, helpless baby. You must stop this."

"I shall." But he had to do something else first.

He gathered Morgan into his arms and brought her close, then slanted his mouth over hers. For an instant, for a blessed, intoxicating instant, she yielded and kissed him back. Then a large hand clamped onto Archer's shoulder and spun him away from Morgan.

"By God, I ought to meet you." Valentine Windham's palm walloped across Archer's cheek, leaving a stinging welt in its wake. "You don't take such liberties with a decent young woman where any telltale or gossip might see you."

"Valentine, damn you," Morgan bit out. "It isn't like that. Why for once couldn't you go play your infernal piano?"

Windham's face showed consternation. "Because this idiot needs to be taught some manners if he's to join the family."

Morgan cradled Archer's cheek against her palm. "He is not joining the family."

"I am too."

"He is too."

Both men spoke at the same time. Morgan dropped her hand and looked like she was about to fly into a scold. Archer could only hope Windham would get the brunt of it.

"Morgan, where did Braithwaite go?"

"He and the other man left through the door we just used, possibly headed for the mews."

"Tell His Grace what's afoot, and have Windham take you home. I love you." He planted a smacking kiss on her mouth, offered Windham a slight, ironic bow, and left his musical lordship warily regarding Morgan's mulish expression.

Six

"A PLOT TO KIDNAP SUCH A YOUNG CHILD HAD TO HAVE BEEN UNDERTAKEN with much forethought," Her Grace observed. "What could Leopold have been thinking?"

His Grace accepted a tumbler of whiskey from the duchess, though the hour was indecently early—or indecently late if such a thing could be said of a summer dawn. "Leopold's hands are spotless, of course. That poor young fellow from the Home Office never knew who exactly was behind the scheme, and his contact probably disappeared back across the Channel before cock-crow. His wife, however, had an infant at the breast."

"I still don't understand." Morgan was perched on the sofa beside Her Grace. The girl looked tired and wore a distracted air, though the all's well had been received from Portmaine's superiors fifteen minutes ago. "Why kidnap a child who might not even inherit the throne? What would Leopold have to gain?"

"I can hazard a guess," said Her Grace. "*If* Leopold is behind this, and *if* his intention was kidnapping his niece rather than something worse, then in a few weeks' time, when the entire nation and half the Continent were in an uproar, he would be the one who 'found' the child. His poor sister, mad with worry, might beg her husband to keep the girl with Uncle Leo, where she'd be 'safer' than on English soil, and Kent, for reasons of his own, might allow it."

"Either that," said His Grace, passing the whiskey back to his duchess, "or at some point later in her life, dear Uncle Leopold might use the leverage of having saved the princess's life for his own ends. The man is brilliant, in his own way, and patient for a young fellow. It's an interesting combination."

Her Grace's smile was impish. "Puts me in mind of another man in his younger years."

Morgan took to fiddling with the cuff of her night robe.

"I'm not young any longer, and staying up the entire night waiting on word of some distant drama is a taxing business." He rose and extended a hand to his duchess. "Morgan, I advise you to take a tray in your room rather than come down for breakfast. I've no doubt before this day is through, you'll receive some correspondence from Carlton House, and you'll want to be well rested when it arrives. Your Grace." He patted his wife's arm. "My thanks for standing vigil with us, but you will accompany me above stairs now and cancel your appointments for the day."

He did not like to leave Morgan alone, looking about eight years old in her night robe and slippers, but there was nothing more to be done.

Or was there? His Grace entwined his fingers through his wife's and paused at the door to the sitting room. "Morgan, do you know what the hardest thing was about recovering from my heart seizure several years ago?"

The duchess cast a curious glance his way and held her peace.

"The fear of another, Your Grace?"

"That would be a nuisance, of course, and an inconvenience to Her Grace, but no. The hardest thing was realizing that I'd gone my entire lifetime believing that if I cared for someone, I need not suffer them to care for me in return. I alone could feel responsibility, loyalty, patience, affection, and so forth as the simple expedients of warm sentiment. It doesn't work like that. The greatest challenge is not loving faithfully, but accepting a reciprocity of such sentiments."

Morgan's brows knit. "If Your Grace says so."

"I most assuredly do, and my duchess would agree with me." The girl was likely so tired, his words were wasted. "And now it's time we all sought our beds."

"Rest well, Your Graces."

The duchess tugged discreetly on his hand and drew him into the corridor. "Percival? An *inconvenience*? What were you going on about?"

He moved along the corridor with her, an old fellow with his bride of several decades, feeling tired and blessed and grateful. "That was about a certain young lady being as proud and stubborn as a certain duke used to be."

Her Grace's smile was lovely, if tired. "Used to be, Percy?"

"Of course, and my duchess would agree with me on this as well."

"She would—provided she was in public."

⁓

"Why the hell didn't you heed my letter, Portmaine?" Valentine Windham strode past Archer like some sort of one-man tempest. "Could you not, in the space of an entire week, find your way out to Oxfordshire?"

"Good day to you, too," Archer replied. "And that's Sir Archer to you, my lord."

Windham leaned back against the sill of the library windows, crossed his arms, and tried for a glower that degenerated into—of all things—a lopsided smile. "I wish you the joy of your knighthood, Sir Archer. Try skulking around the drawing rooms with a knighthood hanging about your neck."

"I just might. May I offer you refreshment, my lord, or will you grant my most heartfelt wish and take yourself off directly?"

"Spare me the tea and crumpets when a man could use decent potation."

Archer took pity on his lordship, who might have simply asked for a tot to wash the dust from his throat. Windham looked like he'd ridden in directly from the shires, and as if he'd gotten as little sleep as Archer had. Archer poured two glasses of smooth whiskey and passed one to his guest.

His uninvited guest.

"My thanks." Windham took a whiff of his drink before sipping, probably without realizing he did it. "Ellen said to give you more time."

"More time before what?"

"I'm not here to apologize, if that's what you're hoping for."

His lordship was here for some purpose known only to himself—and his wife, apparently. "I will manage to survive my dismay at your lack of apology."

Another smile, but softer. No wonder the hostesses liked it when Lord Val graced their salons. "I apologized to Morgan. Ellen said I must tell you that."

"That is between you and Morgan. If you're not going to scamper off to some far away piano bench, shall we be seated?"

"No need. I wanted you to come out to Bel Canto to meet my family." His lordship set his drink on the mantel and began to wander about the room.

"I know your family. I've met them all, including St. Just. They were at Hazelton's wedding to your sister." Though Morgan had not been introduced to him, of that he was certain.

"Not that family." Windham ran a finger down the length of the mantel and then examined it, as if looking for dust. "*My* family. I am a *papa*." His tone suggested this was an honorific somewhere between king and archangel.

Which… it should be.

"One noted the protective inclinations, also the ungovernable temper and complete inability to apply reason. That you would find a female willing to bear your young is the surprising conclusion." Archer took Windham's abandoned drink and set it back on the sideboard.

"Wait until it's your turn, Port—*Sir* Archer." Windham stopped before a bookcase. "*The Decameron*, for example, will move up to higher and higher shelves, until your children are reading, and then it will leave your household altogether."

"It's not even in English, for God's sake."

"And your prized volumes of erotic woodcuts from the exotic cultures of the East?" Windham went on. "Onto the fire, and you won't think twice about it."

"The volume you're holding in your hands is nearly two hundred years old, Windham. What on earth is your point?"

He turned loose of one of Archer's most prized inheritances and stood staring at the bookshelves. "How does a woman know she's a mother, Portmaine?"

"Because the less-than-pleasant occasion of giving birth is indelibly imprinted on her memory, you fool. Surely your wife isn't raising awkward questions at this late date?"

"She'll recall giving birth, of course, but how does she know she's a *mother*? A woman who can provide safety and nurturing to her babies, who can protect them and love them and give them a fair start in this often unfair life?"

He was a musical genius, the son of a wily old duke, and an arrogant exponent of his class—and a pain in Archer's knighted backside. Valentine Windham was also, however, Morgan James's friend. If Archer had learned anything in the long hours of conversation in Morgan's boudoir, he'd learned that Windham alone had earned the privilege of Morgan's friendship.

"Windham, I am about two seconds away from gratifying the need to return to you the blow you struck on my undeserving person a week ago." The damned man began to smile again. "I will restrain myself, however, because you are responsible for finding the physician who restored Morgan's hearing to her three years ago. I suppose a fair hearing now is the least I owe you. Now for God's sake stop dodging and feinting and tell me what it is I must do to get the woman to marry me."

ॐ

Morgan loved the small sounds—the clink and tinkle of fine china when Her Grace served tea, the way a branch might tap a window in a gentle breeze, the song of birds on a summer morning.

Horses' hooves on cobbled streets and the jingle of the harness on a dray. The list had been long before she'd added the sound of Archer Portmaine's voice by firelight to the top of it. The way he groaned with pleasure...

Sir Archer. The Regent had quietly bestowed a knighthood on him for personal service to the Crown. Morgan wondered if Archer had stolen a moment to hold the baby princess in his arms. He'd saved the child from being kidnapped, or worse, possibly by her own maternal uncle.

A pang shot through her, deep inside, as a shadow fell across her little patch of the ducal garden.

"I have wondered about something, about several somethings, in fact."

Archer's voice, casual as you please. Morgan closed her eyes.

"May I join you, Miss James? It's a pretty day to linger among the flowers."

She nodded, speech being beyond her. She'd ordered him to stay away, and then when she had realized he might come to harm, she'd wanted nothing but to see him again.

Still, she kept her eyes closed. More than she wanted to see Archer Portmaine, she wanted to hear his beautiful voice.

"What have you wondered, Sir Archer?" She felt his weight settle beside her, right beside her, teasing Morgan's nose with the fragrance of cedar and making the wooden bench creak.

"When you were in the card room, Miss James, and Braithwaite and his cohort were hatching their scheme, didn't they realize you'd overheard them? You said they were only a few yards away?"

What an odd thing to fret over. "They spoke softly, so I heard little, but Lord Braithwaite told the other man I was known to be deaf as a post and there was no need to worry about me."

Archer crossed his long legs and twitched at the crease of his breeches near his knee. "Interesting."

When had she opened her eyes? "*Interesting?* I thought it insulting, myself. You've gotten some rest."

"Some. It's interesting to me that because they attributed a lack of hearing to you, you were able to listen to their entire conversation. I was quite proud of you, of your calm and your quick thinking, both. You'd make a wonderful investigator."

Another pang, this one worse than one before. "Why are you here, Archer?"

"To propose, of course."

"I wish you would not. I beg you, in fact, not to put that question before me."

"Whyever not? I love you. I believe your regard for me sufficient that the notion of marriage has merit for us. Unless there's someone else?"

Morgan rose and stalked off a few paces. *I love you.* Why had the blighted man gone and said that again? "There's nobody else."

"Well, there might be somebody else, in a manner of speaking." She heard him pace up behind her in the grass, felt the heat of his nearness. "A very small someone else. Vinegar and sponges are not entirely reliable, you know."

Among the bleak thoughts crowding her mind, Morgan seized on a very bleak thought indeed: he wasn't going to go away, not unless she spoke plainly to him. The man deserved reasons, not mute stubbornness from her.

Morgan faced a very solemn Archer Portmaine. "That's why we cannot marry. Because of those little someone elses."

"I met the baby princess." His gaze became softer. "I was charmed to think someday, when I'm an old, old knight smelling of camphor and bay rum, I can tell my queen I've seen her wearing little more than a receiving blanket and kissed her nose."

"You would not."

"Marry me, and you might see if I do. What is the real problem, Morgan? You would love any child resulting from our union, and so would I. Our children would want for nothing, and neither would you."

He stepped closer, making it nearly impossible for Morgan to keep her hands off of him. But she must. She must, or she'd lose the will to answer his question.

"I cannot be anybody's mother."

"Cannot?" His brows drew down. "The mandatory preliminaries seemed to agree with you."

"Oh, blast you to Hades." She paced away again then turned to glare at him.

"The preliminaries were lovely. They were beyond anything, as lovely as Anna assured me they would be."

His frown became fierce. "I suspected you were a virgin, and now you confirm it. I realized in hindsight that there was no scent of vinegar in the room, either. Did you even use the sponges?"

Truth was a painful, painful thing, but it would set him free. "I did not—I very much wanted you to… *be* with me, and I was repeating things I'd heard maids giggle about on back stairs—but surely the first time there can be no chance…?"

His smile was terrible and beautiful—a smile of triumph, possession, and tenderness all rolled into one. "There is *every* chance. Has the female complaint befallen you?"

No, but she'd spent most of the last week assuring herself that was a function of upset, only of upset. "I don't want to speak of that. I want to tell you that no baby should have me for a mother. I cannot hear, Archer."

"You hear, Morgan. Perhaps not as well as others, but you hear well enough."

"I do *not*. Unless I'm facing somebody, unless we're in a quiet room, I often miss words and phrases. I'm likely to lose more of my hearing as I age. Much more."

"That musical bufflehead was right then. You've some fool notion in your head that a woman has to be able to hear to be a mother."

Morgan couldn't feel betrayed—she'd not sworn her friend to secrecy—but she could be surprised that Valentine would share such a thing with Archer. "Valentine overstepped if he told you that."

"Overstepping seems to be one of his two natural talents. Come here, Morgan."

He held out a hand to her. A bare hand, steady, masculine, strong… irresistible.

She stared at that hand. "Archer, I cannot *hear*." She could feel though, feel her insides rocketing about, feel her knees trying to tremble. "I cannot *hear* the cry of a child, not even a b-baby crying in a quiet garden… I could not hear my children if they needed me, and that would be unbear… unbearable."

"Living the rest of my life without you would be unbearable." His fingers closed around hers in a sure grip. "The Regent wanted to commend you publicly, Morgan, but considered that would raise too many curious eyebrows when the matter must be kept quiet. If you hadn't been so clever and so brave and so *deaf*… How can you think you could not be a mother, when no less than a princess of the realm owes her safety to you?"

He spoke nonsense, but such comforting nonsense. "Archer, I couldn't hear Lady Ellen's baby… We were in this very garden, and Ellen flew along the path, while I…" Hadn't heard a blessed thing, and the child had surely been in distress.

"And what does that signify? Lord Valentine says Lady Ellen wakes up from a sound sleep, one floor down and halfway across their house from the nursery, and informs him with unwavering certainty that the child is awake or hungry or otherwise fretful. I don't think the man has been troubled for one damned minute by an inability to hear his own child, and the faculty of hearing is precious to him indeed."

Archer spoke these words against Morgan's temple, which was only possible because she'd at some point wrapped herself into his arms.

"I did not save the princess. You men, with weeks of vigilance, of *listening*, Archer…"

"Listening, yes, but watching, too, Morgan, and thinking. We had fourteen minutes—I timed it—*fourteen minutes* to move that dear, tiny girl before those rogues came stealing into her nursery. If you hadn't been so quick, the princess would at this moment likely still be in flight across the Continent. Hearing be damned." He gathered her closer. "Give me a wife with courage, brains, and the wits to use whatever resources she has at hand. Give me a wife I can love with my whole heart."

Hearing be damned?

Hearing be *damned*? The upheaval in Morgan's middle was shifting, trying to make the leap from dread to hope. She clung to him and grabbed for that courage he seemed to think she had in such abundance.

"I want babies, Archer. I want your babies, but I want them to be safe. I need them to be safe."

"No more than I do, and I want more than that."

She pulled away enough to watch his mouth. What could possibly be more important than the safety of helpless little children? "What do you want?"

"Sit with me." He drew her back to the bench and kept her hand in his. "I've done some thinking, Morgan, about how a knight is going to support his lady and a very large family in style."

"I have a fat dowry thanks to Westhaven and St. Just, and I don't need—a *large* family?"

"We've years ahead of us, and those preliminaries to conception did seem to agree with you."

She tightened her grip on his hand. "They did. Very much."

"Well, then. You were the one who put together that the child I knew as Princess Alexandrina Victoire was in fact Vicky."

"Her Grace mentioned it, just talk among the ladies over tea." And where was he going with this, and was he really, truly going to propose?

"That bit of talk was critical information. Without it, I might have set out for central France, or been guarding a bunch of aging royal dukes instead of stopping a kidnapping. Do you recall I told you weeks ago about a peer's wife who preferred the company of women?"

"I do."

"Maggie said it was common knowledge among the ladies. The woman had a penchant for walking into the wrong dressing room at the dressmakers, and so forth. The other women felt sorry for her, even as they regarded her with some curiosity."

"I know the lady myself, but Archer, if you think I want you lurking in slums and dealing with kidnappers—"

"Us. Not me, *us*. And not in slums. His Grace asked me to get involved in the last matter as a favor. I assure you I have no appetite for that level of intrigue. I'm perfectly content to go after missing diaries, straying spouses, and presuming footmen, but I think the venture is more likely to succeed if I have a partner."

"A partner?"

"Somebody to think things through with, somebody who won't mind that I need to stay up late sorting ideas, somebody who can bring a feminine perspective to situations that often involve women."

"A partner." It wasn't upheaval now, it was clamoring, and it came from Morgan's heart, like the pealing of a thousand church bells and the hallelujah of a throng of joyous choirs. "You want a partner?"

He leaned very close and spoke in a near whisper. "And a mother to my children and a wife and a lover and a friend. A very best friend. Say you'll marry me, Morgan, and be my partner in all things, and the mother of my children."

She heard him, heard every single word, and in all the decades of their marriage, his was the one voice she could always hear. Over the clamor of their nine children, over the chatter of the many social outings they enjoyed, over all the noise and nonsense of a fashionable life and the occasional investigation, Morgan always heard Archer with perfect clarity.

Jonathan & Amy

One

"A GENTLEMAN DOES NOT MAKE ADVANCES TOWARD A WOMAN IN HIS EMPLOY."

Jonathan Dolan's muttering and pacing brought him to the windows of his office, where he could watch his daughter gathering flowers in the back gardens. Her governess sat nearby, nose in a book, a spaniel panting at her feet.

"A gentleman does *not* make advances toward a woman in his employ."

This declaration had become Jonathan's personal Eleventh Commandment, but was no more palatable with the added emphasis.

"A goddamned *gentleman*, does not perishing *make advances* toward his daughter's *governess*, no matter how lovely, well formed, well spoken, gentle, kind, and—bloody hell."

A footman approached the pretty tableau in the garden, and before Miss Ingraham could turn and face the house, Jonathan stalked away from the windows. It would not do for her to know he was staring—though she'd conclude he was merely being a vigilant papa.

And he *was* a vigilant papa, also a doting, loving papa, but not only that.

He was, in addition, a wealthy man in his prime who had no wife with whom to share his life or his passions. A man who had buried his beloved spouse nearly five years ago and was watching his life march along, one lonely night followed by another. A man who had endured enough of that life, a fellow now determined to put into place a plan which—if he were successful—would improve his circumstances immeasurably.

And cast him into an unfathomable darkness if he failed.

He contemplated fortifying himself with a healthy tot of good Irish whiskey, but if Miss Ingraham got close enough for him to catch a whiff of her lemony fragrance, she'd smell the spirits on his breath.

"Mr. Dolan?"

Amy Ingraham stood in the doorway to the office, the picture of genteel English good looks: a shade taller than average, blond hair pulled back into a tidy bun, gray eyes complemented by a sky-blue walking dress several years out of fashion. The intelligence in those eyes was every bit as attractive to Jonathan as the curves filling out the dress.

"Miss Ingraham, please come in. Georgina looks to be enjoying her outing."

"The day is too pretty to keep the child at her lessons without a break, and the dog requires the occasional visit to the gardens as well."

She remained in the doorway, the location having symbolic significance. Amy Ingraham—granddaughter of a viscount, but neither family nor servant in Jonathan's household—excelled at hovering in liminal spaces.

"Have a seat, Miss Ingraham." He'd gestured to the settee near the hearth rather than one of the straight-backed chairs facing his desk. When she crossed the room, he closed the door behind her.

Her chin came up. "Mr. Dolan—"

Merely his name, but crackling with starch and repressed lectures.

"What I have to discuss is private and regards Georgina's best interests. Shall I ring for tea?"

She inhaled through her elegant nose, clearly torn between the need for the door to remain open and the temptation offered by a laden tea tray. To a lady raised in strict propriety, the tea tray would be a singular indicator of hospitality and manners, if not graciousness.

She lowered herself to the edge of the settee. "You may ring for tea. Just tea."

Jonathan went to the door and signaled a footman. *Just tea, indeed.*

He closed the door, the snick of the latch sounding inordinately loud, such was the power of a governess's disapproving silences.

"If I recall aright, your holidays are approaching, Miss Ingraham." Jonathan stalked across the room to stand near a wing chair. "May I take a seat?"

"You are my employer, Mr. Dolan, and this is your private domain. You are entitled to sit where you please, when you please."

She had a strong jaw, a defined chin. The jaw was set, that chin a trifle elevated, even considering he was standing over her. Where he *wanted* to sit was directly beside her on that settee.

He took the wing chair. "Have you a destination in mind for your holiday?"

"I visit family."

Of course, she did. What else was she to do? Pop over to Paris and take a turn dancing at the opera before a crowd of leering young men?

"May I inquire as to where you visit family?"

He could see her debating whether it was manners or deference that required her to answer. The tray the kitchen had been warned to prepare saved her from making an immediate reply.

Jonathan took the tray at the door, and when Miss Ingraham kept her gaze on the flowers beyond the window, he realized he'd fumbled. He should have taken a seat without asking her permission, he should have remained in silent, well-tailored splendor on his rosy backside while the footman brought the tray into the room, and then he should have indicated where the tray was to be set with an imperious wave of his lamentably calloused hand.

When the footman was gone and the door once again closed, Miss Ingraham studied the enormous silver tray and its contents. "Shall I pour?"

"If you pour, Miss Ingraham, then I will make you up a sandwich—or two."

She was trying not to smile—or grimace, he wasn't sure which. She picked up the teapot and made that perfect graceful picture of an English lady dispensing the tea. The curve of the teapot's handle complemented the curve of her body, while the way she kept two fingers on the pot's lid put the finishing touch on the image.

"Do you prefer mustard, butter, or both on your bread, Miss Ingraham?'

"A touch of both. This tea has jasmine in it."

"I was given to understand it's your preferred choice." Her favorite. He purposely did not use that word while he liberally coated her bread with butter.

"I do enjoy it."

That's all. Four small words followed by an enormous silence full of scolds, sniffs, and even a few genteel expressions of exasperation. How she must resent his summons, or possibly her entire life as Georgina's governess.

"You're not going to make this easy for me, are you?" He added a bit more butter and topped it with a dab of mustard.

"A governess does not take tea with her employer."

Jonathan's oldest sister, Mary Grace, had been a governess. "That depends on the household. It's midday, Miss Ingraham. You've been chasing that child around the entire morning, and I'm hungry. Shall I deny myself some sustenance while we're in discussions simply because you are too hidebound to share a midday meal with me?"

She stirred a fat dollop of cream and two lumps of sugar into his tea. "You should not. My apologies." She held the cup out to him, her hand absolutely steady.

And even in those civilities, she managed a hint of a reproach.

"Amy—"

Her gaze flew to his, her eyes betraying more surprise than horror.

His manners were as ragged as his stonemason father's had been, but Jonathan Dolan had never wanted for determination. He tried again from a more honest tack.

"Miss Ingraham, I eat alone at every meal save breakfast, when you and Georgina take pity on me and afford me some company. You visit with the child while I pretend to read the newspaper, because my ability to engage Georgina in conversation is wanting. Would it be imposing too greatly to ask you to break bread with me?"

She poured a second cup of tea and sat back. Jonathan waited for her to put cream and sugar in her cup, but instead she sighed, her shoulders dropping.

"It's much easier for me when you growl and snap, sir. This forthrightness—or charm—whatever it is, it isn't well advised."

"Hunger isn't well advised." He added thin slices of ham to her sandwich and a rectangle of yellow cheddar. "Might we declare a truce while we're eating?"

Her lips quirked up. She had a full, even lush mouth, one usually kept ruthlessly sculpted into a flat, inexpressive line—at least when she was with him. Jonathan held his breath in hopes she might permit herself an honest smile.

"I cannot resist a man who plies with me jasmine tea," she said as the smile bloomed. "It's wicked of you, sir. You must never tell Georgina."

With that smile, Jonathan's control over his own features slipped. He smiled back and passed her a plate bearing her sandwich, some strawberries, two tea cakes, and a slice of pineapple.

"Now that you've handed me something to bargain with, Miss Ingraham, we shall have a very enjoyable meal."

⤴︎

Jonathan Dolan's rare smiles would make angels weep, and Amy Ingraham did not consider herself an angel. The meal would be enjoyable for him—he made this claim sound believable—but for her, it would be both torture and bliss.

She was attracted to her employer. This pathetic, sorry conclusion took no great insight.

She listened for the sound of his voice.

She watched at breakfast to learn exactly how he took his tea.

She defended him as fiercely as she dared to the occasional grumbling young footman, though the maids never complained about Mr. Dolan.

While she practiced French with Georgina over breakfast, Amy studied the way Mr. Dolan's thick, dark hair fell over his brow. She noticed how morning sun sometimes made him look weary, and she saw the utter besottedness with which he beheld his daughter in unguarded moments.

And she *loved* to hear him thundering at some jobber or subcontractor who had delivered late or shoddy goods.

Amy yanked her thoughts back to the present, to this unprecedented midday meal with her employer. *Just tea, indeed.*

"So tell me, sir, what are we to discuss?"

His smile, both mischievous and bashful, faded. "I have a proposition for you."

His tone was brusque, and as soon as the words were out of his mouth, he set his teacup down and rose. "That came out wrong."

The momentary leap in Amy's pulse settled. Of course he hadn't meant anything untoward. Jonathan Dolan was the soul of propriety, a gentleman to his big, handsome bones.

Alas for her. "Come sit, sir, lest you leave me to dine alone."

He ran a hand through his hair and shot her a look that smacked of bewilderment.

"I'll sit in a moment. I'd like you to consider joining me and Georgina for a jaunt out to Surrey. My brother-in-law is insistent that his niece come visit him and his new marchioness. If I drag my heels accepting the invitation, Lord

Deene will get his back up, and we've had plenty enough of that behavior from him to last us lifetimes."

The Marquess of Deene being the brother of Mr. Dolan's late wife, a man of rank and influence, and one who had the power to command his niece to the country.

"You have agreed to bring her to visit her uncle, have you not?"

"May God have mercy upon me, I have."

He dreaded this visit. Amy could tell as much from the wariness in his gaze and the fact that he was standing across the room, keeping furniture and space between them.

"I had thought to visit my family in Surrey, sir." Such as her family was. Drusilla and Hecate put up with her during the few weeks of leave she took from her job.

"And you shall." He closed the distance and resumed his seat. "I shall see that you have time with your family while we heed Deene's summons, and I'm sure Deene's marchioness will make you welcome." He paused to narrow his eyes at Amy. "She's not the fussy sort. Unlike some."

Amy ignored the jibe and tried to still the excitement brewing in her veins. Oh, to be able to come and go at the cottage for once, to see her home but be spared the long silences, the faint disappointment lurking behind every compliment her sisters gave her.

The worry.

"How long would this visit last, sir?"

He sat back and crossed his legs at the knee. The pose made him look elegant and imperious, while his expression gave away nothing. "A few weeks at most. Deene will likely go shooting up North in August, English gentleman that he is."

Amy passed him a plate with two sandwiches on it—sandwiches she'd made not only to keep her hands busy, but also because Jonathan Dolan would neglect to eat, did he not join his daughter for breakfast each morning.

"How long do I have to consider this journey, Mr. Dolan?" Though she already knew what her reply would be.

"Give me an answer now, Miss Ingraham. If you're not to accompany us, I'll have to make other arrangements for Georgina's care while I'm ruralizing with her family."

They were Mr. Dolan's family too, if only by marriage. "Eat your sandwiches, sir, and give me some time to consider this. You have been hatching this scheme for who knows how long, while it's only now been sprung upon me."

His gaze flitted to the window then back to Amy's plate. "Your tea is getting cold, Miss Ingraham. I do not mean to badger you."

Her tea—the exact brand she permitted herself only at Christmas and on her birthday, or when she was feeling particularly low. She raised her cup and closed her eyes to savor the delicate, flowery aroma. Mr. Dolan had a reputation as a superb negotiator. He was honest, but ruthless.

Jasmine tea was ruthless, indeed. "Is this to be a house party?"

He studied her between bites of his sandwich, and he wasn't coy about it, another reason to like her employer. "I gather from your tone that you do not approve of house parties?"

"I left my last position in part because of a house party. Too many gentlemen nearly mistook my room for theirs." Including her former employer.

Mr. Dolan set his plate down with a noisy clink. "It's not a benighted house party. Deene wants to spend time with his niece, and a house full of drunken peers and their ladies would not be conducive to his lordship's ends. Eat your sandwich, Miss Ingraham."

He was on his feet again, standing over at the window in a few strides. Amy took a bite of her sandwich. The bread had been made with white flour that very morning; the crusts had been cut away. The butter was fresh, the cheese tangy and soft; the ham carried a hint of smoke and sweetness.

Mr. Dolan's staff ate well enough, but if Amy went on this visit, she wouldn't be passing up seconds for the sake of peace at the servants' table, or skipping sweets to leave more for the maids and footmen. Three weeks of excellent food—Deene's household would offer commodious hospitality even to a governess—three weeks of away from the other Dolan servants' odd looks and sniffy asides, three weeks of fresh air and freedom from the schoolroom.

Three weeks of proximity to home and all Amy loved there…

"I will accompany Georgina to visit her uncle, but Mr. Dolan, if you and I are to share a meal, it's customary to do so seated in one another's company." And while his profile and his manly physique were well worth study, so was his handsome countenance.

He turned, the wary expression back on his face. "You'll not change your mind? I will compensate you for giving up your scheduled holiday, of course, but if I tell Georgina you'll accompany us, you can't turn around and leave me—*us*—hanging."

She fixed him another cup of tea with two sugars and a fat portion of cream, the way he liked it. "I'll not change my mind. A holiday from Georgina's studies probably has as much appeal for me as it does for her."

Mr. Dolan abandoned his post by the window to resume his seat. "Georgina says you're a slave driver, but her French seems to be coming along."

"She has a gift for languages. Another sandwich?"

"Please, and there's something else you should know." He peered at his teacup as if perplexed as to how it had found its way into those big, capable hands of his.

"Out with it, Mr. Dolan. Prevarication might work with your business associates, but a governess is made of sterner stuff."

He muttered something. Mother of God? Sometimes his voice shaded more toward a brogue, and the words were harder to distinguish.

"I'd like you to take on an additional pupil between now and when we depart for Surrey. I realize it's short notice, but I'll compensate you for the extra effort."

"Mr. Dolan, you compensate me more than adequately, and while I appreciate your generosity, I have to wonder what this additional effort entails. Who is to be my new pupil?"

He continued to stare at his teacup. "Your new pupil is to be none other than myself."

❧

How hard could it be to pass a piece of paper into a woman's hand?

Jonathan asked himself this question as he marshaled his courage and surrendered his list into Amy Ingraham's keeping. Even putting pen to paper had made him queasy.

She scanned the document, and he knew exactly what she saw:

What is proper conduct when serving tea to another man?

How precisely does one offer and render escort to a lady in public?

Where is the order of precedence listed?

Why is thirty the usual number of guests at a dinner party?

How does a man properly assist a lady from a conveyance?

Under what circumstances, *if any*, might a gentleman raise his voice?

On and on the reckoning went, a list of every mistake Jonathan had made since arriving to his wealth, every misstep, and not a few of his regrets. His late wife had tried, gently, for a time, to guide him into genteel behavior, but then even she had given up.

He could only hope Miss Ingraham viewed his list of humiliations as a pile of social straw she could spin into gold behind the closed doors of Jonathan's home.

She wrinkled her nose, which did not bode well for his aspiration as a pupil of gentlemanly deportment. "You want me to teach you to waltz?"

"Most assuredly."

"But not the minuet, the gavotte, the polonaise, the other ballroom dances? Do you know the contredanses?"

"I know the parlor dances, and enough of the ballroom dances to get by. Most of them are such lumbering affairs they can be learned at sight, but the waltz is a recent addition to the ballrooms—" He looked down at his hands. The left bore the most scars, having been half smashed in a quarry accident when he was twelve. "I cannot fathom it."

She started chattering about how simple the waltz was, while Jonathan watched her mouth and pondered the desperation of a man who'd stoop to such a subterfuge. The Irish engaged in several activities without limit—they worked like beasts, but when not working, they danced and sang. Some would say they also procreated, abused hard liquor, and prayed with equal fervor—some English.

"Mr. Dolan, are you paying attention?"

"I always pay attention to you, Miss Ingraham." The words came out sounding like a rebuke, not a compliment or the simple truth, which they were. Given the state of his nerves, a rebuke was probably safest for them both.

"See that you do pay attention. We have only a week, and this is not a short list. I will need time to organize our approach."

While Jonathan would need time to tie his hands behind his back lest he reach forward and touch her pretty, golden hair. In the morning sun, she wasn't merely blond. Her hair was shot with highlights of red, wheat, bronze, and more, indefinable colors that played along each individual strand. Spread out over a pillow, her hair would be an entire palette...

"I have a suggestion, Miss Ingraham."

She arched a brow, all starchy business and brisk efficiency. No wonder Georgina's education was progressing at such a great rate.

"If we are to maximize the time between now and our departure, then it makes sense for you to take your meals with me."

Such a delicate frown had Miss Ingraham. "That...does...make sense."

And so reluctant. Jonathan's despair eclipsed the desire that simmered in his veins whenever he beheld his daughter's governess. "Only for a week, Miss Ingraham, and I assure you I will be on my best behavior."

"Yes, you will." She studied him until the corners of her mouth curved up and an *impish* light gleamed in her eyes. "Keeping you on your best behavior shall be my personal mission."

And thus began his week of heaven—and hell.

She showed him how to tie his cravats in the more fashionable knots, though how she knew such things was a mystery. This exercise required her hands on his person, making it a wonder of biblical proportions that Jonathan mastered anything beyond the fussed-up reef knot he'd been using for years.

She lectured him through three meals a day plus tea—high bloody tea!—and gave him little books to read on the subject of table manners.

She inspected his turnout each morning and each time before he left the house, tugging on a shirtsleeve or adjusting his *boutonniere*. He was no longer permitted to refer to it as a *damned posy*.

And then the real torment began.

"We must do something about your hair." Miss Ingraham made this pronouncement at breakfast on Thursday, and their departure was scheduled for Saturday morning.

"You will not be parading me around all slicked down with grease and perfume, Miss Ingraham. I like my hair clean."

While Georgina grinned at her eggs on Jonathan's left, Miss Ingraham sat back in her chair on his right, her expression alarmingly pensive. "You have lovely hair." He did not roll his eyes, but her compliments always preceded some dire pronouncement, and she did not disappoint on this occasion. "Your hair is in want of a trim."

"Then I shall cut it. More tea?"

She remained silent, until she leaned forward and feathered her fingers through his hair. "You have marvelously thick hair, and the color is unusual. Titian."

Which meant however dark it was, it was still red, and thus the wrong color. She repeated the caress of her fingers through his hair, while Jonathan tried to ignore the pleasure of her touch.

In this, at least, the week had been successful: Amy Ingraham showed no more compunction about touching him than if he were a five-year-old boy and truly one of her charges.

"May I help cut Papa's hair?"

Jonathan spoke a bit too loudly. "Certainly not. Finish your eggs."

"You may keep a curl for a locket," Miss Ingraham said. The females exchanged a look, one Jonathan recognized, as any man with seven sisters would.

"You two are conspiring," he said, pouring more tea for Miss Ingraham. "This does not bode well for my peace of mind. There are laws against conspiracies. Females plotting to overthrow the order of a man's household is likely some sort of felony. Old George sired six daughters. I can't believe he'd fail to address such potential unrest in his kingdom."

"Papa's eggs are getting cold," Georgina remarked to no one in particular.

"So are yours, young lady."

"A gentleman never argues with a lady." Miss Ingraham's expression was positively bored, while her gray eyes danced gleefully.

"She's an imp from h—the depths, not a lady. Not yet." When Georgina grinned at him, Jonathan brushed his finger down her nose in a parody of a reprimand. "And a very pretty imp, too."

He dawdled over his eggs and complained at length about being denied his newspaper at the breakfast table, but in the end, the ram went meekly, even willingly, to be shorn.

&

The week flew by, a whirlwind of moments for Amy to dread and then treasure, tumbling one right after another.

Mr. Dolan studied his own betterment with an intensity Amy found daunting. If she handed him a book on manners after dinner, he had it memorized by morning. If she suggested an outing to the park with Georgina for the sake of variety, he used it as an opportunity to practice everything, from his polite conversation to the proper means of handing a lady down from a vehicle.

"You haven't taught me to waltz, Miss Ingraham. If I'm someday to escort my daughter to social functions, I'll need that skill."

Georgina had darted out of the breakfast parlor to take her dog to the garden, leaving Amy alone with her employer for much of the meal.

"Georgina won't be waltzing for another ten years," she remarked. "You have plenty of time to learn."

"Miss Ingraham—" He sounded as if he were going to sail into one of his well-reasoned, volume-escalating tirades that Amy so enjoyed, provided they were directed at others.

His jaw snapped closed. He touched his napkin to his lips. "Miss Ingraham, it's entirely likely Deene's marchioness will take it into her pretty head to have a da—a deuced ball in honor of this visit or some such rot. I will not be made a fool of for the sake of your faintheartedness."

"Faintheartedness, Mr. Dolan?"

"You do not relish the idea of an Irish bear mincing around the da—the blasted ballrooms of proper—Mother of God." On that exhalation, he leaned forward and used the side of his thumb to brush at the corner of Amy's lip. "You've a crumb...of toast."

One more fleeting caress and he sat back, scowling mightily. "A toast crumb is distracting, and it's not in the rule books."

Amy reached for her tea but didn't trust herself to bring the teacup to her mouth. The feel of his callused thumb grazing her skin so gently—a butterfly-soft thumb-kiss that sent warmth sizzling through her person—was more than a lady should have to bear without swooning.

"Sometimes, one must improvise, Mr. Dolan."

"But a gentleman doesn't touch—"

Before she could stop herself, Amy placed a finger to his lips. "A gentleman can hardly allow a lady to be embarrassed by toast crumbs, can he? Moreover, you would not have used the same measures had Lady Deene been the one sporting a crumb, would you?"

He still looked a trifle tense. "Of course not. Deene would draw my bloo—my very cork. More tea, Miss Ingraham?"

Amy blinked at her teacup. He'd certainly taken to offering her tea, but even she had a limit for how much jasmine-scented libation she could down at one meal. "No, thank you."

"So when do we waltz, Miss Ingraham?"

Amy did not want Georgina underfoot when they danced; she did not want the lesson to be hurried. She also did not want candlelight threatening her good sense beyond all recall. "Now, unless you have other plans?"

"I am at your service." He rose and offered his bare hand as politely as if he'd been to the manor born. Amy made the trip through the house on his arm, allowing him to escort her through the hallways, up the stairs, and into the largest of the public parlors.

The week had seen a shift in this at least: he was no longer so wary of bodily proximity to her. When their hands brushed, when she took his arm, he no longer tensed at each and every contact.

And neither did she. Amy was learning to handle the flood of pleasure she felt when she was near him, learning to ignore the riot of sensations his scent and warmth provoked. His height and size, his expressions and intonations had become wonderfully familiar in a whole new way.

Mr. Dolan stopped in the middle of the parlor. "We'll need music."

"Soon." Amy dropped his arm. "First, we'll need the doors folded back and the rugs rolled up."

While the footmen saw to the arrangements, Amy noted the subtle signs of unease in her pupil. He shot his cuffs, an indication that he'd rather roll them back. He ran his hand through his hair, his shorter locks making him frown each time he repeated the gesture. He paced, he looked out the window, he looked anywhere, in fact, but at her.

When the last footman withdrew to warn the housekeeper she might be needed at the piano, Amy approached the window. "Georgina is a lucky girl, Mr. Dolan. Not all parents are as devoted as you are."

He glanced down at her. "I'm her father, of course I love her."

Amy kept her gaze on the child and the spaniel frolicking in the grass outside. Something about Mr. Dolan's brusque use of the word "love" made Amy regard him yet still more highly.

"Not all fathers can say the same. Are you done stalling?"

His lips quirked up in the fleeting, devilish smile Amy enjoyed so much. The only one she liked better was the one he saved for his daughter, which was so full of affection and approval, it took Amy's breath away.

"I do not stall, Miss Ingraham. I consider my options, I develop strategy, I choose my moment."

"You miss her mother."

The words slipped out, completely inappropriate to the moment, and to Amy's position in the household. Mr. Dolan's smile became wistful, then sad.

"I miss her terribly. But as much as I miss what I had with her, I miss as well what was taken from us when she died."

An inappropriately honest reply to a wholly misguided observation, but Amy couldn't leave it alone. "What was taken from you?"

"We were just becoming friends. She was always my ally, even when I thought she was only carping and correcting to keep me in my place. A man overly endowed with pride doesn't always make a good husband when he marries so far above himself."

He had regrets. That he would carry such sentiments without ever giving a hint of them ought to have occurred to her.

"We all have regrets, Mr. Dolan. One makes choices without being able to guess their consequences, and one can't always choose wisely."

He turned from the window, his gaze betraying a lurking amusement. "Can't *one*? Are you stalling now, Miss Amy?"

Oh, how she liked the sound of her name in his rumbling baritone. How she liked that he looked at her when he teased her and baited her.

"Mr. Dolan—"

He touched her mouth as she had touched his at the breakfast table, with a single, gentle finger. "A gentleman may address a woman familiar to him as Miss Christian Name in informal circumstances if the lady does not object."

His recitation of the rule was word-perfect. Amy removed his finger from her lips and set her hand on his muscular shoulder. "The time has come to dance."

Two

"THE TIME HAS COME TO MARRY." NIGEL HERODOTUS GEORGE INGRAHAM, ninth Viscount Wooster, infused his tone with as much indifference as he could muster—which was considerable.

"Done all the time." His friend, Angel Bonham, the Baron Bonham of Hartley, poured them each a bumper of brandy and passed one to his guest. "Heartiest congratulations. When will you tell your cousin of her good fortune?"

"Second cousin, please." Nigel took a savoring sip of much better libation than he'd been able to stock at Wooster House for some time. "She'll turn twenty-eight on the fifteenth of next month, so my courtship will be precipitous."

Bonham's blond brows drew down. "Because of your violent passion for her, after what, twelve years of not laying eyes on the girl?"

"Nobody is a girl at twenty-eight, Bonny, particularly not after governessing Mayfair's pampered brats for seven years."

Bonham's handsome face screwed up with consternation. "You're to marry a governess? Maria will laugh you to scorn, old man, to say nothing of what the fellows at the clubs will think."

"Maria…" Nigel peered at his drink and pictured his mistress in all her voluptuous Mediterranean beauty. "Maria is a substantial part of the reason this desperate measure must be taken."

Maria and her appetite for pretty tokens played a role, as did the many, many obligations a man of title and taste must meet if he were to have any consequence among his peers. Then, too, Mama's consequence weighed in the balance and drove Nigel to the otherwise unthinkable step of making Amy Ingraham the next Viscountess Wooster.

Bonham lowered his lanky frame onto a leather ottoman. "The solicitors have given up all hope?"

"They've been nattering at me since she turned twenty-five. They have no objection to keeping wealth in the family, lest their own bottomless pockets go untended, but they're nervous and making noises of the wrong sort."

Bonham was a pretty man, all blond good looks and hail-fellow-well-met, but he wasn't stupid. "You're a peer. You can't be tossed into the Fleet for bad debts."

"I can be blackballed from the clubs."

A silence befell them, one indicative of the unfathomable suffering involved in such a fate.

"Best be about your wooing," Bonham said, staring at his drink morosely. "But if she's been governessing for seven years, an Irish tinker on a lame donkey would probably look like a knight in shining armor to her."

"Which does nothing to enhance the lady's charms in my own eyes. A peer of the realm has certain standards."

Bonham got up to fetch the decanter. "Think of Maria, Wooster, and do what must be done. At least your brother has some sons, so it isn't as if you have to get brats on the gi—on your second cousin."

"I will take my consolation from that signal fact while you, dear Bonny, see that for the nonce I get roaring, stinking, knee-crawling drunk, if you please."

Bonham didn't even glance at the clock, which was chiming an obscenely early hour. "What are friends for?"

⟨≈⟩

Waltzing was not difficult. Jonathan's late wife had taught him well, and he'd delighted in being her equal in that, at least.

Relearning the waltz with Amy while arousal tried to blossom in Jonathan's breeches was difficult in the extreme. From some fluffy white cloud, Jonathan's late wife was no doubt laughing her pretty, aristocratic arse off.

"I need music," he muttered. Something to focus on besides the occasional lemony whiff of Amy, the brush of her skirts against his legs, the way she moved his body around, her hands on his torso and shoulder, pushing him this way and that.

"Soon. Do you want your housekeeper to see you step on my feet, sir?"

"I'll not step on your bl—blessed feet, Amy Ingraham."

"Again." She got a solid hold of him, and one-two-three'd him down the room and up the other side. He liked the corners the best, when she pulled him in close and then forgot to turn loose of him for a few steps.

But enough was enough.

"My turn to lead, Miss Amy. You're too good at it for a fellow's peace of mind."

"I am not too good—" She fell silent, the slight, self-mocking smile lurking at her lips. "Oh, very well. You lead, but please don't toss me about like a sack of grain. Take it slowly at first and trust me to follow."

"Right. You'll follow as long as you're giving all the directions."

He danced her in a slow triple meter along the same path she'd taken him, but this time was different. She *did* let him lead. She moved with him, not quite in anticipation of his maneuvers, but in complicity with them.

He could feel her humming softly under her breath, feel her lithe body surrender to his guidance. The lesson became torturous when he pulled her close on the first twirling turn and her breasts fleetingly brushed his chest.

She smiled up at him. "There's hope for you, Mr. Dolan."

Another turn, and he was doomed. "Generous of you to say so, Miss Amy."

"Try to let the rhythm of the dance keep you relaxed. You're stiffening up on me."

Mother of God. He dropped his arms and stepped back. "We need music if we're to accomplish my objective."

Her expression turned mulish. "Do you always accomplish your objectives, Mr. Dolan?"

"No." He ran a hand through hair made a good deal shorter and peculiarly *fluffy* by her damned little scissors. "No, I do not, though that usually only increases my determination. For example, you would not call me Jonathan, no matter how politely I asked it of you."

"It would not be proper. You're my—"

He was glad for the tiff, glad for the distraction of it, but when she pinched up her mouth in that pruny, lecturing way, it made him want to kiss her all the more.

"Music, Miss Amy. Now."

The housekeeper was summoned. She took her place at the piano, back to the room, and launched into a surprisingly competent triple-meter introduction without so much as glancing at the couple for whom she played.

Jonathan bowed, his partner curtsied, and after more than a week of waiting and anticipating, Jonathan had the pleasure of dancing down the room with the woman about whom he dreamed.

He had the odd thought that Amy Ingraham was *real.* Where his hand rested on her back, he felt the slight wrinkle of a chemise and stays beneath the fabric of her dress. When he drew her into his arms, the aroma of lemon verbena mingled with laundry starch and something else—a faint trace of ink, perhaps?—to bring the schoolroom to mind.

And Mother of God, the woman could dance. She'd been keeping her powder dry in the earlier drills, maintaining the fiction that she was a governess even in waltz position. With the music filling the room, she became lissome and buoyant, not a sylph, but a woman with a body a man could worship, given privacy and leave to do so.

So he prolonged the exercise by the few means at his disposal.

"Wrong way, Mr. Dolan."

"Beg your pardon."

Then, "You're a trifle ahead of the music, sir."

"I do apologize."

Several phrases later: "I think we'd best start from the beginning."

On the third attempt he grew daring.

"Not so tight on the turns, Mr. Dolan."

"Your pardon, of course…"

"Not so *many* turns, Mr. Dolan."

Bless her, she was a very patient woman, and very determined to see her pupil succeed, too.

"I think we'd better start again, Miss Ingraham."

Perhaps he was tiring her out, because the feel of her shifted, from competent and graceful to yielding and maybe even…submissive. To Jonathan, her following became instinctive.

This had such a salutary effect on his breeding organs that he finished the final tour of the room without a stumble, a wrong turn, or any other diversion to mar his pure enjoyment of the waltz. When the music came to a close, Jonathan realized that he'd just danced himself out of further instruction.

And maybe his teacher realized it too, for she leaned in a little, as if winded.

"I think you've acquired the knack, sir."

He'd acquired a cockstand, most assuredly, and because a man in desperate straits needed some small token in recompense for his forbearance, he bent down and brushed his lips over her cheek.

She didn't pull immediately away. She sighed, the sound to Jonathan one of long-suffering, redolent of the trials of governessing a grown man on the dance floor.

"You're supposed to kiss the lady's hand, Mr. Dolan, or more precisely, to engage in gestures suggestive of that aim without actually putting your mouth to her person or her glove."

"My mistake." Except it wasn't a mistake. Kissing Amy was the best move he'd made all week. He followed up by raising her bare hand in his, smoothing his fingers over her knuckles, and pressing his lips softly to the back of her hand.

At which moment, the piano lid banged shut, and Miss Amy took a decisive step to the rear.

⁂

"Imagine my frustration when I find the damned woman has hared off to the country." Nigel stormed into Bonham's study, tossed a bouquet of daisies aside, and helped himself to a glass of whiskey.

Bonham picked up the bunch of abused flowers. "I rather thought governesses were supposed to remain in the vicinity of their charges, not go ruralizing at will."

"She's in the employ of Dolan, the quarry nabob. He's gone off to Surrey, taking the child with him, ergo, Amy is in Surrey as well."

"Surrey's right across the river." Bonham fished a penknife out of the desk drawer and began to trim the flower stems. "The Season's mostly over, and I for one am not enthusiastic about remaining in Town for the balance of the summer."

Nigel paused in the contemplation of his drink—and his future—to peer at his friend. "What on earth are you doing?"

"The flowers last longer if you trim the ends up a bit. Nerissa was particular about her flowers."

"You let that woman lead you around by a certain appendage, Bonny." Nigel made this observation as much in commiseration as judgment, for the fair Nerissa was now enjoying the patronage of some duke. "I bloody hate the bloody countryside. Fresh air makes my nose run."

"Well, cheer up." Bonham gathered the flowers and rummaged through the sideboard's cabinets. "I've a little place out in Surrey, probably use it for a dower property for one of my sisters. If you need to track your prospective viscountess down, we can jaunt out there for a few weeks before I take the yacht North for the shooting."

"Bonny, I should love you even if you didn't have such excellent cellars."

Bonham stood back and surveyed the flowers he'd stuffed into a pitcher of water. "Doesn't look quite right."

The daisies stood at various heights, pointing in all directions, with a couple poking up several inches above their confreres, and the whole thing listing badly to starboard.

"When I marry, my wife will busy herself with arranging all the bouquets just so," Nigel said. "Why can I take no solace from this sanguine eventuality?"

Bonham ambled over to the sofa and plucked Nigel's drink from his hand. "Take solace from being able to spend your wife's fortune, Wooster. On Maria, at the tables, at Weston's and Hoby's establishments, at the races, et cetera, et cetera, et cetera."

He took a sip of the whiskey and passed the glass back to his guest. "Surrey signifies a deal of countryside. Where exactly has the quarry nabob dragged your affianced wife to?"

"You recall that match race a few weeks back that had all the fellows aflutter?"

Bonham came down on the sofa beside Nigel. "Fellows don't flutter, but yes. Supposedly a friendly wager, but nobody believed it, except that's apparently exactly what it was."

"Dolan's country place is not far from where the race was held."

Bonham appropriated the glass again and drained the contents. "Ergo, your cousin is off to Surrey, ergo, you are off to Surrey."

"Ergo, you are off to Surrey as well."

"Be still my beating heart. More whiskey?"

"Of course."

⤝⤞

"You look different." Lucas Denning, the Marquess of Deene, scowled at his brother-in-law. "Evie will know what's changed."

"We Irish only grow more handsome with time." Jonathan sauntered into

Deene's library, affecting a nonchalance he didn't feel. Deene had more books in one room of his country retreat than Jonathan had seen prior to leaving Ireland. Though the man was several years Jonathan's junior, he had centuries of aristocratic breeding to his name, and blond, blue-eyed good looks to go with them.

Deene wrinkled his patrician nose and made a circumnavigation of Jonathan's person. "You appear to be thriving. Is that jacket from Weston's?"

"It is, though I'll not patronize them again."

Deene's glower eased. "They've grown too popular and thus charge too much and take too long to make a simple garment. Would you like a drink?"

That Jonathan would share even something as basic as an opinion regarding a tailor with the handsome marquess was vaguely disturbing. "What have you got?"

"My marchioness said you'd be a man of uncomplicated tastes, and thus the sideboard boasts only brandy, whiskey, chilled hock, and, um, cold lemonade."

Deene's fair countenance colored slightly at the mention of this last beverage.

"Lemonade, Deene? Does your marchioness think I'm an eight-year-old man of uncomplicated tastes?"

The marquess swung away from the sideboard and spoke with cool civility. "What can I get you, Dolan?"

Insight struck with an unaccustomed shaft of compassion for Lord Deene. "Your marchioness is breeding, isn't she? She's avoiding spirits, and you're humoring her. I'll have the lemonade then, and so will you."

Deene looked sheepish, relieved and not a little surprised. He passed over a tall, sweating glass, then poured one for himself.

Jonathan lifted his glass. "To the lady's health."

Deene followed suit. "To her health and my nerves."

Jonathan remembered not to gulp his drink, though the ride out from London had been hot and dusty. "I assume you'll want to establish some sort of schedule for Georgina's visits in future?"

Deene set his glass aside—empty. "You assume correctly. When last you and I spoke of the matter, you agreed that Georgina should have regular visits with me and my marchioness. Your idea of regular is no doubt at variance with my own."

Every five years could be quite regular. "At some variance, I'm sure. How far along is your wife?"

"She keeps saying 'not very.'" Deene went to take another swig of his drink then scowled at his empty glass. "I realize these things happen in the ordinary course, but one doesn't... I mean to say...if one can't...it's all very well in theory, but..."

"In reality," Jonathan said gently, "the notion of childbirth scares a man to death. Raising children is very much in the same line. I suggest we get out a deck of cards, repair to the billiards room, or otherwise engage in the fiction that we're *getting along*, lest your marchioness work her wiles on you any further."

"Evie has no wiles. She's quite forthright, and I'll not put off the matter of an agreement regarding visits with my niece."

What a shame Marie had not lived long enough to see her brother fall so hard and so wonderfully in love.

"Your determination has me quaking in my dusty boots, Deene." Jonathan went to the sideboard, topped up his own drink, and poured a fresh one for his host. "In case you are dreading the prospect, I have no intention of getting along with you, though your marchioness is charming beyond endurance. In your presence, however, I'm happy to shout and carry on at great length regarding the days Georgina spends in your house—"

"Weeks, at least!"

"—But the womenfolk will have the matter quite in hand by the time they finish ambling down the barn aisles. They might need until teatime to contrive a way to make us think the terms they reach are entirely our idea."

Deene blinked, accepted his drink, and muttered, "My thanks." His lordship drank half of this glass as well, then paused, one side of his mouth quirking up. "Billiards or cards?"

"Billiards."

Deene remained quiet until they reached the game room on the second floor. "Have you deputed Miss Ingraham to negotiate on your behalf?"

"With some women, it isn't a matter of delegating authority, it's a matter of managing on the crumbs of dignity they leave us." Jonathan took down a cue stick from the rack on the wall, and put his choice back as too light.

"Evie would never threaten my dignity."

Jonathan eyed the lemonade in the younger man's glass. "Not intentionally, of course. The only consolation is that you manage on those crumbs of dignity willingly to ensure her happiness and safety."

Deene chose his cue stick and sighted down it toward nothing in particular that Jonathan could determine. "Would you have me believe this is how it was between you and my sister?"

So casual, but behind the question was a younger brother's worry, and a surviving sibling's guilt. Without planning to, without *wanting* to, Jonathan addressed both.

"Deene, I loved your sister very much. I took years to understand what a gift the Almighty and your impecunious father put in my hands, but I am confident that by the time she was taken from us, she was at least certain of my regard. Now prepare to suffer a sound drubbing in the name of hospitality."

Whether in the name of hospitality or as a function of a new husband and expectant father's nerves, Jonathan's host did in fact lose to him handily.

All three times.

And perhaps because Jonathan was feeling expansive in victory, but more likely because he could see that Deene's anxiety over the marchioness had robbed him of even the ability to concentrate on a game of billiards, Jonathan hazarded a question.

"You consider yourself a gentleman, don't you, Deene?"

Deene looked up from a table devoid of easy shots. "Are you contemplating calling me out, Dolan? It's a bit late for that."

"I will take that as a yes, and thus I will put a question to you: Is there any circumstance under which a gentleman may make advances toward a woman in his employ?"

The vague air of distraction left Deene's countenance. He straightened without making a shot and regarded Jonathan with a half smile. "Advances of a romantic nature? No, there is not. Is this about that blue-eyed governess?"

"Miss Ingraham's eyes are gray, and do you think I'd admit to *you* that I enjoyed an attraction to the lady?"

"You just did, but the answer is still no, not if a fellow wants to keep his honor in good shine. Alas for you." Deene grinned evilly, bent over the table, sighted down his cue stick, and by virtue of skillful use of the bumpers and a judicious application of spin on the cue ball, managed to sink two balls and leave Jonathan not one decent shot.

❧

The waltzing had about killed Amy's self-discipline, left it a miserable, whining mess of shoulds and oughts cowering in the dingiest corner of her conscience. Mr. Dolan brought to waltzing the same intensity of focus he brought to his business endeavors and his parenting, which meant he'd not simply swayed around the room with her, he'd *danced*.

"Mr. Dolan's lack of refined antecedents isn't what gives him such a feel for the music."

Charles cocked his head, his big brown eyes conveying both concern and curiosity.

"I've danced with country lads by the score, and they lack Mr. Dolan's... grace."

They also lacked his height, his muscle, his blue eyes, his aquiline nose, his particular lavender-and-fresh-air scent, his smile, his way of narrowing those eyes when he became determined on something, his way of moving a woman around on the dance floor like she was both safe and cherished in his embrace.

"I'm an idiot." More than twenty-four hours after turning down the room with her employer, and Amy still wanted to close her eyes and recall the moments she'd spent in his arms.

Charles rose from the hearth rug and parked his hairy chin on Amy's knee.

"I will see much less of Mr. Dolan now that we're ensconced here with Lord and Lady Deene. I shall recover my equilibrium. You may depend upon it."

A knock on her door had the dog looking askance at her.

"Come in."

She would recover her equilibrium later, because at that moment, Jonathan Dolan appeared in Amy's doorway, looking windblown, sun-browned, and delectable in shirtsleeves and riding attire.

"Mr. Dolan." Amy nearly startled off the settee at the foot of her bed. "If you're looking for Georgina, Lady Deene tarried with her in the stables to see this year's foals."

"Kidnapped her, you mean. I expected you to be a more ferocious body-guard, Miss Ingraham."

He ambled into her room without an invitation and took a place beside her on the small settee.

"Hold your peace, my dear." He leaned back and crossed his feet at the ankles. "A gentleman does not take a seat without a lady's permission, a gentleman does not presume on a lady's private environs, a gentleman does not—in my opinion—get to exercise a great deal of common sense. Do you mind if I take a seat? I was up late last night seeing to business and woke early to make the journey here on horseback."

Amy cast a minatory glance at the open door. "If you are tired, of course you should sit."

"Walk with me in the garden, Amy Ingraham. I have matters to discuss with you." He heaved out a sigh, and it was all Amy could do not to touch him. Weariness was evident in the way he rolled his shoulders, the grooves bracketing his mouth, and the informality of his posture.

"I was about to change for dinner."

"We have plenty of time. I'm not sure whether Deene is hovering more closely over his marchioness or his niece, but he was no damned—I beg your pardon—no challenge at all at billiards. I sent him out to the stables lest he embarrass himself further."

Mr. Dolan rose and extended a hand down to her.

Were she at home—at Mr. Dolan's home—Amy would have pointedly ignored that hand and even glared at her employer for his presumption. But the marchioness had been so friendly, and his lordship so welcoming, Amy had been given to understand that in this household, she would be treated like a guest. The idea that this visit was a holiday in truth, a small holiday from the strictest observance of the most inconvenient rules, was too attractive to ignore.

She took Mr. Dolan's hand.

"Are you content with the arrangements here, Miss Ingraham?"

Not Miss Amy. Ah, well.

"I am. The maid detailed to the nursery is cheerful and the oldest of seven. She'll manage Georgina quite easily."

"Your room looks commodious."

Amy's employer was trying to make small talk, but coming up against a reality that emerged whenever people of different stations attempted to move beyond civilities: they had, in truth, little in common.

"My room is lovely. Are you concerned that Lord Deene will charm his way into Georgina's heart?"

Mr. Dolan let out a bark of laughter. "He'll have to wedge past his marchioness to accomplish that, and he's too besotted to manage such a thing. The woman rides like a demon, you see, and Georgina has been pestering me for a pony since she could gallop across the playroom. Her mother loved to ride."

The last observation was offered contemplatively, as if being around Lord Deene stirred a bereavement Mr. Dolan hadn't anticipated.

"Are you missing your late wife, sir?"

He paused with her on the steps of the back terrace. "I miss her every day, of course, though the first time I realized I'd gone a day without thinking of her specifically, I wondered if..." His gave traveled over the back gardens, which were sporting their full, colorful summer glory. "I did not come out here to discuss my status as a widower, not directly in any case."

A retreat from such a painful topic ought to be allowed, though Amy couldn't help but think of how he might have finished the sentence.

"When I began to get over the loss of my parents, I wondered if letting them go wasn't somehow disloyal."

He walked along beside her in silence for a few moments, past bobbing daisies, on to fragrant red roses. "Just so, but then you recall the departed bestirring themselves in their last hours to admonish you sternly to be happy, to love again, and it is that topic I wished to broach with you."

Mr. Dolan spoke in such calm, reasonable tones that the content of his comments took a moment to sort itself out in Amy's mind.

He wanted to speak to her of *love*?

"About Lord Deene, sir. You must not worry that he could ever replace you in Georgina's affections. You are her papa, her only parent, and she adores you."

"She adored me the day I got her that dam—that dratted dog. When I insist she learn French and refuse her a pony in Town, she is not at all convinced of my value. I suspect she is in want of a mother. Shall we sit?"

Amy liked very much that Mr. Dolan's view of his daughter was unsentimental, but she liked even more that he loved the child as fiercely as he did. She took her seat beside him and made no objection when he rested an arm along the back of the bench.

His arm wasn't around her, exactly, but when she sat back, she could pretend Mr. Dolan's posture was one of affection.

"What exactly are we out here to discuss, Mr. Dolan?"

"They are lovely gardens, are they not?"

The roses were in quite good form, including some heavily scented damask beds a few yards away. Pansies enjoyed a shady corner, and beyond those, poppies grew, and something tall and purple—foxglove?

"Whitley's gardens are much like these. A treat for the nose, the eyes, and the soul." She'd spent enough summers with Georgina at the Dolan country property to recall every corner of the expansive gardens. "Will we go there this summer?"

"Very possibly, though I will procure a pony first if I treasure my daughter's happiness, which I do. But let me tell you now, Miss Ingraham, while we have some privacy, that I am feeling very much betrayed by your recent attempts to instruct me."

Amy left off staring at the flowers to risk a glance at Mr. Dolan. For all he was fatigued, he didn't seem angry, nor was his tone irritated.

"In what regard have I betrayed you, sir?"

"Behold, my late wife's brother, the young and handsome marquess. A gentleman by birth, breeding, and behavior. He came to the front door of his own home to admit us, Amy Ingraham, and you did not scold him for the oversight."

"Of course, I didn't. The man's a marquess, and his wife—"

Mr. Dolan stopped her words with a finger to her lips and a shake of his head. "He was in riding attire, my dear. You showed not the least sign of being scandalized."

My dear? "Are you mocking me, sir?"

"I am mocking myself." He shifted beside her, and while he probably didn't realize it, this brought his arm in direct contact with Amy's shoulders. She savored the closeness and tried to attend his words.

"In what regard would you mock yourself?"

"Very few of those rules matter, do they, Amy? I can still be a gentleman if I forget my top hat on a sunny day. I can still be a disgrace if I have perfect table manners. I sincerely hope this is so. In the alternative, I must conclude that I am not now, nor will I ever be, a gentleman."

Amy? "But you are the most honor—"

She broke off when he turned toward her. The arm resting on her shoulders was no longer a casual weight; it encircled her person in a gentle but clearly intentional semblance of an embrace.

He brought his free hand up and used two fingers to caress Amy's jaw.

"A gentleman does not make advances toward a woman in his employ, Amy Ingraham. I must conclude I cannot be gentleman." He brushed her hair back from her temple with the callused pad of his thumb. "My relief at this realization is boundless."

❦

"More tea, my lords?"

"Oh, come now." Bonny's eyes twinkled in the most nauseating fashion as he passed his cup back to dear cousin Hecate. "Wooster here is your cousin. Surely the milording can keep for more formal occasions?"

Nigel roused himself from dismal contemplation of the stale half cake on his plate. "I insist. We cousins must not stand on ceremony. I cannot think why you haven't called on us in Hampshire of a summer. Mama would be delighted to have the company."

Mama would turn the hounds loose on him for suggesting such a thing.

Women above the age of twenty-two ought never simper, but neither Drusilla nor Hecate demonstrated awareness of this universal truth.

"We couldn't," said Hecate at the same moment Drusilla cooed, "We'd love to."

"Then I'll send the traveling coach to fetch you as soon as you establish a date with Mama. But tell me"—he made himself take a sip of his tea, the better to appear nonchalant—"where is Cousin Amy and might we persuade her to join your visit to the family seat?"

If Bonny took exception to the imperial we, he was too well-bred to show it.

The sisters exchanged a look incomprehensible to Nigel by virtue of it being a look exchanged between females, and also a look exchanged between *twin* females.

"Amy is tending to her charge," Drusilla said. "I understand the family rusticates this time of year."

Either Amy hadn't told her sisters she was at Dolan's country holding, or Drusilla and Hecate were exercising a touch of discretion on their older sister's behalf.

Bonny cast a puzzled glance at Nigel. "If Miss Ingraham is employed in the household of Mr. Dolan—do I have that right?—then I believe he might be related to your distant neighbor, the Marquess of Deene. I can never keep all these Society connections straight, but perhaps you ladies can untangle it for me?"

No wonder Bonny had the prettiest, most accommodating mistresses, because without even a conniving glance between them, Drusilla and Hecate were racing each other to explain that the dear baron had it exactly right.

"And while Amy might certainly by rights find a position in a more exalted house," Hecate said, "it must be allowed that Mr. Dolan's family connections are impeccable."

Drusilla nodded sagely over a plate of cakes, which Nigel had found to his regret were at least a day old. "Deene married a duke's daughter, no less, and it's said to be a love match."

More simpering, which had the weak tea and stale cakes threatening to rebel.

"We ought to call on her," Nigel announced, though this was the very purpose of his exile to the countryside. "Extend the invitation, let Dolan know the woman has family."

"She'd like that," Drusilla replied. "Dolan is a cit, but quite well fixed from what we hear. It wouldn't hurt him to understand that the old families, the *best* families, can be protective when it comes to their young women."

Bonny paused in the midst of chewing on a cake, and Nigel had to wonder if a criticism hadn't just been served up with the tea and crumpets. He got to his feet rather than ponder such an improbability.

"We'll check in on her at Dolan's estate early next week. Ladies, it has been a pleasure, and you must write to Mama posthaste."

Bonny bowed over their hands, patted their knuckles, stood a shade too close in parting, and twinkled his damned eyes until Nigel wanted to wallop his friend with a riding crop, but then—thank God—they were trotting down the lane toward Bonny's country retreat while Hecate and Drusilla waved them on their way with monogrammed handkerchiefs and admonitions to come by again soon.

"What lovely cousins you have, Wooster. I liked the little brunette in particular. They might have made decent matches if somebody had seen to their come-outs."

"Second cousins, and Drusilla's smile hides a world of feminine cunning. Mama wasn't inclined to present them. I rather thought Hecate turned out well enough." Better than a cousin of any degree ought to have turned out, and he'd never thought himself partial to blonds with mischievous smiles.

Bonny regarded Nigel for a long moment. "Your mama doesn't hold the title, and your mama must learn that you are the head of the family. I went through the same thing with my mother. To set matters on the proper course takes a firm hand and nerves of steel—probably very good preparation for holy matrimony."

"Bonny, are you censuring my treatment of my cousins?" The very notion stung.

Bonny shrugged broad shoulders. "You haven't exactly *treated* them, so what is there to criticize? Besides, you're marrying the fair Amy, and that will give you the means to make provisions for the other two, won't it?"

This realization stung a good deal more. The addition of not one but three women to the family dole was a lowering thought. "Suppose it will." Nigel whacked his mount on the quarters and cantered away from the stale crumpets, the weak tea, and the obligations connoted thereby.

Three

A MAN WHO'D SPENT MUCH OF HIS CHILDHOOD ON NODDING TERMS WITH starvation knew better than to plunder or steal what must be bargained for, regardless of how dearly he desired the prize. The past week had shown Jonathan one thing at least: he could not go on worshipping from afar, he needed to resolve matters with Amy Ingraham one way or another before he parted with his reason.

And *either* way, he was determined to at least have a kiss to show for his efforts.

Jonathan settled his lips over Miss Ingraham's with…authority. He struck a balance between entreaty and demand that required him to ignore both the male-animal jubilation coursing through his veins and the terror roiling in his gut.

She'd be horrified at his expression of honest desire.

She'd say nothing, but in the morning he'd find a tidily penned notice of intent to vacate her post.

She'd simply vanish…

This notion made him gather her more closely in his arms and take a glancing taste of her lips with his tongue. So plush and soft, so…

Amy Ingraham made the sweetest little moan in the back of her throat, and through the haze of his building lust, Jonathan felt her hand fist in his hair and her breasts press firmly, even desperately, to his chest.

She might vanish in the morning, but right now, *she was kissing him back.*

The relief of that realization had him gentling his approach so he might savor the pleasures of the moment—

The heat of her tongue when it made a slow sweep over his bottom lip.

The particular sound of their clothing shifting and rubbing in close proximity.

Her leg hooked across his knees, adding a nice little clutching gesture below their waists.

The lovely, pungent fragrance of lemon verbena on the summer air.

Jonathan was contemplating the necessity of shaping her breast under his palm when Amy's mouth withdrew from his.

"This is wicked."

She breathed the words against his neck, her fist still closed around the hair at his nape. He felt the rising and falling of her chest against his sternum while her leg slid back to a more decorous position.

"Not wicked." Jonathan cradled her jaw and marveled at the contrast between his stonemason's hands and her soft cheek. "Lovely. Sweet. Precious beyond words."

Gaelic endearments bubbled up, but rather than blemish the moment with his heathen tongue, he settled for kissing her temple. "You kissed me too, my dear." Gaelic would have been better than that smug pronouncement, cursing would have been better, and yet, it was a truth he wanted her to acknowledge.

She tried to sit up. "*Any* woman would have been helpless to resist such skill, sir…"

"Mother of God, can you not say my name, Amy Ingraham?"

The effort to sit up, to stiffen her spine, lasted another three seconds, while Jonathan gently thwarted her. He kept his arms around her, tucked his chin over her crown, and held her loosely until she subsided with a sigh.

"This was very bad of us." She sounded more bewildered than outraged. At least she wasn't amused.

"I'm sure you'll tell me why a little kiss is so very bad, long before I have any interest in hearing your sermon. For now, might I please have the pleasure of simply holding you?"

She straightened enough to look him in the eye for an instant. "That was your idea of a *little* kiss?" She tucked herself against him, muttering something that sounded like "Mother of God."

After another moment, and another weighty sigh from the woman in his embrace, Amy's arm stole around the back of Jonathan's waist.

"How shall I face you at breakfast, Mr. D——"

He dipped his head and bit her earlobe. "Jonathan." Speaking through teeth clenched around a delectable bit of female flesh while that female tried not to laugh was an effort.

"You are horrid, *Mister Dolan*." She did laugh, the slight tremors of her body making Jonathan want to lay her out flat beneath him on the bench, shove their clothing aside…

He wrestled his thoughts away from that image. "Jon-a-than. Say it."

Her free hand came up to cradle his jaw, her palm soft and warm against his skin. "Jonathan. Jonathan Patrick Joseph Dolan."

"Thank you." *Bless her*, for giving him this small boon and for knowing his full name. "I've wanted to kiss you forever, you know."

The admission was probably stupid, a bad miscalculation that would have her thinking he'd been lusting in dark corners since the day he'd hired her, which wasn't the case at all.

She snuggled closer. "I've been wanting to kiss you since you bought

Georgina the spaniel. My papa would never let me have a dog, said they were too much fuss and bother, as if..."

In her silence, Jonathan heard the rest of the thought: as if a daughter weren't bother enough.

"I'll buy you an entire kennel."

She un-snuggled.

She didn't exactly stomp off, but *now* Jonathan knew he'd miscalculated. He was certain of it when she straightened, kissed his cheek, and sat up. "You needn't buy me anything, sir. This was a delightful lapse, but a lapse nonetheless. Shall we agree to forget it happened?"

He'd been smug in victory a moment ago, and now the ground beneath his feet was treacherous. "I can agree never to mention it without your invitation."

The look she gave him was hard to fathom. "My thanks."

She sounded like Lord Deene, her words bringing to mind the aristocrat implying something besides thanks. While Jonathan sought for some means of arguing her conclusions, she leaned in again and kissed him on the mouth lingeringly.

When she rose and headed back toward the house, Jonathan marshaled frustration that wasn't entirely physical. That last kiss, the one she'd taken from him, had been a kiss of parting.

Or had it? The damned dog had joined the household at least a year ago—no, two years ago.

At least.

∽≠∾

Hecate Ingraham stuffed her handkerchief back into a pocket as the dust on the drive dissipated into the summer air. "We have been wicked, Sister."

Drusilla tucked her handkerchief away as well and paced over to the porch swing. "Naughty, indeed. The stale tea cakes were an inspiration. I do like the look of the baron though."

Hecate took a seat beside her sister and gave the swing a push with her slippered foot.

"I think it a shame that Cousin Nigel has grown so handsome. He was a crashing bore when we were forced to visit in Hampshire as children."

"A good-looking crashing bore," Drusilla agreed. "But only a second cousin, thank God. Do we have a proper pot of tea now, or is a medicinal tot of the raspberry cordial in order?"

"A tot. Definitely a tot." Another push, while Dru heaved out a sigh that portended a mind at work on a Problem.

"We must warn Amy, you know. Nigel is up to something, and it won't be something as tame as putting toads in our beds."

"We put them in his boots first, alas for the toads. What are you fretting at, Dru?"

Drusilla took a turn toe-pushing the swing, rather vigorously. "Amy is our sister."

A statement of the obvious from Dru was nothing more than an opening feint. "She is."

"She sends us money frequently, and she has suffered at the hands of the Witless Gender."

"Suffered grievously," Hecate replied, though it was years ago, and many women had suffered the same fate. She was about to rise and fetch the cordial when Drusilla went on speaking.

"Amy probably won't even notice the baron's shoulders."

Ah. "And you saw him first, so you think it only fair that he fall in love with you. Honestly, Dru, that's not a sacrifice Amy would expect you to make."

"I do not think the baron will be falling in love with anybody. I think if we warn Amy that Nigel is sniffing about the gate, she might conclude it's her responsibility to see that he'll make provision for the two of us—though God knows he's had years to do that. Nigel would be a deal of work if she took him on, while Amy's present circumstance seems to make her happy. As happy as she'll allow herself to be."

Nigel would be a deal of handsome work. Hecate got the swing moving again.

"Amy is happy with her Mr. Dolan, whose household she might forsake if we're impressed to go to Hampshire." Amy wrote little regarding her employer, but the very absence of contumely suggested that she approved of the man.

"Mr. Dolan and his dear Georgina. Men do occasionally marry their children's governesses." Drusilla was not wrong in this. They'd had occasion to make lists of the men they knew who'd married their children's governesses.

"We've had no indication such a match is in the offing, Dru, and Amy has worked for Mr. Dolan for years."

"A few years. A widower has things to deal with, and Amy says Mr. Dolan is shy."

The swing creaked to a halt. "Amy can be shy too." Also stubborn, loyal, proper to a fault, and in her highly educated way, not very bright.

A widower was better than nothing, of course. Both twins had been approached by widowers—men who weren't in the market for schoolgirls or stepchildren. Such attention wasn't quite flattering, but it was better than being ignored altogether, particularly when the widower was youngish, wealthy, and handsome, and the lady had long since lost her heart to the widower's small daughter.

"Amy and her Mr. Dolan will find their way," Drusilla said. "I shall find the raspberry cordial." She rose, but Hecate caught her by the wrist.

"Pour me a glass, and we'll compose a note to Amy warning her that Nigel has recalled his family connections after all these years. We can post it the first of the week—assuming we can find her direction, and assuming she hasn't gone back to Town without telling us."

Such a note would ensure that Amy would be underfoot when next Nigel came around oozing charm and wearing boots badly in need of new heels. Somebody needed to take Nigel in hand, because Dear Cousin was up to an adult version of putting a toad in a young lady's bed.

"Mr. Dolan might better comprehend the treasure he's been harboring if a titled, handsome swain shows Amy some attention," Drusilla said. "But Amy might consider it her responsibility to fall in with whatever scheme of Nigel's will see us settled. We must consider strategy, Sister. We owe it to Amy to consider our strategy before we summon her from Mr. Dolan's side."

Drusilla did not tarry long enough for Hecate to start listing considerations and possibilities, but instead disappeared into the house.

"Strategy! And bring the bottle out here, if you please," Hecate called after her, "with the fresh tea cakes!"

≈

Amy awoke to a flash of lightning and a rumble of thunder. A nice, here-comes-the-storm sort of rumble that meant a brisk breeze was likely to kick up soon. Grabbing for her dressing gown, she pushed her feet into slippers and headed across the corridor to Georgina's room.

The curtains beside the girl's bed were already dancing in the freshening breeze, while the bed itself was empty.

And this, more than the coming storm, was what had awakened Amy—a sixth sense that all was not well with her charge. The same instinct had alerted Amy to more than one nightmare, as well as the child's inchoate bout of influenza.

Amy closed the window except for a half-inch crack and inspected the room. No dressing gown and no slippers, and Georgina was very good about observing a nightly routine that would have had both at the foot of the bed.

"Wandering, then." And Georgina wandered to one destination when she wanted comfort. Not to her governess, not if Papa was anywhere to be found.

Amy knew exactly where Jon—where Mr. Dolan's room was. Georgina had insisted on seeing it, and had made an inspection of it. The dog, Charles, was sternly admonished not to eat Papa's slippers, "lest Papa be cross."

As if Jonathan Dolan could ever be cross with his daughter. Gruff possibly, and stern, of course, but not cross. The door to his room was cracked a few inches, and soft light spilled into the corridor. Amy tapped twice on the door.

"Come in." Mr. Dolan's voice, but speaking softly rather than issuing orders and ultimatums.

He sat in a capacious armchair, Georgina curled against his chest. His hand stroked slowly over her back while her breathing followed a regular rhythm.

"She couldn't sleep. Deene has recruited her to assist the marchioness with naming the foals, of which I can tell you, there are at least two dozen."

The picture of the small child dozing peacefully in her father's arms caused a queer ache in Amy's chest. When Georgina had been ill, her father had slept on the floor of the nursery until her fever had abated. He'd read to his daughter, played cards with her, taught her how to shoot marbles, then turned around and interrogated the physicians he'd hired—the best to be had—until they either produced intelligible answers or were shown the door.

Amy pushed the memory aside and advanced into the room. "I think she's enjoying her visit."

His smile was rueful as he gathered Georgina and rose with her cradled in his embrace.

"Must you? Of course she's enjoying her visit. Deene has cozened his wife into ensuring it's so. My only consolation is that without his marchioness, he'd be reduced to stashing his pockets with horehound sweets and performing card tricks the same as any other uncle."

"I am more than capable of tucking her in, sir."

"Of course you are." He leaned over and kissed Amy's cheek, angling the child slightly away to effect his thievery. "Soon, she'll be too grown up to bring the events of the day to Papa. Fetch us the candle, if you please. Let me have what cuddles I can before my daughter outgrows her regard for me."

"You'll miss her." Amy picked up the candle, resenting that his claim on the child was as far superior to her own as his physical strength was to hers.

"Perhaps we'll both miss her."

Rotten man.

But as Amy illuminated his progress down the corridor to Georgina's room, she admitted part of her pique was a function of the kiss they'd shared three days earlier. He hadn't brought it up in conversation, but he'd repeated the offense in its misdemeanor varieties.

He'd kissed her hand when he escorted her up to her room at the end of the day.

He'd kissed her cheek when he'd collected her from the library prior to dinner.

He'd claimed a kiss as his prize when the adults had indulged Georgina in a game of forfeits, causing the child to groan and the marchioness to posit that any lady would want to lose her round to Mr. Dolan if that was the boon he sought.

And Jonathan had laughed and cast such a look at Amy, she'd been put to the blush in company.

Dratted, man. Dratted handsome man, looking weary and slightly disheveled and perilously dear.

"If you'll put her on the bed."

His lips quirked up, as if he wasn't fooled by Amy's businesslike air. He settled the child gently on the mattress, then drew the blankets up and straightened. "She'll sleep soundly now, but what about you? Will the storm keep you awake?"

Amy passed him the candle and tucked the covers more closely around Georgina. She smoothed a hand over the child's brow, then realized what she was doing.

"I'm sorry."

He cupped his hand around the candle to shield it from the draft, but this also reduced the available light. "What could you be sorry for?"

"I don't mean to imply... Georgina is not my daughter."

While Amy forbid herself to fuss at the sleeping child any further, Jonathan held the candle up a few inches, closer to Amy's face. "Your mood is not sanguine, my dear. Are you angry with me? Marie could be irritable too, at certain predictable intervals."

"At certain—!"

"Come along, my dear." He took her hand in his and led her from the room, closing the door quietly behind them. "I suppose a gentleman wouldn't allude to such a notion? Marie was hardly reserved about her bodily rhythms."

"A gentleman would most assuredly avoid such topics." Though *damn* him, he'd suggested a plausible excuse for why Amy had felt a sense of melancholia over the past several days.

"Then husbands aren't gentlemen, because without fail, if my wife were screeching at me one moment and weeping in my arms the next, there was only one explanation. I took to marking my calendar so I'd know when to bring home flowers."

Amy stopped but didn't retrieve her hand from his grasp. "You brought her flowers?"

"I brought you flowers."

He tugged on her hand, and she started walking again. "When?"

"When you had that head cold, in the winter."

"The card said they were from Georgina." But Amy had had her suspicions, of course she had. And one of the red roses gracing that bouquet—roses in January!—was pressed between the pages of her Bible. "Where are we going?" The question answered itself as they came to a halt. "This is a bad idea, Mr. Dolan."

And yet, she followed him into his bedroom and said nothing when he closed the door behind them, set the candle down, and turned to face her, his hands on his hips.

"I'll tell you what is a bad idea, Amy Ingraham. A bad idea is when you watch me like I'm about to pounce on you, to the point that Deene has remarked the situation."

The last thing, the very last thing Amy had expected was a lecture—and a deserved lecture. "I do apologize, but if you'd keep your lips to yourself, perhaps I wouldn't maintain such a close eye on you."

He glowered, and without moving, seemed to grow taller and broader. "If my advances are wholly unwelcome, you have only to so inform me."

To get away from the indignation in his gaze, and the hint of vulnerability lurking beneath it, Amy ducked aside and began to pace. "Your attentions are not wholly unwelcome, but you leave it to me to exercise sound judgment, and I am not as reliable in this regard as you might think."

"You have very sound judgment, my dear Amy. I wouldn't entrust you with my only child if you lacked judgment."

Now he sounded amused, the wretch, and he'd called her Amy.

Also *my dear*. Again.

"There, you see! You call me Amy, and I want to smile. Not a condescending smile, as if I had some perspective on such a presumption, but a real, genuine smile, *at you*—simply for using my name."

"Say my name."

He made no sense. "Jonathan."

And while she was studying him, trying to fathom what he was about, he smiled—*at her*. His smile harkened to the way he looked at Georgina, full of tenderness and approval, but it was a swain's smile, not a papa's smile at all.

"Yes," Amy said, taking a seat. "I want to look at you in precisely that manner. This is, this is *folly*." And that she remained right there beside him, in his bedroom, late at night, worse than folly.

"You are flustered." He lowered himself beside her. "I am sorry for it. Tell me what I can do to calm you."

He took her hand, and despite all sense to the contrary, it helped steady Amy's nerves—until she saw where they were sitting. "This is a bed."

"My bed. It's comfortable too, which suggests Deene is emerging from the perpetual adolescence common to his peers. Tell me what's really bothering you. You know if it's in my power to do so, I'll address it."

He kissed her forehead, and that obliterated Amy's scanty reserves of composure. The scent of him, the proximity of his throat to her mouth, the realization that he was without neckwear... *This would never do.*

"You think I am proper enough to resist what you offer, because you assume I don't precisely *know* what you offer. I wish... That is, you must consider..." She was gripping his hand and knew she should untangle her fingers from his. "I have *experience*," she went on, "such that I am more susceptible to temptation than you suppose. I know where kisses can lead. I know what use beds can be put to."

Jonathan withdrew his fingers from her grasp at that confession—now, when she wanted to drag his hand against her heart and hold it there.

"You have experience?" His voice was painfully neutral, as cool as the rain beginning to patter down outside the window. "What variety of experience?"

"The kind no true lady ought to have."

❧

"Your shot." Bonny yawned and cracked his jaw. "And make it count. I'm for bed once I've beaten you again."

"I'm distracted. I rode over to Dolan's country retreat—the place is the size of a palace—but no Amy. Seems they're enjoying the company of the Marquess of Deene, whose hospitality even includes Dolan's brat." Nigel considered the billiards table as thunder rumbled off to the south. "And that storm doesn't help my concentration."

"You're dithering, or possibly whining."

"Both." The table held not one decent shot, and any more brandy would mean a bad head in the morning, which—given his plans—Nigel could not afford. "Where did you get off to today?"

Bonny's smile was wicked. He leaned on his cue stick as if it were a shepherd's crook. "I paid a call."

"Upon whom? There's precious little decent company hereabouts, not like Kent."

"Seems I forgot my gloves when we last visited your cousins."

Nigel squatted to sight a potential shot at eye level. "*Forgot* your gloves? You paid a call on the Misses Ingraham over a pair of gloves? Subjected yourself to more stale tea cakes and weak tea over an item of apparel?"

"No." Bonny twirled his cue stick like a baton. "My gloves are all accounted for. I used the pretext of a missing pair to enjoy some very impressive raspberry cordial and a few sandwiches on the porch in the company of Miss Drusilla. Miss Hecate was off to the lending library."

"Raspberry cordial cannot *be* impressive." Nigel rose, feeling a crick in his back, also a peculiar relief that Bonny hadn't aimed his charms at Hecate. She was too substantial a woman for a man as good-hearted as Bonny. She'd chew him up and spit him out in the space of a single waltz.

"Raspberry cordial can be quite impressive," Bonny said, "unlike your billiards game. If you were to forfeit, I might be persuaded to keep your disgrace to myself."

Bonny was good-hearted. He was not an idiot. "You'd keep it to yourself—if what?"

"If you dower your cousins."

Abruptly, they weren't bantering. They'd progressed to that delicate ground where friendships could flounder and challenges might be issued.

Nigel took his shot, which sent balls bouncing all over the table, but sank not a one. "Bonny, if I could dower them, I would. Mama wouldn't have it."

Bonny skewered Nigel with a look that announced contempt for the fiction that Nigel's mother had vetoed dowries.

But Bonny *was* good-hearted, so no challenge—no overt challenge—was issued. "Perhaps when you win the hand of the fair Amy, you might bring the topic up with your wife, for she will want to see her sisters provided for. A dowager viscountess would not have a say in such a discussion, would she?"

Bonny leaned over the table, aimed, and took his shot. As a crack of thunder sounded directly overhead, three balls dropped, just like that. One, two, three.

❧

"Were you willing?"

Jonathan put the question quietly, but the lady's answer made such a difference. Mother of God, if she'd been forced... And here he was, cadging kisses from her at every opportunity.

"Oh, I was far from forced. I was eager."

Amy was disgruntled, and she could be only *Amy* when he beheld her in her night-robe and slippers, her hair a golden rope over one shoulder.

"Eager is a good thing." Jonathan slipped his arm around her waist. "A woman ought to be eager, especially her first time."

She shook her hand free of his and toyed with a button on the sleeve of her robe. "What about her second or her third?"

A story lurked here, and late at night with a breeze whipping up and only one candle lit was the time to wrest the story from her. Jonathan nudged Amy's head to his shoulder—where it did not stay, until she returned it there herself. "Tell me, dear heart. I told you about my calendar."

"You should not have."

A glimmer of amusement laced her words, so he didn't push. He stroked her back and savored the feel of her right next to him, *on his bed*.

"There was a boy. His name was Robert."

A boy, not a man. "Go on."

"He was the squire's son, a suitable fellow, and he had a wonderful smile." She fell silent for a moment while Jonathan focused on her use of the past tense. "But he was seventeen and restless, needing to see the world if not conquer it. His indulgent papa bought him a commission, and off he went for a soldier on the Peninsula."

"But first he charmed you with his smile, as boys in their regimentals are wont to do."

"You make it sound prosaic. He and I had an understanding—we truly did—except he would not let it be an engagement, given that he was going off to war." She sounded weary, as if she'd told herself this aspect of the tale many times.

"You want to believe he was honorable." Jonathan turned her, so she was in his embrace more than merely sitting beside him.

"When he died, his commanding officer sent to me the lock of hair Robert had carried everywhere. The letter was very nice, going on about how thoughts of me must have comforted the fallen hero, but that lock of hair was several shades darker than mine has ever been."

"He might have been carrying it for a comrade, a comrade fallen in battle."

Jonathan brought his arms around her, and she burrowed into him with a gusty sigh. "You are so kind. I was furious."

He propped his chin on her crown, closed his eyes, and inhaled a bouquet of lemon verbena. "Because?"

"All that eagerness? I wanted...I don't know...the philharmonic in swelling crescendos, poetry beneath the full moon, something besides him pushing my skirts up to grunt and sneeze over me for a few moments in a haymow."

Jonathan did not laugh, not at her pique, not at the sneezing. The man Robert was dead—the *boy* was dead—and even in her innocence, Amy hadn't been the least bit impressed.

"My wife was not eager to fulfill her marital responsibilities, not at first." Whatever the moment called for, Jonathan suspected it wasn't that.

Amy drew back, her expression puzzled. "You loved her. I know you did."

He gently maneuvered her head back to his shoulder. "I did—very much— but we married for the wrong reasons. Her family needed money, which I had; I wanted respectability for my children, which she could guarantee. A merciful God granted us friendship after a few years, but childbearing was dangerous for her, and her passions were not...they were not of the body."

Not for *his* body, in any case. She'd been loving, affectionate, and dutiful, also anxious to have more children, but never *eager.*

"I'm sorry."

Two ordinary words, but in them, Jonathan heard an understanding and consolation he'd never sought from another.

"It was difficult, when she died. One feels grief, but also guilt, and that anger you referred to. And then one feels simply sadness."

Amy said nothing, but she did slip her arms around Jonathan's waist. They were sitting on a bed by candlelight, and their embrace was no longer simply a matter of him holding her.

For she was holding him, too.

"Amy?"

Her hold on him became a trifle more...fierce. That fierceness told him she did not want to return to her room any more than he wanted her to go. But how, how on earth, did a *gentleman* make love to a *lady*?

"I should leave." Still she did not pull away.

"I want...I want your eagerness. I want to give you my eagerness. I want you to hear poetry by moonlight and the philharmonic right here in this bed. With me. Now."

Now and forever. He didn't say that. Let her consider the moment, and as the moment went, so too, the forever could go.

She turned her face to his shoulder, and Jonathan tried not to breathe. His offer was precipitous, headlong even, but he felt compelled to establish his place in her affections, and this interlude under Deene's roof was an ideal opportunity for advancing his suit.

Probably the only opportunity.

"Yes, Jonathan. Please." The tremor in her voice mirrored the unsteady beat of his heart. "Yes" alone would have been enough to thrill him, but, "Yes, Jonathan, please..."

He wanted to recall each detail of this night for decades to come, so for a procession of instants, he did nothing but savor the embrace: rain pattering down on gusts and soft billows of summer air, lemon verbena teasing his nose, the perfect satisfaction of Amy in her nightclothes against his body while the candle shadows danced on the breeze.

And eagerness, a lovely passionate eagerness simmering through his veins.

"Jonathan? You're not changing your mind, are you?"

"Never. I am trying to decide if you'd want the candle to remain lit."

She lifted her cheek from his shoulder. "I want to see you." Her smile was the hesitant, beautiful smile of a woman new to expressions of passion. Jonathan rose off the bed, brought the candle to the night table, and began to disrobe.

"See me, you shall."

Her smile softened, and he had to focus instead on removing his clothing. His hands didn't shake, exactly, but rather than fumble with his shirt buttons, he pulled the thing over his head and tossed it on a chair. His boots and stockings followed, and then he was down to breeches and underlinen.

Now, he hesitated.

"You are familiar with the evidence of a man's desire?" Said evidence had been growing since the moment she'd sat on the bed. The etiquette books had provided exactly no guidance regarding how an aroused man dealt with the effects of base urges in the presence of an eager lady.

Amy stroked a hand over his bare belly. "I want to see you." She slid her hand lower to cup him through his breeches. "Robert was always in a hurry. Always worried somebody would catch us…"

In which case, the sorry pup would have had to marry her and give up his silly notions of the glory of war. "Undo my falls, Amy. Please." He added that last word because now his hands *were* unsteady.

Amy's were not. She dispatched the buttons on his breeches, then sat back. "You'll have to do the rest."

"My heartfelt pleasure." He shoved the rest of his clothing to the floor and stood, hands at his sides. The look on Amy's face was precious—stern, curious, and not a little nonplussed.

"Robert wasn't built on quite the same scale you are."

Which might account in part for the boy's inability to inspire bodily poetry or soaring music. "Touch me, if it pleases you to do so."

He could see the longing in her gaze at war with trepidation, so he decided the matter for her by taking her hand and curling her fingers around his shaft.

"You're warm."

While her hand was cool, wonderfully cool.

"Robert wanted me to kiss him." She sounded dubious. "Here."

"We can save that for another day if you'd rather." Many other days, days when Jonathan had developed a great deal more restraint than was available to him at that moment. "Amy, I want to see you too."

She left off fondling him, which was a mercy and a grief, then rose to stand beside the bed. "I'm old, you know."

"Ancient, I'm sure, and yet I am older than you by several years." He kept his hands at his sides lest he tear her clothing from her body and reveal her in all her glorious maturity. In his imagination, the sound of ripping fabric was drowning out the violins, and yet, Amy did not hurry.

She held his gaze while she unbuttoned her dressing gown—the thing had fourteen buttons. When he married her, he'd make sure all her nightclothes had only three buttons. Or two.

Or a simple sash around her middle on those few occasions when he permitted her to don a dressing gown.

She passed him the dressing gown, and he brought it to his nose to inhale the flowers-and-lemon aroma of her. "Do you need my assistance with that nightgown, Amy?"

She nodded, which he interpreted as an admission that her courage had deserted her. He took pity on them both and drew the nightgown over her head, his ability to count beyond three in any language having abandoned him.

"I wish you would not stare at me, sir."

"Jonathan. The bed is behind you. The covers are available to soothe your modesty, but, Amy?" The impulse to lash his arms around her was a palpable, writhing thing.

She stopped peering around the room to cast him a glance.

"My dear, you are gorgeous. You are beautiful, and if you do not get into that bed this instant, I will fall on my knees to worship what I see of you by the light of this candle."

Not poetry, but it put a hesitant smile back on her face. She scooted under the covers, and he followed her into the bed, crawling across the mattress to poise over her on all fours.

"Dear heart, how eager are you?"

She regarded him earnestly. "Quite."

"Spread your legs a little."

She might have recalled a similar importuning from the departed Robert, because she frowned when she complied. "Now what?"

Now nothing came between them but his self-restraint. "You might kiss me."

By dint of iron self-discipline, he remained crouched above her under the covers, close but not touching, while she considered his suggestion. A gentleman would know flowery speeches and pretty words; Jonathan knew only lust and an abiding regard for his lady.

No—not *regard*. In those moments while Amy's gaze traveled from his eyes to his forehead to his lips and back to his eyes, Jonathan faced a truth: he had loved his wife. He described the feeling to himself as part duty, part deep fondness, part fast friendship.

He loved this woman too, but the mix was different—it included eagerness and panting lust, and while a gentleman wouldn't likely be pleased to admit it, this was in Jonathan's estimation an improvement over the marital relationship.

A brush of soft lips obliterated his ability to ruminate. "Do that again, Amy. *Please*, do that again."

She smiled this time, smiled right against his mouth. He wanted to growl—would she consider that grunting? Her hand sank into his hair and without thinking, Jonathan allowed his arousal to brush against her sex.

He did growl—and she moaned, and the kiss turned into an oral wrestling match involving their entire bodies—tongues, hands, torsos, legs, and lips. In the melee, he came perilously close to penetration, and they both went still.

"Jonathan, you must..." She swallowed and found his free hand with her own, then laced their fingers. "Please. I can't bear to wait any longer."

He'd wanted to make her come at least once before suffering the pleasure of joining their bodies. The plan was selfish, intended to hedge a bet against his flagging self-control and their mutual *eagerness*. The plan was also insupportable, given the feel of her naked body beneath his and the way she said his name.

"Listen for the violins, my love." He laid his cheek against hers, and in silence, found the opening to her body. She drew in a quick breath at the first nudge of his cock, so he waited until she'd relaxed again to push against her heat.

From somewhere, he found the resolve to move slowly. To listen to *her*—violins, be damned—to her breathing, to the way her body lifted into his deliberate thrusts then subsided, to the feel of her fingers closing more tightly around his.

He brushed his thumb across her palm. "Relax, my lady. I'm not going to sneeze, and this will take us more than a few moments."

As he set up a voluptuous rhythm in the sweet heat of her body, he prayed joining this way would in a figurative sense take them the rest of their lives.

Four

At her first sight of Jonathan Dolan, Amy had liked that he was a brute of a man. Not only tall, but broad shouldered and braced with an ungenteel complement of muscle. He had calluses and scars, he raised his voice on occasion with his business connections, and did not suffer fools. Such a man would take up his responsibilities with competence and determination.

He would dower his poor relations, and from the portraits and sketches on the walls of his office, he had a number of those. As her interview with her prospective employer had progressed, Amy had found him keenly intelligent, a conscientious parent, and unflinching when it came to discussion of difficult subjects—his daughter's safety, money, Amy's character. He'd even made her sign a dauntingly lengthy contract.

In a manner many women would not have comprehended, Jonathan Dolan was a brave man.

In the ensuing months, Amy's estimation of him had risen further. He was not merely conscientious where Georgina was concerned, he was devoted to the child. He could not only discuss money, he could quietly share it with any numbers of charities, and was gruffly generous with Amy herself.

Now she found he was also, beneath his finely tailored attire, *gorgeous*, a breathtaking specimen who made poor Robert, with his skinny chest and soft hands, look like the mere boy he'd been.

And Jonathan Dolan knew things about generosity that had nothing to do with coin, and everything to do with patience. He brushed his thumb across her palm again.

"I like when you do that."

"This?" He repeated the gesture, a slow, sweet slide of flesh on flesh.

She turned her head and kissed his forearm. "When you do that with your thumb, you say you want to touch me every way you can."

He spoke very near her ear, so close she could feel the shape of his breath against her neck. "I want to touch you in ways that haven't been dreamed of yet—not by you, not by the naughty angels themselves. I want to put my mouth and hands to places on your body that will shock and delight you equally. I want to embolden you with my passion such that you shock and delight me with your own."

A hint of a brogue had slipped into his voice, giving it a musical quality that counterpointed the undulations of his hips.

"Jonathan, I want to cry."

He rested his forehead on hers and slowed his thrusts even more. "Hold on to me."

She wanted to tell him the tears would have been for that girl in the haymow, the one whose back was itchy, who'd watched the wooden pulley hanging from the roof beam creak in the breeze while a selfish boy had fumbled and sneezed over her.

"Hold onto me, Amy." Jonathan's voice had taken on a rasp as he repeated the words. She locked her ankles at the small of his back, clutched his hand in hers, and focused her awareness on the slow thrust and retreat of their joined bodies.

A sense of vertigo stole over her, of gravity slipping its moorings. She closed her eyes and clung to him, begging with her hips for less deliberation and more passion.

He hitched up, shifted the angle, and abruptly, passion was too much.

Amy's body went into a frenzy of pleasure, a rejoicing in itself that transcended her skin and dissolved the boundaries between her and her lover. She could feel his body as if it were her own, could feel pleasure ricocheting between them and expanding until she was weeping against his throat and bucking madly beneath him.

And then...a resonant stillness, broken only by the feel of Jonathan's hand smoothing over her hair and their breathing finding a complementary rhythm.

Long, contented moments went by while Amy simply marveled at what her body was capable of in Jonathan Dolan's arms.

"Do you cry for your soldier boy, Amy?"

His voice was as gentle as the touch of his hand on her hair. Amy turned her face into his throat. "I cry for the girl who yearned. She wasn't wrong: there is astounding poetry, there are gorgeous symphonies."

"Dear lady, that was merely the opening movement."

❧

Maybe he'd forgotten this soul-deep postcoital peace, or maybe it had never been like this before. As a younger man, Jonathan had been too restless and self-important to appreciate the pleasure of simply holding a woman in his arms. As a husband, he hadn't wanted to presume or overstay his welcome. As a widower, his encounters had been about sexual relief, with neither party seeking any entanglement.

He was entangled now. He'd arranged Amy over him, so she straddled his hips and cuddled against his chest. She used the end of her braid to tickle his mouth in a distracted way, as if her body wanted to play, but her mind was intent on serious matters.

"You are thinking, Miss Ingraham." He kissed her crown. "These are not moments one ought to waste on thinking."

She raised a troubled expression to his gaze. "Do you hold me in less esteem now for knowing what you do about me?"

Ah, women. Certain women. "What do I know about you? I know passion makes you brave and generous. I know you move me to forget myself. I know I am happy at this moment."

"Be serious." A hint of the governess laced her inflection. He envied schoolboys as he traced the arch of her brow with his thumb.

"I will be what you call serious. Marry me, Amy Ingraham. Please marry me. I will procure a special license, Deene and his lady will stand up with us, Georgina will be ecstatic. We can be married by sunset tomorrow and spend all our nights composing symphonies to passion."

She did not smile at him. If anything, her countenance became more solemn. Jonathan debated the wisdom of arousing her again as a distraction, ran an experimental hand down the elegant curve of her spine, and discarded the notion.

A single caress of her bare flesh, and *he* was the one distracted.

"You needn't offer for me, sir. I am no more or less chaste than I was when I got into this bed."

Her words held a chilling sense of purpose, and Jonathan divined that along with her blue blood, Amy Ingraham had inherited a dose of the martyr. She would preserve him—son of a stonemason, climbing cit, upstart social nothing—from what she perceived as marrying beneath himself.

"Amy, I did not withdraw." He kept his voice even, when what he wanted was to roll her beneath him and prevent her bodily from leaving the bed. "Neither time did I take the simplest measure to reduce the likelihood of conception. I am one of twelve. I have nieces and nephews without limit. I would not have climbed into this bed without intending to marry you."

She stroked her fingers over his mouth. "I am not sure I would have climbed into this bed if I'd known your intent."

"*Why the hell not?*" He was about to remind her that he could provide for her handsomely, buy her all the pretty things and fine horses she wanted, but something stopped him. Poetry and symphonies, maybe.

She looked hesitant in the flickering candlelight. "It isn't what you think—it isn't that I don't…that I would not care to be your wife."

"Then what is it?"

"I had not thought to be anybody's wife, not ever, not now… I must discuss this with my sisters, I think."

"Amy, are you ashamed of me? Is that it? Because my first wife was ashamed of me, and I bore it for years. If that's how—"

"Hush." She kissed him on the mouth, a solid, you-listen-to-me kiss followed up with a stern glare. "I am not ashamed of you. I could *never* be ashamed of you. You are the most worthy, honorable man I know. I adore Georgina, and *she* adores you." Amy's brows drew down as if in puzzlement. "I adore *you*. I must think about this though."

He wanted to make love with her all over again, simply for admitting she adored him—he would think about the rest of her words later—but he instead posed a question. "Do you want to consider terms?"

This, he could understand. She had bargaining power now that every woman thought she gave up at the altar—only to find she held even higher cards after the wedding.

"I want to consider everything. I really did not foresee forcing an offer from you."

"Mother of—Amy, did you suppose I could be this intimate with you, hold you while your tears wet my chest, bury myself inside you not once but twice, and then greet you over breakfast as if nothing had changed?"

"Many men suppose just that, and carry it off quite well. I visit with other governesses in the park, abigails, and companions. Ours can be a perilous existence."

"And you think I'd condemn you to that?" He wanted to shake her, and he wanted to use his fists on the men who'd justified these notions of hers with such dishonorable behavior.

"You look so fierce, Jonathan Dolan." Her smile was slow and knowing, not a smile he'd seen on her before, and it made her positively, rivetingly beautiful. "You would not take advantage of me—of anyone. You are far too much a gentleman to behave so disgracefully."

He did not comment on the error of her observation. "So you'll marry me?"

"Give me time to adjust to the notion. I'll give you an answer before we must go back to Town."

He wanted to tell her they'd leave for Town at dawn, but his negotiating instincts told him not to let her see how desperate he was—not to put it into words yet again. "Take your time, then, Miss Ingraham, but I know a few things about music and poetry."

She brushed her hand over his chest, then stared at his right nipple as it reacted to her touch. "What do you know?"

"I adore you, too. I have for quite some time. I also know that symphonies typically have at least three movements, and poems can have many stanzas. They can go on for pages and pages."

His behavior in the next hours wasn't gentlemanly, but he made a decision in favor of hope and trust and adoration. As he explored all those extra stanzas and orchestral finales with Amy, Jonathan again took not the simplest measures to reduce the probability of conception.

Nor did she ask him to.

⚜

Nigel did not allow himself to peer around the Marquess of Deene's foyer until the footman had withdrawn, bearing Nigel's hat, riding gloves, and crop, and the butler had toddled off with Nigel's card on a salver.

Cousin Amy was no doubt overwhelmed by such grand surrounds. To have a card delivered to her on a silver tray would likely fluster the woman nicely.

"I beg your pardon, sir." A petite blond bearing a bowl of roses halted abruptly in the doorway to the foyer. "May I be of assistance?"

She was pretty enough, and as Nigel's gaze traveled over her person, he noted generous curves in the best places, particularly those places north of her waist and south of her chin.

"I am Wooster." He infused his voice with a hint of hauteur.

"Mr. Wooster." She bobbed a curtsy, roses and all. The woman wasn't even wearing a cap, which suggested Lord Deene overlooked a bit of laxness from his more attractive domestics.

Nigel studied her bosom, which truly was perfect. Not vulgarly generous, but abundant and well displayed by a fetching pale green dress. "*Lord* Wooster."

"Are you here to see his lordship?"

If she was the housekeeper, then such a question wasn't exactly rude. "I will pay my courtesies to him, certainly, but I am calling upon a guest, Miss Amy Ingraham. The butler has been dispatched to fetch her."

The woman's gaze dropped to her roses. "I'll wish you good day then." She popped another small curtsy and withdrew.

Deene was said to be recently wed. His marchioness must be the tolerant sort, or she'd have dismissed the likes of the curvy little blond immediately upon getting Deene up to scratch. This idea put Nigel in a good humor. A man with a tolerant wife would be disposed to understand Nigel's own circumstances, which might come in handy if Dolan grumbled about the loss of a governess.

Which he would not. Even a mushroom like Dolan had to know governesses were available on any street corner.

The butler reappeared through the doorway the housekeeper had just vacated. "This way, my lord."

The house smelled good, of flowers, lemon, and beeswax. The place was full of summer sunshine too, the windows sparkling clean, and the drapery tidily folded back. Nigel abruptly decided that upon his marriage to Amy, the family seat in Hampshire would get a good scrubbing—the present viscountess not being inclined to trifle with household matters.

"Miss Ingraham has been informed of your arrival, my lord."

The butler bowed his way from the pretty parlor into which Nigel had been shown. From somewhere in the house, a woman's laughter rang out, then the lower tones of a man's voice. Morale was apparently good among Deene's servants, though decorum sadly wanting.

"Cousin Nigel." A woman spoke his name a few moments later, a willowy blond with lovely gray eyes, a perfect complexion, and soft masses of shiny hair caught back at her nape. Standing inside the doorway, she was prettier than the housekeeper by virtue of greater height. For that matter, she was prettier than many women by virtue of some unnameable luminous quality to her whole bearing.

And this was Jonathan Dolan's *governess*?

"Dear Cousin Amy." He held out his hands to her, and when she crossed a few steps to take them into her own, he tugged her in close enough for an embrace.

The moment—the entire situation—called for boldness.

She allowed him a brief, chaste hug then stepped back. "This is a surprise and a pleasure. May I ring for tea?"

She'd probably enjoy such a small gesture of standing, to have a titled relation call on her, and to be able to offer him tea. "Tea would be lovely, but not half so lovely as you, dear cousin.

This compliment earned him a quizzical glance—Amy would not be used to drawing-room flatteries—and then she went to the door to order the tray. Nigel was pleased to note the view of the back of her was as lovely as the view of the front. Amy wasn't as curvaceous as her sister Hecate, but Nigel would reconcile himself to that disappointment eventually.

"Won't you have a seat, Nigel? I can't stay long. Georgina has her heart set on a picnic this afternoon, and I disappoint her at my peril."

Nigel affixed a look of sympathy to his features, took a seat on the sofa, and patted the place beside him. "Is your charge a spoiled little beast? I am grieved to hear it."

Amy took a ladder-backed chair near the hearth, and sat so her spine did not touch the chair. Perhaps she hadn't understood the proximity he'd offered; more likely she could not afford to act familiarly with a caller.

But no, she was smiling. "Georgina is a treasure, the day is gorgeous, and the marchioness has declared that we will abandon the house and go wading. How does the summer find you, Nigel, and what brings you this way?"

Boldness, he reminded himself. "I am in good health, but as for what brings me to Surrey, you do. Surely you must know that."

Her brows drew down. "I'm glad to see you, of course, but my circumstances are very comfortable. You need have no concern for me."

The tea tray arrived, and Nigel was pleased to see Amy could navigate it without fumbling. He accepted a cup and set it aside after a single sip. "Amy, your birthday approaches."

"In a few weeks. You will not tease me into revealing which one it is, either. I've had rather a lot of them." Her rueful smile was fleeting.

Boldness. "My dear, I can wait no longer. The issue of our betrothal has become urgent."

Her head came up, and she set her cup on its saucer with a little clatter. "Our *what*?"

"Our betrothal. Might I have a few of those cakes?" They looked delicious, draped in frosting and arranged just so.

"Nigel, you can't blithely announce—" She fell silent, which was wise of her. She'd been on the verge of raising her voice, something Mama would not approve of at all. Nigel accepted a plate with three cakes on it.

"You're not having any?"

She got up to pace. "For God's sake, Nigel. We are not now, nor have we ever been, engaged."

"Well, this makes one thing clear." He popped a cake in his mouth, letting chocolate sweetness spread over his palate. "I'm reassured you weren't being coy, or—heaven forbid!—trying to avoid your duty. You really didn't know?"

She whirled toward him from across the room and stopped, her arms crossed over her middle. "Didn't know *what*?"

"Didn't know of our engagement. Surely somebody…" He pretended to assess her heightened color, her tense posture. "But I can see they did not. Finish your tea, Amy, and contemplate how many women enjoy exchanging a governess's lot for that of a titled lady. Consider it my early birthday present to you."

She did not do exactly as he bid. She went to the window and stood for a long moment with her back to him, which allowed Nigel to consume two more tea cakes. He waited, expecting she'd soon start weeping with gratitude and demanding that he promise he was not jesting.

If only.

Amy was a pretty enough woman that Nigel would manage to do his marital duty by her, but she wasn't…*warm*, not like her sister Hecate. Her eyes held no laughter, no light of devilment. She wasn't…approachable, and she didn't look at all like she'd become the sort of viscountess to meekly pacify Mama day after day.

"I brought you a ring, though I can't vouch for its size. Shall I put it on your finger?"

She turned, her features remarkably composed considering the good fortune befalling her. "That would be rather hasty, wouldn't it? You might consider us engaged, but I have heard no proposal, and you haven't heard an acceptance."

He hadn't seen her for twelve years, but even as an adolescent, she'd had a sort of sternness about her. When Nigel had heard Cousin Amy was at work in the schoolroom, he'd considered it a natural fit for her and pitied any unruly children in her care.

Nonetheless, boldness meant he should slap an indulgent smile on his face and jolly her past her incredulity.

"Come, Cousin, are we to descend into dramatics? Shall I go down on one knee? The documents require that we are to marry by your twenty-eighth birthday if Grandpapa's provisions aren't to be largely lost to you."

"Our *grandfathers* set this up? I cannot believe such a thing."

Mulish woman. She'd likely inherited that from their great-grandfather, whose stubbornness was legendary.

"You are in shock." He rose and moved closer to her, and caught a whiff of lemons from her. She would wear lemon, though a hint of brimstone wouldn't have surprised him. "I have had years to accustom myself to these terms, and years to hope you were merely indulging in an independent nature when you went into service—"

"An independent nature? For God's sake, Nigel, I wanted to eat. I wanted to provide for my sisters. I wanted to survive. I wrote to your mother repeatedly, begging for her assistance and guidance, and I even wrote to you."

"I never saw your letter." His mother had burned it unread, saying it couldn't include anything other than all its predecessors had. "I am sorry, and the post is notorious for being unreliable."

"It is not." Her voice cracked like a whip.

Would he have to *argue* her into accepting a title? Nigel's gaze fell on Amy's prim mouth, and he felt a sinking sensation regarding his marital future.

"So you thought yourself abandoned? Why didn't you come to us, Amy? We're your family, and you must have known we'd be in Town during the Season? A post chaise out to Hampshire shouldn't have been beyond you, and Mama would never turn away family."

Nigel was congratulating himself on the concern and hint of reproach in his voice—as well as the smoothness of his lying—when the petite blond came barging into the room.

"Miss Ingraham, I'm sorry to interrupt your little tête-à-tête with his lordship, but Georgina is growing inpatient. Your duties call."

The little idiot beamed encouragingly at Amy, which was the outside of too much.

"My good woman, you are rag-mannered indeed to interrupt a gentleman when he's calling on a lady, much less on a relation, much, much less when he's calling on his intended for the purpose of solemnizing their engagement. You will take yourself off immediately. Tell the dratted child to go copy some prayers, and be very certain that I will inform Lord Deene of the rudeness countenanced among his help."

Amy's jaw snapped closed with an audible click, though if she were to become a viscountess, then she'd need to know how to deliver a proper dressing down. God knew Mama had the knack of it.

"Why don't I fetch Lord Deene?" the blond volunteered. She had a gleam in her eye Nigel did not in the least approve of. "And Amy Ingraham, you are coming with me." She grabbed Amy by the wrist and towed Nigel's cousin from the room.

Clearly, Amy was oppressed in her present circumstances, even by so dubious an authority as her host's housekeeper. But of course, the woman was likely Deene's leman, which put a different light on the situation.

Deene was to be admired, really, if he could keep wife and mistress both content under the same roof. Nigel resumed his seat before the tea tray and popped another cake into his mouth.

A wife, a mistress, and a jolly good cook, too. Perhaps married life might not be so bad after all.

❦

"Get the hell in here." Jonathan's brother-in-law grabbed him by the elbow and all but dragged him into the library.

"Deene, is this how you treat guests now? I'll have a word with mine hostess that your disposition is in want of—"

Deene closed the door behind them with a kick of his boot. "Shut up and listen, Dolan."

"I do not respond well to the imperative voice, Deene." Jonathan shrugged out of his lordship's grasp. "I'm to join Georgina and her governess for a picnic down by the stream, where I will no doubt be splashed without mercy and consoled for the abuse I suffer by being pelted with strawberries and—"

"Drink this." Deene shoved a glass of whiskey at Jonathan. "You've trouble brewing, unless I much mistake the situation."

Jonathan peered at his drink. "Even for you, Deene, this is odd behavior. Explain yourself."

"Evie came across a Lord Wooster lurking in our foyer, a pink of the *ton* idling about in high fashion without an invitation from me. He said he came to call upon your Miss Ingraham, and when Evie couldn't find me to alert me to his presence, she took it upon herself to chaperone his call."

"Lord Wooster." The name rang a bell, not a pleasant one. "Where is Amy right now?"

Deene nodded, as if Jonathan's response confirmed something in the marquess's mind. "Evie dragooned Miss Ingraham into joining Georgie on their planned outing."

"*Our* planned outing. I gather you were not invited?" Jonathan took a fortifying drink of excellent potation, but it did little to ease his distress at the thought of a titled gentleman calling upon Amy.

"What would be the point of my joining the picnic? Evie was going to distract the child, while you…"

"While I what?

"Wooed your child's governess."

This sip was necessary to give Jonathan time to think. "I was under the impression, Deene, that you regard me as the presuming Irish cit who kidnapped your sister into holy matrimony by taking advantage of both her and your mercenary father. You hate me, and you tolerate me under your roof only because you do not want to offend your niece."

"I do not hate you." Deene muttered this, and turned away to pour himself a drink. When he'd tossed back two fingers—and not of lemonade—he rounded on Jonathan with a determined expression. "I resented you." He ran a hand through his hair. "I resent you."

Jonathan saluted with his drink. "Present tense, duly noted. I resent you, too. Marie thought you could do no wrong, while I was a constant source of shame to her."

"Ashamed of *you?*"

"Certainly." Even with Deene's best libation on hand, the admission wasn't easy. "I all but bought her, Deene, or so she believed, and no matter that she was mistaken, I was not her choice. I was her duty."

Deene poured himself another half glass. "She bloody loved you, you fool. She was ashamed of her family, of the way her own father sold her off to pay his gambling debts—and my tuition bills. That's what she resented."

The marquess glowered at his drink while insight warmed Jonathan's insides more than the best whiskey ever would.

"Looking after Georgina is the only way you can absolve yourself of the sacrifice your sister made for her family—for you."

Deene's glower intensified. "I'm Georgina's uncle, her only adult male relation on her mother's side worth the name. I will not neglect my responsibility, but we can argue that point some other day. I'd say at present we have a more pressing concern."

"Lord Wooster." And wasn't it interesting, that Wooster was *our* problem?

"He announced to Evie that he's some relation of Miss Ingraham's and he's come to seal their betrothal. Georgina won't like this development at all, and I can't say I approve of it either."

As a boy, Jonathan had experienced the shock on a hot summer day of leaping from the broiling sun into the still, frigid depths of the water filling an abandoned quarry. The same sensations went through him then settled in a leaden ball in his guts.

Among the upper-class English, there was no such thing as an informal betrothal.

"To hell with your approval," Jonathan spat. "I loathe the very notion of Amy marrying another."

"Thought you might." Deene looked marginally relieved. "I've run Wooster off for now, but he'll be back tomorrow. He told me in confidence that their grandfathers set it up, so the marriage has to take place in the next few weeks or Amy's portion will be greatly reduced. What shall we do about him?"

Jonathan attributed the frisson of weakness in his knees to Deene's blasted whiskey.

"He's titled, Deene, and he's a gentleman. I'll bet he's such a damned gentleman he wears gloves to bed and has some fussy little maggot shine his boots with champagne."

Deene set his drink down with a thump.

"So you'll cede the field? You'll withdraw from the lists, when you can't take your eyes off that woman? For God's sake, you *fought* for Marie when you hardly knew her. You bludgeoned, bribed, and brawled your way into the best clubs, tricked out your handsome Irish arse to perfection, courted her at every ball and breakfast in Mayfair... And you'll toss Miss Ingraham over at the first sign of competition?"

Deene in a tirade was an impressive sight. He was usually so much the English gentleman that his sheer size and brawn tended to fade from notice, but not when he was breathing fire and spitting indignation.

"Let me tell you something, Dolan. If you think I'll stand idly by while some prancing ninny makes off with my niece a few years hence on the strength of his papa's title or his mama's blue blood, you are sadly mistaken. *One doesn't treat a female he loves in such an asinine fashion.*"

At some point in Deene's diatribe, Jonathan had taken up residence on a leather sofa. Deene came down beside him. "What will you do, Dolan?"

Jonathan passed Deene his glass. "I resent you, Deene, because I'm stubborn about these things, and you are too, but in the present instance—and in the present instance only—I must admit I find a particle of sense amid all your blustering."

"You're saying I'm right." Deene finished Jonathan's drink. "So what, for the love of God, shall you do about Lord Rooster?"

"I'm going wading." Jonathan rose and headed for door, but paused with his hand on the latch. "And, Deene? I loved your sister. From the first time she made herself stand up with me, I loved her, though I took far too long to make this evident to the lady herself."

He kept his back to his host when Deene spoke softly from his place on the sofa. "Duly noted."

❧

Never before had Amy resented Georgina, but for two hours in the afternoon, it was as if the child had known Amy sought privacy with Jonathan. The marchioness could not tempt the girl to make daisy chains; the marquess could not distract Georgina with offers to show her the best climbing tree.

Eventually, Amy had given up. Jonathan had not met her gaze, not at the stream, and not over dinner. He probably thought she'd deceived him, had accepted his advances in bad faith while engaged to another.

Boldness got her nowhere. When she'd suggested a walk in the garden after dinner, Jonathan had declined, murmuring something about tucking Georgina in. In every other regard, he'd been his usual, punctiliously polite if somewhat irascible self.

Boldness be damned, *desperate* measures were called for.

Amy buttoned her dressing gown, picked up her candle, and headed for her lover's bedroom—assuming he still considered them lovers—only to find his bed empty. She was sitting on Jonathan's bed, pondering what came after desperate measures when the door opened and the object of her determination stepped into the room.

He closed the door behind him and set his candle on the bureau. "There you are."

Amy remained on the bed. "There *you* are."

"Am—" He remained rooted by the door. "Miss Ingraham, please be mindful that you look quite fetching in your present location, and given how we comported ourselves in that location not twenty-four hours past, you might consider placing your person elsewhere."

Miss Ingraham?! "You want me to leave?" The possibility that Jonathan would not want her if she were engaged to another had haunted her since she'd heard Nigel's awful pronouncement.

"Leave?" Still he made no move to approach her. "I was rather hoping..." He glanced around the room. "May I be honest?"

"Honesty would be appreciated." She steeled herself for a polite tongue-lashing about women who fled engagements and frolicked under false pretenses.

"I was thinking, Miss Ingraham, that you might remove to the settee, where I could take the seat beside you without risking—" Another sigh. His gaze fell on Amy's face, his expression somber. "If I might be *very* honest, I was rather hoping you might let me hold you."

She flew across the room into his arms, lashing her own around his waist. "I am *not* engaged to Nigel. I cannot *be* engaged to Nigel." She repeated what had become her private prayer over and over, her face pressed to Jonathan's chest.

His hand settled on her hair. "Amy, please don't cry."

She did not oblige his request. While he walked her to the bed—not the blighted settee—she accepted his handkerchief and his physical support.

"I cannot fathom what Nigel is about." She dabbed at her eyes with Jonathan's linen, the lavender scent of it soothing. "He leaves my sisters and me to eke out an existence on the edge of poverty for years, then comes strutting around condescending, as if... Oh, I could just *slap* him, Jonathan. Him and his infernal mama."

"I am more relieved than you know to hear this." Jonathan murmured these words against Amy's hair, and the very sound of his voice calmed her further. "When you were so standoffish at the stream today, I began to wonder, and then when you did not come up to the nursery..."

She reached for his hand. "You declined to walk in the garden."

"I did not want Deene's lady to haul his perishing lordship out for a breath of fresh air along with us."

So they'd both been in an agony of uncertainty. This comforted Amy a very great deal, but not quite enough. "Jonathan, what am I to do?"

"You'll not marry that buffoon."

"But he spoke as if there were documents."

"Then we'll demand to see them." He sounded not simply resolute, he sounded as if he relished the whole idea of brangling with Nigel.

"Jonathan, you must be careful. Nigel has a nasty streak."

"This is about money, Amy. I'm almost sure of it. When it comes to money, trade, and dirty business, I have a nasty streak too."

In contrast to the ferocious undertone in his voice, his hand on Amy's back was gentle.

She let her head rest on his shoulder and put his handkerchief aside. "How can you know money is at the root of this? Nigel thought I went into service to indulge my independent nature. Even if I had—which is an *absurd* notion—that doesn't explain why he let poor Hecate and Drusilla languish without any dowry at all."

"All the more reason to conclude the man is eyeing his exchequer."

"Or his mama is. She's a dragon."

"Then you will allow me to slay your dragons, but can we please be more comfortable while we discuss the particulars?"

"You want to remove to the settee?"

"No, my dear. I want to remove your clothes."

He'd brought his arms around her, and at his words, the last of Amy's anxiety abated to a manageable level. "There's more we need to discuss, Jonathan. My sisters must be informed of these developments."

"We'll discuss anything you wish, *later*."

"In that case"—she kissed his cheek—"I want to remove your clothes too."

Five

A MAN WITH ELEVEN SIBLINGS UNDERSTOOD FAMILY. WHEN SEVEN OF HIS SIB-lings were female, he also had a healthy dose of respect for the sororal bond, which served Jonathan well when he took Amy to call on her sisters the following morning.

Over strong tea and fresh crumpets, he observed several salient facts, which he discussed with his intended as he drove her back to Deene's holding.

"You miss your sisters, Amy. I would not have begrudged you more frequent visits out here had you asked, and your sisters would certainly have been welcome to see you in Town."

"We do meet occasionally, but you had me sign a contract that elucidated in detail when I was to have leave."

He'd forgotten about her contract, though it was no doubt filed tidily away in some drawer. "I wanted someone steady for Georgina's governess."

She gave him an indulgent look that had him recalling the previous night. "One understands your devotion to your only child, Jonathan."

"She might not be my only child for long. You will marry me, won't you?"

When her indulgent smile might have muted to the lambent expression of a woman in love, her lips pursed, and her brows drew down. "To plight my troth to one man when I'm engaged to another tempts fate."

Jonathan urged the horse, a handsome bay gelding on loan from Deene's stables, to pick up the pace of its trot. When he wanted badly to argue, he instead fell back on the guidance of one of Amy's preachy little books.

"We will deal with your cousin's unfortunate misperception. I liked your sisters, liked them very much. They're protective of you, and they look forward to repaying your generosity."

Now, her smile softened. "You, sir, have changed the subject, though I'm so very glad you liked Dru and Hecate. They liked you too, or they would never have brought out the cordial." But then the smile disappeared. "I haven't been generous with them, please understand that. They are very stubborn, those two. They refuse to see that I'm the oldest and it's my duty to provide for us as best I can."

From what Jonathan had observed, Hecate and Drusilla were managing well enough. Their surroundings were humble but comfortable. They had a maid of all work, a man of all work, and a mule of all work, who was as near to fat as a mule could get.

"What they see, my dear, is that you have gone into service to punish yourself for lapsing with the late Robert, and they have had quite enough of your penance. You refuse to admit your sisters are grown women—very pretty, capable grown women—and they are waiting for you to settle before they change their own prospects."

Beside him, Amy was silent for a moment while the tilbury spun along between green hedgerows. "I am not pleased to think you might be right. They are that loyal. What did Hecate want to ask you?"

Hecate, the one who looked most like Amy, had drawn Jonathan aside in the small stable and whispered a few pointed comments in his ear.

"Your sister asked me, among other things, if I my intentions toward you were honorable. I assured her they were. The question remains, though, whether your intentions are honorable toward me."

"Do you really want me to answer that?"

Her expression, frowning again and distracted, was answer enough.

"When we've sorted your cousin out, you will give me an answer, Amy."

Though as to *how* they would sort dear Nigel out, Jonathan himself did not yet have as many answers as he might have wished.

❦

"I have a plan, but I'd like your opinion on it." Jonathan kept his tone neutral, because despite the recent thawing in his relations with Deene, the younger man was an integral part of the plan—if he allowed himself to be.

"You want my opinion?" Deene paused while running his stirrup irons up their leathers. "Is this why you let me beat you?"

"We weren't racing." Jonathan loosened his horse's girth while he offered that bouncer. "We were merely having a good gallop."

Deene patted his stallion's sweaty neck. "A very good gallop. I suspect Evie put you up to it, because we've agreed I'm not allowed to race her these days."

The charming little marchioness *had* put Jonathan up to it, cornering him in the breakfast parlor when Amy had departed for the upper reaches of the house. "I put me up to it. A hard ride clears a man's head, and you have the perfect property for it."

They handed their mounts off to grooms, and as the clip-clop of shod hooves faded into the barn behind them, Deene stripped off his gloves. "Did you just pay me a compliment, Dolan?"

"Cut line. I paid your property a compliment. Where can we talk without interruption?"

Jonathan slapped his gloves against his thigh, knowing Deene might well refuse him aid. The impending discussion would be difficult, not a negotiation but a flat-out session of begging, for which Jonathan had spent much of the night preparing.

Deene gestured toward a pair of benches set up beneath a spreading oak. "Let's sit. How is Miss Ingraham faring?"

"She is a stoic woman. It's difficult to tell." Though in the middle of the night, when she clung to Jonathan even in sleep, it wasn't difficult at all.

"The ladies keep much more to themselves than we give them credit for. Evie is squarely in your corner, though." Deene took a seat on one bench, resting his back against the tree and crossing his legs at the ankle.

Jonathan came down beside him. "It's the mothering instinct. When they're on the nest, women can become quite fierce."

"Do they also become affectionate?"

Jonathan did not give in to the impulse to study Deene, whose question had been offered most casually. He considered a proper answer instead.

"I speak not only as Georgina's father, but as a man with seven married sisters, into whose confidence I am frequently dragged, and I can tell you, Deene, some of them become hopelessly wanton. My brothers-in-law, stout men all, theorize this gives a fellow a chance to store up some goodwill for when the lady's attentions will be usurped upon the arrival of the Blessed Event."

"Keeps a fellow motivated to grow his family, I suppose."

Deene was smiling the idiot smile of man in love. Jonathan smiled too. "Wait until you hold the child in your arms, Deene. You think you love your marchioness now..."

He trailed off, missing Georgina's mother, though with a sweetness to the ache, a peace that had been lacking previously. Absolution, perhaps, or the knowledge that Marie would want Jonathan to ask for Deene's help.

"I do love Evie. I suspect you love Miss Ingraham, and I can tell you, Dolan, if your intentions toward the woman aren't honorable, I am to take you apart with my fists, her ladyship's orders."

"I am atremble at the prospect." Jonathan leaned back against the same tree. "I must dispose of the peacocking cousin first though, and for that I need some assistance."

Deene closed his eyes and crossed his arms, as if preparing for a nap. "Say on."

Jonathan spoke for quite some time, and for the entire length of his discourse, My Lord Deene appeared to enjoy a pleasant nap with his friend, the oak tree. When Jonathan fell silent, Deene roused himself with a leisurely stretch.

"You put your domestics under written contracts?"

Of all the things to seize on, Deene would choose this detail. "A servant gains no consequence working in the household of a cit like me, Deene. I'd lose staff to the greater houses of Mayfair constantly if I didn't insist on terms with the upper servants."

"Evie will like this plan."

Jonathan held his silence, hoping dear Evie's buffleheaded husband would be persuaded by his wife's preferences.

"I like this plan, Dolan. Mind you, I still don't like *you*, but about this plan, I can find nothing to criticize. I will assume Miss Ingraham had a hand in coming up with your scheme?"

"She did not. I think it imperative that she have no idea what I'm about, else Wooster will call my bluff."

Deene's smile now was diabolical. "One condition, Dolan."

Jonathan steeled himself to swallow a visitation schedule for Georgina that parted him from his daughter for half the year. He waited for Deene to demand financial consideration; he tormented himself wondering if Deene would obliterate the Dolan racing stables.

"You have to let me watch."

Relief sang through Jonathan's body. "Referee. I'll let you referee—and I'll let you buy Georgina a damned pony, provided it's at least twenty years old."

"Dolan."

In the quiet of the club's reading room, Jonathan's name was spoken very softly. Worth Kettering was big, handsome, a dark-haired favorite with the ladies, and privy to nearly every financial secret ever to leak out of Mayfair.

"Kettering. Shall you join me?"

"It's a lovely day. I was hoping you'd walk me home."

Kettering was not a friend. He was a man of business serving only such members of the aristocracy as Kettering himself deemed worthy of his attention. Jonathan had done business with him on occasion, finding him ruthless, clever, and honest.

And not one to socialize needlessly.

Jonathan rose and put aside the newspaper he'd been staring at for the past hour. They gathered top hats, gloves, and walking sticks at the door and went out into the brilliant sunshine of a summer day.

"So how comes your little project, Dolan?" Kettering's tone was blasé, his pace relaxed.

"I gather you've been in communication with Deene?"

"Among others. Some of my clients have taken an interest in your situation. Tell me about your lady."

Jonathan hadn't anticipated this line of inquiry, but according to Deene, Kettering was in a position to obtain certain documents Jonathan was desperate to have. "My daughter's governess, you mean?"

"Word is, Miss Ingraham is the granddaughter of a viscount." Kettering used his walking stick to decapitate a daisy in a planting around a lamppost. "An earl lurks not too far back on her mother's side."

"I hadn't known that."

Kettering stooped to pick up the daisy and slipped it into his buttonhole. "Deene has decided that I'm in a position to assist you, Dolan, but there will be conditions."

The tension that had been roiling in Jonathan's belly since he'd left Amy in Surrey a week ago eased fractionally. "I'd like to hear them."

"Seems Wooster is not particularly liked, but there's sympathy for him because of who he has for a mother. She, however, is uniformly held in dislike, to the extent the ladies of Polite Society are now enlisted in support of your cause."

"A man can't help his antecedents."

Kettering's smile was not one Jonathan would have enjoyed seeing over a negotiating table. "I've heard that sentiment rather a lot lately, from people in very high places." He reached into his pocket and thrust a stack of folded notes at Jonathan.

Jonathan took them and tucked them into his own pocket. "How much?"

"Face value," Kettering said, "but then there are those conditions."

"I'm prepared to meet them." Whatever they were, whatever they cost him, Jonathan would meet the conditions placed on him by his titled neighbors, as long as he could marry Amy first.

Kettering launched into a list of terms, and he did not stop talking until they'd reached the front stoop of Jonathan's town house.

❧

"Your dear cousin has come to call again." The Marquess of Deene sounded downright impish when he informed Amy of her fate.

"Must you sound so pleased, my lord?" Amy let him help her to her feet, then watched while his lordship swung Georgina up for a piggyback ride. "And it isn't well done of you to show your face in the nursery. A proper lord would have sent a footman."

A week under Deene's roof had made Amy very bold indeed, also nigh beside herself with anxiety over Jonathan's continued absence.

"You sound like my wife, Miss Amy, which is as high a compliment as I can pay without risking a round of fisticuffs with my brother-in-law. Her ladyship has very much enjoyed chaperoning Wooster's calls."

"Thank God for that." Nigel hadn't renewed his suit, but chose instead to shower Amy with obsequies that were as false as they were distasteful.

"And your sisters have been invited for dinner."

Amy halted at the head of the stairs. "My lord, that was hardly necessary, but I thank you."

Georgina paused in the middle of braiding a hank of her uncle's blond hair. "I like your sisters, Miss. I think Papa would like them too."

Before Amy could respond, Deene shook out the braid. "I like Miss Amy's sisters, and so does your Aunt Eve. And as for your papa, I can take you to him, if you like."

"Oh, yes, please!" Georgina bounced in place. "Charles and I have missed him *so* much!"

"Miss Amy, your caller awaits you in the guest parlor, and her ladyship has tea and crumpets at the ready. Go repel boarders, and I'm sure Dolan will be along presently to meet your cousin."

Lord Deene wasn't a formal man. He'd treated Amy as a guest from the moment he'd welcomed her to his house, and his regard for his niece was sincere. Still, Amy was taken quite aback when Deene leaned in and kissed her cheek.

"You are not without supporters, Amy Ingraham. The next time I take this liberty, I'll be kissing the bride."

He winked at her and left, Georgina's fingers again busy with his hair.

Kissing the bride—but whose bride would she be?

If Jonathan were back from Town, he hadn't sent Amy a note to apprise her of his return. Perhaps he was tossing her on Cousin Nigel's mercy after all, which notion caused Amy to shudder in the corridor outside the guest parlor.

For the sake of her sisters, she couldn't laugh off such an idea, and if Jonathan were disinclined to risk the scandal of breaking the engagement, then what other option would she have besides marrying Nigel?

"My dearest Amy!" Nigel rose from the sofa and approached Amy with outstretched hands the moment she crossed the threshold. "How lovely you look. Come join me."

He towed her over to the sofa by keeping her hand gripped in his own— and what soft hands Nigel had. Amy sat and accepted a cup of tea from the marchioness, whose green eyes bore as much mischief as sympathy.

"Lord Wooster was telling me that his dear mama has been dying to renew her acquaintance with you, Miss Ingraham, and with your sisters too. One wonders why the woman isn't this minute in her traveling coach, preparing to journey from Hampshire to your sisters' doorstep."

Amy took a sip of her tea while the marchioness pinned Nigel with an unblinking stare.

"I've already invited my cousins for a visit," he replied. "In the heat, one can't expect a woman of advanced years to be gadding about. Excellent cakes, Lady Deene."

After the bad start Nigel had made with his hostess, her ladyship had slipped into the role of chaperone with unholy glee. The situation would be hilarious, except—

Amy lost her train of thought as Jonathan Dolan came strolling into the room, followed by the Marquess of Deene.

"Your ladyship, Miss Ingraham, good day."

This wasn't any version of Jonathan she'd seen before. He was dressed to the nines, sporting an abundance of subtle indicators of wealth and sophistication. Bond Street tailoring was only the start, followed by gold cuff links, and a cravat pin topped by a small, cheery emerald winking from amid his lace-edged jabot. His waistcoat was embroidered silk, and his boots positively gleamed.

Jonathan Dolan was turned out as a pink of the *ton*, every inch a gentleman, a wealthy aristocrat, even. Amy took another fortifying sip of her tea, lest Nigel notice how desperately glad she was to see Jonathan.

"Mr. Dolan, please have seat," the marchioness said, then turned her beaming smile on her husband. "Deene, you must join us as well. Lord Wooster is *such* an amusing guest. My Lord Wooster, may I make known to you our brother-in-law, Mr. Jonathan Dolan. He's brought our niece to visit us, and, Jonathan, may I present to you Lord Wooster, Miss Ingraham's second cousin."

The men exchanged nods, and Jonathan bowed to his social superior, a gesture Amy could not recall seeing him make in any other situation. Such deference did not bode well for her future, but then she caught a sly wink from Lady Deene.

The marquess took a seat next to his wife and accepted a cup of tea from her. "I understand you aspire to be more than a second cousin to Miss Ingraham, Wooster. May I offer you my congratulations?"

Jonathan fussed with the lace at his wrists. "That would be premature, would it not?"

"I beg your pardon, sir?" Beside Amy, Nigel sat forward, closer to the edge of the seat. "I don't believe the matter concerns you."

"Concerns me? Not directly, of course not." His gaze traveled over Amy in an alarmingly dispassionate fashion. "But if Miss Ingraham allows you to sweep her off her feet, then my daughter will have to give up her governess, will she not?"

"She most certainly shall! My viscountess will not be kept in service—of all the ridiculous notions." Nigel reached for Amy's hand, as if he had every right. Amy picked up her cup and saucer, dodging Nigel's attempted grab and wondering what in creation Jonathan was about.

"Deene, you will have to explain this to me." Jonathan waved away a proffered cup of tea in a gesture Amy was sure would have done the Regent proud. "Miss Ingraham is free to toil away in my nursery as long as she's Wooster's cousin, but forbidden such activity when she's his wife. I do not understand the aristocracy's convoluted notions of family, and probably never shall."

"All quite puzzling," Lady Deene murmured.

"Well, be that as it may," Jonathan said, "if you're to marry the woman, then I'll expect you to assume responsibility for her debts."

What? "Mr. Dolan," Amy said slowly, "I have no debts."

He shot her a pitying glance. "If you seek to leave my household, Miss Ingraham, you will have at least one very substantial debt to me."

His expression told her nothing, leaving Amy to think she'd been given a part in a melodrama but never shown her lines.

"I do not see how I can be in your debt, sir."

Nigel patted her hand. "Neither do I, and in any case, I am most assuredly unwilling to allow some pin money to stand between me and my intended. State your business, Dolan, and then perhaps you all will allow Miss Ingraham and me some privacy."

Jonathan extracted a gold watch from a pocket, flipped it open, studied it for a moment, then closed it with a snap.

"I'll wish you both happy then, but prior to the nuptials, I'll expect payment in full of the liquidated damages sum named in Miss Ingraham's employment contract."

Nigel was on his feet. "That is absurd. Amy is not your bond servant."

Jonathan rose slowly, shooting his cuffs before he flicked an impassive gaze over Nigel.

"My daughter is precious to me, Wooster, *as is my entire family*. At the time Miss Ingraham joined our household, Georgina was half-orphaned, withdrawn, and a shadow of the happy child who'd graced my nursery for nearly three years. I was grieving and at a loss as to how to help my daughter, but I knew Georgina's governess had to be an extraordinary person."

He fell silent, but Amy was too busy swallowing back the lump in her throat to meet his gaze. *What* was he about?

"I knew, in Miss Ingraham, I had found a treasure, and so I added a liquidated damages clause to her contract. If she quit before I was ready to dismiss her, she'd have to repay all her wages and then some."

"That cannot be legal," Nigel said, hands clenched into fists. "Deene, disabuse this glorified shopkeeper of his confused thinking."

"It's legal," Deene said between bites of chocolate cake. "If Dolan cuts Miss Ingraham loose, he's obligated to pay substantial severance. I read the document myself and thought it quite ingenious. Tell him how much, Dolan."

Jonathan named a staggeringly high figure, one Amy vaguely recalled seeing in her contract. At the time, she'd been more concerned about keeping her sisters fed than any peculiar legal language, though Jonathan had explained to her exactly what the words meant.

Nigel dropped like a brick onto the sofa beside her. "*That* much?" His normally pale countenance became ashen. "Amy, did you sign this document freely?"

"I did. I could have sold the cottage instead, I suppose."

Or she could have presented herself and her sisters on Nigel's doorstep as charity cases. She'd heard Jonathan Dolan worrying for his daughter, and signed the contract the same day, the best decision she'd ever made.

Nigel's chin came up. "Then I'll pay the debt. I will pay it, by God, and you will find some other woman to take orders from you and deal with your daughter."

"Careful," Deene said softly around another mouthful of cake. "I am pleased to count Dolan among my family, Wooster."

"I will *not* be careful. This…this bog-trotting cit thinks he can buy Amy's service, and she a lady to the bone. Dolan, you should be ashamed of yourself."

"I am." Jonathan resumed his seat. "Frequently, but at least I don't run up gambling debts I can't pay off. They have a way of coming back to bite a man at the worst times."

Nigel went absolutely still, like a rabbit busily munching clover, who too late hears the pack over the very next hill.

"Gambling debts," Jonathan drawled. He took a sheaf of papers out of his pocket and put them on the coffee table before Nigel. "Excessive gambling debts, belonging to you—and to your darling mother."

Nigel opened his mouth, then shut it with a snap. He reached out toward the little pile of papers, but drew his hand back without touching them, as if they might indeed bite him.

"My love," the marquess purred, "perhaps you'd order more cakes?"

Her ladyship rose and clamped a small, surprisingly strong hand around Amy's wrist.

"Come along, Miss Ingraham, we must see what the kitchen has to offer."

As Amy let herself be removed from the parlor, she heard Jonathan speaking again.

"I am not a man who would interfere with the course of true love, Wooster, but tell me, can you pay these debts *and* the sum owed me by Miss Ingraham?"

And then the door clicked shut.

❧

The food was probably marvelous, but Amy could hardly taste it.

"What did Nigel say then?" Drusilla asked from across the table.

"He said he was going to kill his mother," Deene replied. "A touching display of filial devotion, absolutely in keeping with his high regard for family generally. But enough said on that unfortunate subject. I propose a toast."

Under the table, Jonathan kept Amy's hand in his, while in view of the company, he reached for his wineglass.

"To family." The marquess's gaze fell on his wife at the opposite end of the table. "And to true love."

Glasses were raised all around, though her ladyship's held barely a sip. Drusilla and Hecate, along with Deene and Lady Deene, carried the conversation through dessert, while Amy could focus only on the pleasure of Jonathan's presence beside her.

The men had been closeted in the parlor for almost two hours, while Amy had been hard put not to pace a hole in the carpet of her ladyship's private sitting room. Then Nigel had left, begging Amy's pardon but informing her that he could not consider them engaged, though he hoped she "understood."

She did *not* understand, not entirely, but she grasped that Jonathan had indeed slain her dragons.

The marchioness gave a signal to the footman at the sideboard, then exchanged a glance with her husband. "Deene has suggested we might withdraw to the billiards room, ladies. I'm sure this will inspire the gentlemen to make haste over their port."

Billiards? With her sisters? Amy rose, which necessitated that Jonathan stand to hold her chair.

"If the company will pardon me," she said, "the day has left me fatigued. I'll pass on the billiards and thank both his lordship and her ladyship for all their kindnesses."

Beside her, Jonathan might have expelled a sigh of relief as he winged his arm at her. "I'll light you up to your room."

She left the dining parlor with him, almost needing the support of his arm, so drained did she feel.

"Jonathan, the stairs are that way."

"The stars, my dear, are this way."

⁂

The day had been long and fraught, with Amy's sisters arriving just as Jonathan had sought to find his lady and some privacy. Perhaps what he had to say ought to wait until morning, but from the way Amy shifted her grip on him, she'd been as anxious for a moment alone as he had.

The instant they gained the back terrace, Amy stepped into his embrace. "I was so worried."

"I'm sorry. I thought it best not to warn you, and there wasn't—"

She put her hand over his mouth. "Now is not a moment for thinking, Mr. Dolan."

Never argue with a lady.

He gently took her hand in his and settled his lips over hers. "Missed you, my love."

"Mm."

She let him have more of her weight, and Jonathan spent the next five minutes reacquainting himself with every lovely, warm, curvaceous blessing Amy possessed.

"You even taste like lemons," he whispered.

"Lemon tarts for dessert will…oh, *Jonathan*."

Jonathan drew back and, with the part of his brain still capable of functioning, made a note that Amy Ingraham—soon to be Amy Dolan—had sensitive earlobes.

"My most adored love, if we do not desist immediately, then I will soon have you against the nearest wall, saying my name repeatedly in that exact tone."

Bless her, she looked more than tempted, but then the governess asserted herself. "I have some questions for you, Jonathan."

"I'm sure you do." He could not possibly let go of her hand, so he led her through fragrant moon shadows to a bench among the roses. "Ask me anything."

She folded her hand around his once they'd sat. "Why didn't you warn me you'd be confronting Nigel with that contract clause?"

"Two reasons. First, I did not want you talking me out of my strategy. The only means I could think of to keep you out of his lily-white hands were financial, and that was hardly gentleman—"

She cut him off with a shake of her head. "You were brilliant. I almost felt sorry for him. What was the other reason?"

"I did not want you to appear to be colluding with me. If Nigel got wind that my interest was personal, then he might have threatened to start rumors regarding your conduct with me when you resided under my roof, and that would not do."

She turned a thoughtful gaze to him. "He might have done exactly that. You are very shrewd."

"Your cousin had other terms for it." *Conniving, sneaking, underhanded.* Deene had approved of Jonathan's tactics as appropriate to the party they dealt with, and had turned up righteous over Nigel's sneering condescension, too, almost as if Jonathan were…family. He set that startling possibility aside for further consideration.

"Jonathan, how did you leave things with Nigel?"

"Does it matter?"

"Yes. He's still my cousin, and from some things Hecate said, I gather she rather pities him."

Jonathan shifted, putting an arm around Amy's shoulders, but keeping his hand in hers too. "Hecate might be willing to take him on, which would make him your brother-in-law as well as your second cousin, but it's you who stood to inherit the largest sum, my dear."

She tried to wiggle away, but Jonathan was having none of that.

"Inherit? From whom?"

"Your grandfather. He left significant sums in trust for you, which the family solicitors have been managing. If you had reached the age of twenty-eight unwed, the money would have all come to you, along with instructions to use it as you see fit. If you were wed before your twenty-eighth birthday, then the money would be disbursed to your spouse, with a requirement that your sisters be adequately dowered from the proceeds, providing they were yet unwed."

"I see."

Jonathan was fairly certain she did not see all the ramifications. Had Nigel been her husband, he would have had absolute control over the funds, and her sisters would have been dowered only in so far as necessary to pass each one off into some grasping fellow's keeping.

"I have a question for you, Amy Ingraham."

She brought their joined hands up and kissed his knuckles of his left hand, the one with the most scars. "Ask."

He slid off the bench to one knee, keeping her hand in his. "Will you marry me?"

She did not hesitate, she did not prolong the moment, and if he hadn't been top over tail in love with her before, he was when she gave him a crisp, confident, "Certainly."

He bent to kiss her hand and felt her palm smooth over his hair.

"Certainly, I will marry you, Jonathan Dolan, and as soon as you can arrange it."

Lest he drag her down into the grass, Jonathan resumed his place beside her. "We have a challenge before us in that regard."

"A small wedding will do very nicely, Jonathan, and I'm sure the marchioness will keep an eye on Georgina if you want some sort of wedding journey."

"You've been forming conspiracies again." Though it warmed his heart that she'd been making such plans. "You and the marchioness will have to be patient. When the good gentlemen of the beau monde surrendered Nigel's vowels to me, they placed conditions on the exchange."

"What sort of conditions?"

"Nigel's mother is due a public set down. We shall be married in St. George's at Hanover Square. Lady Eve's papa will give you away, and Nigel will escort your sisters. All of Polite Society shall be invited except Nigel's mother. You are to have bridesmaids from several of the best families, and Deene and his lady will stand up with us. The wedding breakfast will be scandalously lavish, and also, I'm sure, very well attended."

"Lady Eve's papa..." Amy's free hand cradled Jonathan's jaw. "She's the daughter of a duke, Jonathan. This is not about Nigel's mama, not entirely."

"Of course it is."

"No, it is not, trust me on this. This has to do with Deene taking up for us, and with you, with who you are."

She was looking at him with such intensity, Jonathan could not look away.

"I'm a stonemason's son, Amy. Shrewd, as you put it, and desperately in love with you, but no more than that. That you will have me..."

He broke off, words being inadequate, but when he would have kissed her again, she drew back.

"*They* will have you. *They will have us.* This demand to attend the wedding, it's a way of saying you're one of them, Jonathan, a gentleman, a man of honor whose cause is more deserving of their loyalty than Nigel's title or his mama's consequence."

"A gentleman." He wanted to pretend it was merely a word, but the warmth spreading in his chest belied that notion. For Marie's memory, and for Georgina, but mostly *for Amy*, he wanted to be a gentleman. "Perhaps I am a gentleman, if you say so."

"I say so, and I am your lady."

It was much, much later when the lady and the gentleman sneaked into the house, but Jonathan had been right: their wedding went down in history as one of the best attended ceremonies ever to grace Mayfair, and their union one of the happiest.

MARY FRAN & MATTHEW

One

One glimpse of Lady Mary Frances MacGregor, and Matthew Daniels forgot all about the breathtaking Highland scenery and the misbegotten purpose for his visit to Aberdeenshire.

"For the duration of your stay, our house is your house," Lady Mary Frances said. She strode along the corridor of her brother's country home with purpose, not with the mincing, corseted gait of a London lady, and she had music in her voice. Her walk held music as well, in the rhythm and sway of her hips, in the rustle of her petticoats and the crisp tattoo of her boots on the polished wood floors.

Though what music had to do with anything, Matthew was at a loss to fathom. "The Spanish have a similar saying, my lady: *mi casa es su casa.*"

"My house is your house." She either guessed or made the translation easily. "You've been to Spain, then?"

"In Her Majesty's Army, one can travel a great deal."

A shadow creased her brow, quickly banished and replaced by a smile. "And now you've traveled to our doorstep. This is your room, Mr. Daniels, though we've others if you'd prefer a different view."

She preceded him into the room, leaving Matthew vaguely disconcerted. A proper young woman would not be alone with a gentleman in his private quarters, and Mary Frances MacGregor, being the daughter of an earl, was a lady even in the sense of having a courtesy title—though Matthew had never before met a *lady* with hair that lustrous shade of dark red, or a figure so perfectly designed to thwart a man's gentlemanly self-restraint.

"The view is quite acceptable."

The view was magnificent, including, as it did, the backside of Lady Mary Frances as she bent to struggle with a window sash. She was a substantial woman, both tall and well formed, and Matthew suspected her arms would be trim with muscle, not the smooth, pale appendages a gentleman might see at a London garden party.

"Allow me." He went to her side and jiggled the sash on its runners, hoisting the thing easily to allow in some fresh air.

"The maids will close it by teatime," Lady Mary Frances said. "The nights can be brisk, even in high summer. Will you be needing a bath before the evening meal?"

She put the question casually—just a hostess inquiring after the welfare of a guest—but her gaze slid over him, a quick, assessing flick of green eyes bearing a hint of speculation. He might not fit in an old-fashioned bathing tub was what the gaze said, nothing more.

Nonetheless, he dearly wanted to get clean after long days of traveling. "If it wouldn't be too much trouble?"

"No trouble at all. The bathing chamber is just down the hall to the left, the cistern is full, and the boilers have been going since noon."

She peered into the empty wardrobe, passing close enough to Matthew that he caught a whiff of something female... Flowers. Not roses, which were probably the only flower he knew by scent, but... fresher than roses, less cloying.

"If you need anything to make your visit more enjoyable, Mr. Daniels, you have only to ask, and we'll see to it. Highland hospitality isn't just the stuff of legends."

"My thanks."

She frowned at the high four-poster and again walked past him, though this time she picked up the tartan draped across the foot of the bed. The daughter of an earl ought not to be fussing the blankets, but Matthew liked the sight of her, snapping out the red, white, and blue woolen blanket and giving it a good shake. Her attitude said that nothing, not dust, not visiting English, not a houseful of her oversized brothers, would daunt this woman.

Without thinking, Matthew picked up the two corners of the blanket that had drifted to the blue-and-red tartan rug.

"Will you be having other guests this summer?" He put the question to her as they stepped toward each other.

"Likely not." She grasped the corners he'd picked up, their fingers brushing.

Matthew did not step back. Mary Frances MacGregor—*Lady* Mary Frances MacGregor—had *freckles* over the bridge of her nose. They were faint, even delicate, and they made her look younger. She could have powdered them into oblivion, but she hadn't.

"Mr. Daniels?" She gave the blanket a tug.

Matthew moved back a single step. "You typically have only one set of guests each summer?" Whatever her scent, it wasn't only floral, but also held something spicy, fresh like cedar, but not quite cedar.

"No, we usually have as many guests as the brief summers here permit, particularly once Her Majesty and His Royal Highness are ensconced next door. But if your sister becomes engaged to my brother, there will be other matters to see to, won't there?"

This question, alluding to much and saying little, was accompanied by an expression that involved the corners of the lady's lips turning up, and yet it wasn't a smile.

"I suppose there will." Things like settling a portion of the considerable Daniels's wealth into the impoverished Balfour coffers. Things like preparing for the wedding of a lowly English baron's daughter to a Scottish earl.

"We'll gather in the parlor for drinks before the evening meal, Mr. Daniels. The parlor is directly beneath us, one floor down. Any footman can direct you."

She was insulting him. Matthew took a moment to decipher this, and in the next moment, he realized the insult was not intentional. Some of the MacGregor's "guests," wealthy English wanting to boast of a visit to the Queen's own piece of the Highlands, probably spent much of their stay too inebriated to navigate even the corridors of the earl's country house.

"I'll find my way, though at some point, I would also like to be shown where the rest of my family is housed."

"Of course." Another non-smile. She glanced around the room the way Matthew had seen generals look over the troops prior to a parade review, her lips flattening, her gaze seeking any detail out of order. "Until dinner, Mr. Daniels."

She bobbed a curtsy and whirled away before Matthew could even offer her a proper bow.

❧

"Miss MacGregor?"

Mary Fran's insides clenched at the sound of Baron Altsax's voice. She pasted a smile on her face and tried to push aside the need to check on the dining room, the kitchen, and the ladies' guest rooms—and the need to locate Fiona.

The child tended to hide when a new batch of guests came to stay.

"Baron, what may I do for you?"

"I had a few questions, Miss MacGregor, if you wouldn't mind?" He gestured to his bedroom, his smile suggesting he knew damned good and well the insult he did an earl's daughter by referring to her as "Miss" anything. A double insult, in fact.

Mary Fran did not follow the leering old buffoon into his room. Altsax's son, the soft-spoken Mr. Daniels, would reconnoiter before he started bothering the help—though big, blond, good-looking young men seldom needed to bother the help—not so with the skinny, pot-gutted old men. "I'm a bit behindhand, my lord. Was it something I could send a maid to tend to?"

The baron gestured toward the drinking pitcher on the escritoire, while Mary Fran lingered at the threshold. "This water is not chilled, I've yet to see a tea service, and prolonged travel by train can leave a man in need of something to wash the dust from his throat."

He arched one supercilious eyebrow, as if it took some subtle instinct to divine when an Englishman was whining for his whisky.

"The maids will be along shortly with the tea service, my lord. You'll find a decanter with some of our best libation on the nightstand, and I can send up some chilled water." Because they at least had ice to spare in the Highlands.

"See that you do."

Mary Fran tossed him a hint of a curtsy and left before he could make up more excuses to lure her into his room.

The paying guests were a source of much-needed coin, but the summers were too short, and the expenses of running Balfour too great for paying guests alone to reverse the MacGregor family fortunes. The benefit of this situation was that no coin was on hand to dower Mary Fran, should some fool—brother, guest, or distant relation—take a notion she was again in want of a husband.

"Mary Fran, for God's sake, slow down." She'd been so lost in thought she hadn't realized her brother Ian had approached her from the top of the stairs. "Where are you churning off to in such high dudgeon? Con and Gil sent me to fetch you to the family parlor for a wee dram."

Ian's gaze was weary and concerned, the same as Con or Gil's would have been, though Ian, as the oldest, was the weariest and the most concerned—also the one willing to marry Altsax's featherbrained daughter just so Fiona might someday have a decent dowry.

"I have to check on the kitchens, Ian, and make sure that dim-witted Hetta McKinley didn't forget the butter dishes again, and Eustace Miller has been lurking on the maids' stairway so he can make calf eyes at—"

"Come, you." Ian tucked her hand over his arm. "You deserve a few minutes with family more than the maids need to be protected from Eustace Miller's calf eyes. Let the maids have some fun, and let yourself take five minutes to catch your breath. Go change into your finery and meet us in the family parlor. I'll need your feminine perspective if I'm to coax Altsax's daughter up the church aisle."

Ian had typical MacGregor height and green eyes to go with dark hair and a handsome smile—none of which was worth a single groat. In Asher's continued absence, Ian was also the laird, and well on his way to being officially recognized as the earl. While neither honor generated coin, the earldom allowed him the prospect of marrying an heiress with a title-hungry papa.

Mary Fran did not bustle off to change her dress for any of those reasons, or even because she needed to stay abreast of whatever her three brothers were thinking regarding Ian's scheme to marry wealth.

She heeded her brother's direction because she wanted that wee dram—wanted it far too much.

᙮

Matthew enjoyed a leisurely soak in a marble bathing chamber that boasted every modern convenience, then dressed and prepared to find his way down to the formal parlor. As he moved through the house, he noted the signs of good care: a faint odor of beeswax and lemon oil rising from the gleaming woodwork, sparkling clean windows, fresh flowers in each corridor, an absence of fingerprints on the walls and mirrors.

Lady Mary Frances, or her minions, took the care of Balfour House seriously. A swift drum of heels from around the next corner had Matthew stopping and cocking an ear. A man did not lose the habit of stealth simply because he was no longer billeted to a brewing war zone.

The hint of acrid cigar smoke warned Matthew that his father was in the vicinity.

"Miss MacGregor, perhaps you'd allow me to provide you an escort down to the parlor?" Altsax spoke in the unctuous tones of a man condescending to an inferior, though Lady Mary Frances was arguably the baron's social superior.

Matthew eased far enough down the corridor to see that the lady was attired in a dinner gown of green-and-white plaid that did marvelous things for her eyes—and riveted the baron's attention on her décolletage.

"That's gracious of you, Baron." Her smile was beautiful, though it did not reach her eyes. "I hope Mr. Daniels will escort your womenfolk?"

The baron winged his arm. "I'm sure Matthew or your own brothers will see to that duty."

As the lady tucked her fingers around the baron's elbow, Matthew's gut began to churn. Altsax was never polite to anybody, much less to pretty young women, unless he was maneuvering toward his own ends.

"So why aren't you married, Miss MacGregor?" Altsax stroked his fingers over her hand. "You're comely enough, wellborn, and intended for better than spinsterhood as your brothers' household drudge."

The observation was Altsax's version of flattery, no doubt. Matthew felt a familiar urge to scream, or find a fast horse and gallop straight back to the Crimea.

"Marriage seems to be the topic of the day, my lord." While Matthew watched in a conveniently positioned mirror, Lady Mary Frances smiled back at her escort, revealing a number of strong white teeth. "You are blessed with two comely daughters. It's a pity your baroness could not accompany them on this journey."

As if Altsax would have allowed *that*. Matthew's mother knew better than to come along when her husband had decreed it otherwise, and quite honestly, Matthew envied his mother her freedom from Altsax's company.

"My wife and I have been married for thirty-some years, my dear. I hardly need to keep her underfoot at all times. Marriage is, after all, still a business undertaking among the better classes. I'm sure you'd agree."

Altsax walked with her toward the sweeping main staircase, a monument to carved oak that suggested at some bygone point in the MacGregor family history, coin had been abundant.

Matthew had an instant's premonition of the baron's intent, a gut-clenching moment of knowing what was about to take place. The baron took his opportunity at the turn in the hallway where carpet gave way to gleaming bare floor. He made a show of catching his toe on the carpet and jostling his companion sideways with enough force that she fetched up against the wall.

This allowed Altsax to mash into her bodily, and his hand—like one of the big, hairy spiders common to the tropics—to land squarely on the lady's generous, fashionably exposed bosom.

"I beg your pardon, Miss MacGregor." Altsax made an effort to right himself which of course involved clumsily, almost roughly, groping the lady. Matthew was about to reveal himself to his disgrace of a father, when the baron flew across the hallway as if propelled out of a cannon.

"Baron, do forgive me!" Lady Mary Frances was standing upright and looking creditably dismayed. "I did not mean to step on your foot, I sincerely did not. Are you all right, my lord?"

Her strategy left Altsax trying to look dignified and innocent of his crimes while not putting much weight on one foot. "The fault is mine, Miss MacGregor. I beg your pardon most sincerely. Shall we join your family downstairs?"

"Of course."

As they moved toward the stairs, Matthew noted that this time, Altsax did not offer the lady his arm.

First skirmish to Lady Mary Frances, though as Matthew waited for a silent moment at the top of the stairs, it occurred to him that rising to the lady's defense would have been enjoyable.

Tricky, given that he'd be defending her from his own father, but enjoyable.

※

"A word with you, if you please, Lady Mary Frances."

Mary Fran tore off a bite of scone and regarded Mr. Matthew Daniels where he stood next to her place at the breakfast table. The baron had taken a tray out to the terrace, there to read his newspaper as he let a perfectly lovely repast grow cold at his elbow, while Ian and Miss Augusta Merrick, the younger of the two chaperones, had disappeared to the library.

And now Mary Fran's favorite meal of the day—sometimes her only decent meal of the day—was going to be disturbed by this serious gentleman waiting to assist her to her feet. No doubt Mr. Daniels's shaving water had been too hot, or not hot enough. Perhaps he objected to the scent of heather on his linen, or he'd found a footman using the maids' staircase.

Mary Fran folded a napkin around the last of her scone and put it in her pocket, then placed her hand in Daniels's and let him assist her to her feet. Thank God her brothers weren't on hand to see such a farce.

"In private." The gentleman kept his eyes front as he appended that requirement, as if admitting such a thing made him queasy.

"Shall we walk in the garden, Mr. Daniels? Pace off some of our breakfast?"

"That will serve." He tucked her hand around his arm, which had Mary

Fran about grinding her teeth. They skirted the terrace and minced along until they were a good distance from the house, and still Mr. Daniels said nothing.

"Is there a point to this outing, Mr. Daniels? I don't mean to be rude, but I've a household to run, and though you are our guest, my strolling about here among the flowers isn't going to get the beds made up."

He stopped walking and gazed down at her with a surprised expression. "You do that yourself?"

"I know how. I expect you do as well."

Something flashed through his eyes, humor, possibly. He was one of few men outside her family Mary Fran had to look up to. She'd been an inch taller than Gordie, and she had treasured that inch every day of her so-called marriage.

"I do know how to make up a cot," he said. "Public school imbues a man with all manner of esoteric skills. The military does as well. Shall we sit?"

He was determined on this privacy business, because he was gesturing to a bench that backed up against the tallest hedge in the garden. They'd be hidden from view on that bench.

Even if she were amenable, Mary Fran doubted Mr. Daniels was going to take liberties. Good Lord, if he was this serious about his dallying, then heaven help the ladies he sought to charm. Though as she took a seat, it struck her with a certainty that Matthew Daniels needn't bother charming anybody. For all his English reserve in proper company, he'd plunder and pillage, devil take the hindmost, when he decided on an objective.

Former cavalry could be like that.

"You are smiling, my lady."

And he was watching her mouth as he stood over her. Mary Fran let her smile blossom into a grin as she arranged her skirts. "I'm truant, sitting out here in the garden. I suppose it's fair play, given that my brothers—save for Ian—are off gallivanting about with your sisters and your aunt." And Lord knew what Ian was up to with the spinster cousin—probably prying secrets from the poor lady.

"About my womenfolk." He took the place beside her without her permission, though she would not have objected. "I have sisters."

He had two. The lovely Eugenia Daniels, whom Aunt Eulalie had spotted as a possible wealthy bride for Ian, and the younger, altogether likable Hester Daniels. Mary Fran held her peace, because Mr. Daniels was mentally pacing up to something, and he struck her as man who would not be hurried—she was familiar with the type.

"I have sisters whose happiness means a great deal to me," he went on, leaning forward to prop his elbows on his thighs. "You have brothers."

"My blessing and my curse," she said, wondering *when* he'd get to his point.

"My sisters are dear to me." He flicked a brooding glance at her over his shoulder. "As I'm sure you are dear to your brothers."

"Their hot meals and clean sheets are dear to them."

He sat up abruptly. "They would cheerfully die for you or kill for you. Not for the hot meals or the clean sheets, but for you."

She regarded him for a quizzical moment, trying to fathom his intentions. Insight struck as she studied the square line of his jaw and the way sunlight found the red highlights in his blond hair. "They won't kill your father while he's a guest in our home. Rest easy on that point."

"I cannot *rest easy*, as you say." He hunched forward again, the fabric of his morning coat pulling taut across broad shoulders. "My father's regard for women generally lacks a certain…"

"He's a randy old jackass," Mary Fran said. "I don't hold it against him."

Whatever comment the situation called for, it wasn't that. No earl's daughter, not even a Scottish earl's daughter running a glorified guesthouse ought to be so plainspoken.

"I'm sorry," she said, gaze on her lap. "I don't mean to be disrespectful. Your da's a guest in my home, and I'm responsible…"

"Hush." His finger came to rest on her lips, and when she looked up at him, he was smiling at her. He dropped his finger, but the smile lingered, crinkling the corners of his eyes and putting a light in his gaze that was almost… gentle.

God in heaven. The man was abruptly, stunningly attractive. Mary Fran felt a heat spreading out from that spot on her mouth where his bare finger had touched her.

"My father *is* a randy old jackass, I was searching for those very words. He can offend without meaning to, and sometimes, I fear, when he does mean to."

"He's not the first titled man to show uncouth behavior toward women." She linked her fingers in her lap lest she touch her lip as he had.

"No, but he's my father. If he should come to a premature end, all the burdens of his title will fall upon me, and that, rather than filial devotion, makes me hope your brothers will not have to challenge him to pistols at dawn."

The daft man was genuinely worried. "My brothers are Scottish, but they don't lack sense. If Ian took to dueling with his guests, God Almighty could live next door, and the most baseborn coal nabob wouldn't give a farthing to spend a day with us. Her Majesty has just about frowned dueling out of existence."

Plain speaking wasn't always inappropriate, and Mary Fran sensed Matthew Daniels could tolerate a few home truths.

"I fear, my lady, you underestimate your brothers' devotion to you, and"—he held up a staying hand when she would have interrupted—"you underestimate the depths of my father's more cross inclinations."

Mary Fran studied him, studied the serious planes of his face, and noted a little scar along the left side of his jaw. "I can handle your father, Mr. Daniels. I won't go running to my brothers in a fit of the weeps because he tries to take liberties."

"Tries to take liberties again, don't you mean?"

He had blue eyes—blue, blue eyes that regarded her with wry sternness. "He's too slow, Mr. Daniels. He can but try, and I shall thwart him."

He peered at her, his lips thinning as he came to some conclusion. "Your brother had the opportunity to take my father very much to task the other evening for a verbal slight to you. Balfour instead suggested I see my sire to bed. I'd suspect the reputation of the Scots' temper to be overrated, except I've seen Highland regiments in action."

"Our tempers are simply as passionate as the rest of our emotions."

As soon as the words were out of her mouth, she realized she'd spoken *too* plainly. Ungenteelly, though that was probably not a proper word.

"I agree," he said, rising and extending his hand to her. "Having fought alongside many a Scot, I can say their honor, their humor, their valor, and their tempers were all formidable. Still, I am asking you to apply to me rather than your family should my father's bad manners become troublesome. I assure you, I'll deal with him appropriately."

She wouldn't be *applying* to anybody. If the baron overstepped again, he'd face consequences Mary Fran herself was perfectly capable of meting out. God had given each woman two knees for just such a purpose.

"I can agree to bring concerns regarding your father's conduct to you, Mr. Daniels, before I mention them to my brothers." She placed her hand in his and let him draw her to her feet.

And there they stood for a long, curious moment. His blue eyes bored into her as if he were trying to divine her thoughts.

"My name is Matthew," he said, still holding her hand. "I would be obliged if, when we are not in company, you would do me the honor of using it."

He was so grave about this invitation, Mary Fran had to conclude he was sincere. He would be *honored* if she addressed him familiarly—there was no accounting for the English and their silly manners. She nodded, put her hand on his arm, and let him escort her back to the house in silence.

She did not invite him to address her as Mary Frances.

◈

Maybe being born with red hair, slanting green eyes, a mouth that personified sin incarnate, and a body to match made a woman sad—for Mary Frances MacGregor was a sad woman.

Matthew drew this conclusion by watching her at meals, watching the way she presided over the table with smiles aplenty and little real joy. He drew further evidence of her sadness from the way her brothers treated her, verbally tiptoeing around her the way Matthew had learned to tiptoe around his wife when she was tired, fretful, or in anticipation of her courses.

And Mary Frances worried about her brothers. The anxiety was there in her eyes, in the way she watched them eat and kept their drinks topped up. To Matthew, it was obvious the MacGregor clan was not happy about having to trade their title for English coin, but the Scots as a race could not often afford the luxury of sentiment.

Because she was sad, and because he genuinely enjoyed dancing, when the middle brother, Gilgallon MacGregor, challenged Aunt Julia to a waltz—those were his words, he *challenged* her to a waltz after dinner—and Julia had laughingly accepted, Matthew joined the party adjourning to the ballroom.

"Who will play for us if I'm to show Gilgallon what a dance floor is for?" Julia asked the assemblage.

Before Genie could offer, and thus ensure she wouldn't be dancing with Balfour, Matthew strode over to the big, square piano. "I will provide the music for the first set, on the condition that Lady Mary Frances turns the pages for me."

Genie shot him a disgruntled look, but stood up with the youngest brother, Connor MacGregor, while Balfour led a blushing Hester onto the floor.

"What shall we play for them?" Matthew asked. "Three couples doesn't quite make a set."

"I believe my idiot brother demanded a waltz," Lady Mary Frances muttered as she sorted through a number of music books stacked on the piano's closed lid. "Take your pick."

She shoved a volume of Chopin at him, which wasn't quite ballroom material.

"I take it you don't approve of dancing?" Matthew flipped through until he found the Waltz in C-sharp Minor and opened the cover shielding the keys.

"Dancing's well enough," the lady said. Her tone was anything but approving.

"Maestro, we're growing moss over here!" Julia called, but she was smiling up at her partner in the manner of a younger, more carefree woman, and for that alone, Matthew would dust off his pianistic skills.

He launched into the little waltz, a lilting, sentimental confection full of wistful die-away ascending scales and a turning, sighing secondary melody.

"You play well, Mr. Daniels."

Lady Mary Frances nearly whispered this compliment, and Matthew could feel her gaze on his hands. "That's Matthew, if you please. I've always enjoyed music, but there wasn't much call for it in the military."

Out on the dance floor, by the soft evening light coming through the tall windows, three couples turned down the room in graceful synchrony. Beside Matthew, Lady Mary Frances was humming softly and swaying minutely to the triple meter. He finished off the exposition with another one of those tinkling ascending scales, which allowed him to lean far enough to the right that his shoulder pressed against the lady's.

"Page, my lady."

She flipped the page, and Matthew began the contrasting section, a more stately interlude requiring little concentration, which was fortunate. Lady Mary Frances had applied a different scent for the evening. That fresh, cedary base note was still present, but the overtones were more complicated.

Complicated enough that Matthew could envision sniffing her neck to better parse her perfume.

"What scent are you wearing, my lady? It's particularly appealing."

"Just something I put together on an idle day."

Matthew glanced over at her to find she was watching the dancers, her expression wistful. "You haven't had an idle day since you put your hair up, and likely not many before then."

"A rainy day, then. We have plenty of those. Your sisters are accomplished dancers."

"As are your brothers." For big men, they moved with a lithe grace made more apparent for their kilts. "You should take a turn, my lady."

"No, I should not. I've things to see to, Mr. Daniels, but it is nice to watch my brothers enjoying themselves on the dance floor."

"Page."

She turned the page for him, and Matthew had to focus on the recapitulation of the first, delicate, sighing melody. The final ascending scale trickled nearly to the top of the keyboard, which meant Matthew was leaning into Lady Mary Frances at the conclusion of the piece.

And she was allowing it.

"Oh, well done, my boy, well done." Altsax clapped in loud, slow movements. "I'd forgotten your fondness for music. Perhaps you'd oblige us with another waltz, that I might have the pleasure of dancing with Lady Mary Frances?"

"When did he slither into the room?" Lady Mary Frances muttered, resignation in her tone.

Matthew rose from the piano bench. "I'm afraid that won't serve, your lordship. My compensation for providing music for the ladies is a waltz with my page turner. Perhaps Hester will oblige at the keyboard?"

Gilgallon turned a dazzling smile on Matthew's younger sister. "And I'll turn the pages for her."

"My lady, may I have this dance?" Matthew extended his hand to Lady Mary Frances, who smiled up at him in a display of teeth and thinly banked forbearance.

"The honor would be mine, Mr. Daniels."

He led her to the dance floor, arranged himself and his partner into waltz position, and felt a sigh of recognition as Hester turned her attention to Chopin's Nocturne in E Minor. The piece was often overlooked, full of passion and sentiment, and it suited the woman in Matthew's arms.

"I hate this piece." Lady Mary Frances moved off with him, speaking through clenched teeth.

"You dance to it well enough." This fulsome compliment—certainly among the most lame Matthew had ever offered a lady—had her scowling in addition to clenching her teeth.

"It's too—"

"Don't think of the music then. Tell me what it was like growing up in the Highlands."

She tilted her head as Matthew drew her through the first turn. "It was cold and hungry, like this music. Never enough to eat, never enough peat to burn, and always there was *longing...*"

Her expression confirmed that she hadn't meant to say that, which pleased Matthew inordinately. That he could dance Mary Frances MacGregor out of a little of her self-containment was a victory of sorts. "What else?"

"What else, what?"

"What else was it like, growing up in these mountains?"

He pulled her a trifle closer on the second turn, close enough that he could hear her whisper. "It was lonely, like this blasted tune."

"Your brothers weren't good company?"

"They are my *older brothers*, Mr. Daniels. They were no company at all."

She danced beautifully, effortlessly, a part of the music she professed to hate.

"And yet here I am, my lady, an older brother along on this curious venture for the express purpose of providing my sisters and their chaperones company."

She huffed out a sigh. "I appreciate that you're preserving me from your father's attentions, Mr. Daniels, but I assure you such gallantry is not necessary."

"Matthew, and perhaps I'm not being gallant, perhaps I'm being selfish."

He turned her under his arm, surprised to find he'd spoken the truth. A man leaving the military in disgrace was not expected to show his face at London's fashionable gatherings, and had he done so, few ladies would have stood up with him.

"What was it like growing up in the South?"

Her question was a welcome distraction. "I didn't. I went to boarding school in Northumbria. I was cold and hungry for most of it."

Her gaze sharpened. "Why the North?"

Another turn, another opportunity to pull her a bit closer and enjoy the way her height matched with his own. "The North is cheaper, and Altsax isn't what anybody would call a doting father. I made some friends and spent holidays with them to the extent I could."

Though those same friends would probably be careful not to recognize him now.

"So you weren't lonely."

He distracted her with a daring little spin, one she accommodated easily, and from there, conversation lapsed while Matthew tried to enjoy waltzing with a gorgeous, fragrant woman in his arms.

Her last comment bothered him though. In boarding school, he'd been lonely. The schoolmates who'd taken pity on him for a holiday here or there had not been the sort of companions to provide solace to a boy exiled from his home and family. The military had been a slight improvement, for a time, and then no improvement at all.

As Matthew bowed over the lady's hand to the final strains of the nocturne, he admitted to himself that he'd been lonely for most of his boyhood as well as most of his military career.

And he was lonely still.

Two

MARY FRAN HAD A SOFT SPOT FOR WOUNDED CREATURES, AND THE TALL Englishman was nothing more than another wounded creature. The loneliness came through in his silences, in the grim quality of his expression around his father, in the way he watched his sisters as if bandits might seize them and carry them off.

A severely handsome, grave, quiet, broad-shouldered, wounded creature with beautiful, tanned hands. Matthew Daniels's hands embodied both grace and strength, and even on this family outing through the woods, Mary Fran had occasion to admire them often. Matthew—*Mr. Daniels*—was a solicitous escort, not like a brother who'd pelt along willy-nilly, dragging her forward as if she were a reluctant bullock.

He would shift his hold on her, grip her hand, link their fingers, or grasp her wrist to guide her over logs she'd been hopping since childhood, or past boulders that were hardly going to rise up and roll directly into her path. This solicitude was… lovely. His attention was also largely silent, and his gaze never suggested anything inappropriate.

She rather wished it would.

"That was a heartfelt sigh, my lady. Shall we tell the others we're turning around?"

He'd apparently forgotten he had taken hold of her hand, and she wasn't going to remind him.

"It's a beautiful summer day, I'm free of my chores, and I have a handsome escort for wandering my own property at my leisure. Maybe it was a sigh of pleasure."

He liked that answer. She could tell by the way he flattened his lips as if suppressing a smile, and the way his blue eyes lit briefly with humor.

"You regard this land as your property, don't you?" He shifted his grip again, so their fingers were linked. "Your brothers are almost here at your sufferance."

"They're good brothers, but no, I don't regard the place as my own, really. I wasn't raised here. None of us were. We spent our childhoods farther west in the mountains and came here from time to time to learn the English and have some schooling. The boys had to go to university. I, of course did not."

"You would have terrified the professors."

"Is that a compliment, Mr. Daniels?" *And when was he going to release her hand?*

"Yes, you may be assured it was." He reached up with his free hand and held back a drooping branch, so Mary Fran had to duck very close to him to pass. He didn't step back, and it occurred to her the man was quite possibly doing some English approximation of flirting with her.

Ah, to be flirted with. Not propositioned, not chased, not groped and pinched and leered at... A place in her heart that had been growing cold since her farce of a wedding night felt a small, curling warmth spread through it. To be flirted with...

But the rules of fair play—the English were very big on fair play—decreed she really ought to spare him the effort.

"You could have me, you know. Or I think you could."

Some subtle, smooth innuendo had been called for—an Englishwoman might have known how to dangle her interest coyly—but worse, far, far worse than Mary Fran's blunt declaration, was the awful longing she heard in her own voice.

The despair.

He did drop her hand then and turned to face her. "*Have* you?" His face betrayed nothing. Not shock, not pleasure, not judgment. But that was good, Mary Fran decided. She would have hated to see that calculating, lustful gleam in his eyes, despite her awful, bold words.

Hated to see him glancing around, choosing a tree to brace her against as he rucked up her skirts and unfastened his trousers. Hated it and longed for it. *God in heaven.*

Her chin came up, but this did little to reestablish her dignity when he was taller than she. She opted for bravado, her usual choice in difficult moments. "I'd dally with you, I think. I'm almost sure of it, in fact. I'm a widow—have been for years. I know all about being a widow."

He looked... perplexed as he peered down at her. "You know about being a widow." He regarded her searchingly then lifted his hand to trace her hairline with the side of his thumb. Mary Fran closed her eyes to absorb the unexpected pleasure of that slow, simple caress.

"You know about being lonely," he said, dropping his hand. "I know about that as well, and while I'm flattered you're *almost* sure you'd *consider* importuning from me, I am *not* sure I'm willing to settle for merely that. I hear Hester very obligingly whistling up the path so as not to surprise us. Let's join her, shall we?"

He put her hand on his arm, wrapped his fingers over hers in an odd little display of gallantry, and led her in the direction of Hester's off-key whistling.

While Mary Fran blinked back the damnable and stupid urge to cry.

When a man who'd been celibate for some time declined a beautiful woman's almost, conditional, not-quite invitation to dally, that man was entitled to consider the situation afresh, when his wits were not sent begging by the way dappled sunlight danced across auburn hair. Matthew assured himself of this as he approached his hostess.

"Lady Mary Frances, a word with you, if you don't mind a small interruption of your breakfast?"

She glanced over at him as he slid into the chair next to hers, but didn't quite hide the impatience behind her smile. "Of course, Mr. Daniels. Are we to racket about the garden while we chat, or perhaps take another turn in the woods?"

"If you'd prefer, but I was hoping you'd show me some of the property, assuming the stable can spare us a pair of mounts."

The idea had come to him in the middle of the previous night, when recollection of the feel of her waltzing in his arms, the feel of her hand clasping his, and the sound of her musical burr had necessitated two occasions of self-gratification.

"You're inviting me for a ride?" Her brows knitted, suggesting the prurient interpretation of her question had escaped her notice.

"It's a lovely day, and I've heard rumors that visitors to Balfour might chance upon Her Majesty if they spend enough time in your woods."

As if he ever again wanted to report to his Queen face-to-face.

"A short ride, then. I've—"

"Things to see to," Matthew finished for her. "Shall we meet in the stables in an hour?"

Those delicately arched brows came down. "I hardly need an hour to pop into a habit, Mr. Daniels."

Matthew leaned near to top up her teacup. "You would have made an excellent officer, my lady. You are disciplined, organized, and decisive, also indifferent to your own comfort."

She watched while Matthew added cream and sugar to her tea. "I'm not indifferent to my own—"

He lifted the cup close to her nose, so she could see the fragrant steam curling up and catch a whiff of rich black tea. "You have not yet taken a single bite of your breakfast, and I would not hurry you through your meal. Part of the challenge Her Majesty's forces face in the Balkans is the simple logistical difficulty of defending our interests so far from home. This is the same factor that eventually defeated Napoleon. Drink your tea and eat a proper breakfast."

She took a sip. "The Russian winter had a hand in things, as I recall my history."

He couldn't help but smile. "You know some military history."

She smiled back, a small but genuine smile that fortified Matthew every bit as much as a stout cup of breakfast tea might. "Four older brothers, Mr.

Daniels, and more than a passing respect for Highland winters. I'll see you in the stables in an hour."

Matthew rose, intent on changing into riding attire, but was arrested by the gaze of Ian MacGregor, Earl of Balfour. His lordship was leaning against the doorjamb to the breakfast parlor, the look in the man's eyes speculative.

"Daniels."

"My lord." Matthew hoped that would be the end of it, but the earl ambled along beside him as Matthew headed into the corridor.

"Ach, must we be milording so early in the day? If you're going to flirt with my sister, MacGregor will do, or Ian, since we've several MacGregors underfoot."

The earl wasn't just tall, he was broad, well muscled, and exuded the fitness of a man of the land. Dark hair made a handsome contrast to mossy green eyes, and his smile would have felled many a debutante in the ballrooms to the south.

"I'm going riding with the lady," Matthew said, pausing at the foot of the stairway.

The earl paused right along with him. "Riding is always a nice place to start. Can't get up to too much mischief when you're on separate horses, can you? You will be on separate horses?"

"For God's sake, Balfour, your sister is hardly going to content herself riding pillion behind an Englishman."

"Her husband was English." Balfour studied his big, blunt fingernails, while Matthew absorbed that Balfour was trying to warn him of something.

"It is not a crime to be English." *And why, come to think of it, did Lady Mary Frances eschew her married name?*

"It isn't any great advantage, either, at least not when a fellow is sniffing around Mary Fran's skirts." Balfour's face creased into a grin that wasn't exactly merry. "Enjoy your ride."

With that cryptic comment, the earl spun on his heel and disappeared in the direction of the breakfast parlor.

Matthew repaired to his room, laid out his riding clothes, and tried to determine what Balfour had been telling him. The Scots were deuced canny, of necessity. By virtue of famine, clearances, service on various fighting fronts in Highland regiments, or by operation of prejudicial law, a stupid Scot was historically a dead Scot. This reality had been impressed upon Matthew by the Scottish officers he'd shared campfires with, and by his own family's Scottish history.

But the typical Scot was also fair-minded to a fault.

Balfour really had been warning him, he decided. Warning him that only a stupid Englishman would do more than flirt with the fair Mary Frances.

"Or perhaps," Matthew told his reflection in the cheval mirror, "an Englishman who relishes a challenge and recognizes another lonely soul when he sees one."

Though maybe dallying with Mary Fran was the aspiration of an Englishman who was both lonely *and* stupid.

❦

"I haven't been up to this lookout since…" Mary Fran paused to take in a great lungful of heather-scented air and tried to think back.

"Then it has been too long. A view like this restores the soul."

Matthew Daniels sat a horse like a man born to the saddle. His horsemanship was a relaxed, natural thing, not a set of skills he'd honed just to show off, and his boots and breeches weren't in the first stare of fashion. They looked comfortable, like Mary Fran's old green velvet riding habit.

He gestured to the west, to the gleaming gray edifice under construction farther up the River Dee. "I take it that's Balmoral?"

"None other. Albert had it designed for his Queen—and their children, of course. It seems a shame to use such a lovely property only a few months of the year."

"It seems a shame that you are moldering away here in the countryside the year round, my lady. Doesn't some part of you long for the society of Edinburgh?"

If he'd been flirting with her the livelong morning, if his efforts to boost her into the saddle had been the least forward, if he'd done anything except appreciate the beauty of her home, Mary Fran might have launched a barbed retort discouraging his suggestion that her life was somehow incomplete.

But he'd been a perfect gentleman. Polite and friendly without a hint of impropriety. His demeanor reminded Mary Fran of the way all the gentlemen had treated her prior to her marriage.

"I might like to see a bit of the South, but then I'd have to leave my Fee, wouldn't I?"

"I beg your pardon?" He stood in the stirrups then settled back into the saddle, an equestrian at his leisure. "Your fee? I can't imagine your brothers would begrudge you wages should you take a short holiday."

Too late, Mary Fran realized that the barrier she vigilantly maintained between her role as hostess and her role as mother had fallen. Oh, the female guests usually got wind of Fiona at some point—the child was outright pestering the spinster cousin, Augusta Merrick—but Mary Fran kept her daughter away from the gentlemen guests.

Far, far away, particularly from the English ones.

"Not that kind of fee, but my Fiona."

Daniels's expression didn't change.

"My *daughter* Fiona." Mary Fran pretended to study Balmoral, a brand-new building intended to resemble something medieval, at least from a distance. She knew the place well—Her Majesty was a good neighbor, and His Highness an avid sportsman—but she did not know why she kept talking.

"Fiona is my heart. I love her dearly, but she's impossible sometimes. She says the most confounding things, and she has no sense except at the oddest moments. Her uncles dote on her, and I worry that isn't a good thing, then I worry that I ought to be doting on her."

She fell silent, wishing not that she'd kept her mouth shut, but that her companion would say something.

"You sound like my commanding officers, fretting over the troops. Doubting yourself for coddling them, doubting yourself for enforcing the discipline an army needs to function, despairing over the best soldiers when they do the most idiot things on leave." He offered her a smile, a slow tipping up of his lips, the same smile that crinkled the corners of his eyes. "It's the very devil when one can't help but care, isn't it?"

She realized something about him then. He was not only a former military man at loose ends in the civilian world, not only an Englishman, not only a paying guest whose sister might well be the next Countess of Balfour.

He was a man, a human being, a fellow creature. A man who had refused Mary Fran's invitation to sin simply because he was decent.

She basked in his smile, in the understanding of it, and offered him her own smile in return. "The very devil, indeed. I want to brain my brothers most days. They must wear their muddy boots in the house, swear in front of Fiona, and tell lewd jokes when they think I'm not listening."

"Sounds like life in the military—though you might also have alluded delicately to the noisome bodily functions one doesn't speak of in Polite Society."

He was pretending to study Balmoral now too, but Mary Fran couldn't help it. She laughed, a chuckle at first, then a great big belly laugh that had the horse shifting beneath her.

"Tell me more about military life, Matthew Daniels. I might have some useful suggestions for its improvement."

They let their horses amble down the hillside while Matthew told one tale after another of pranks and skirmishes, though gradually, his tone became more serious.

"You did not want to leave," Mary Fran guessed. "You hated it, and you loved it."

He stroked a gloved hand down his horse's crest. "I think most career military have mixed feelings, but no, I didn't love it. I felt useful, though, and it grates upon me daily that I must idle about, my father's much-vaunted heir, when I could be of real service in a part of the world that's quickly heading for war."

Useful. She knew what a cold comfort that was. *Useful* became an acceptable way to go on only when the alternative was to be useless.

"Could you go back?"

Mary Fran might have missed the expression on his face, but she liked watching the way emotion would flicker through his blue eyes. The happy emotions—humor, joy, pleasure in the scenery—were fleeting, while the other emotions faded more gradually.

"I cannot go back. Not ever, and I do not want to."

Despair—profound despair—but also resignation crossed his features.

"I wish we'd brought a picnic." The observation was as close as she could come to admitting she did not want to go back either—to the housework, the squabbling maids, her swearing brothers, and sometimes even to her own confounding, exhausting, endlessly dear daughter.

"A picnic sounds like a lovely idea for another day, my lady. Tell me, how do you think your brother is faring with his courting of my sister?"

The change in topic was welcome, and it was a relief to think that if Ian married Eugenia, then Matthew Daniels might become a relation of some sort to Mary Fran—and to Fiona.

"Ian must be studying the terrain before advancing his troops," Mary Fran replied. "I can't say as I'd be very impressed with his efforts thus far, though you English do delight in your mincing about. He can hardly pounce on the lady and carry her off to his castle."

"Mincing about. I take it mincing about would not meet with your approval were a man to court you?"

They were back to his version of flirting. It made the prospect of her duties at Balfour a little more bearable and suggested that Matthew had had enough of shadows and regrets for one morning. "Mincing about would not impress me one bit. Shall I race you back to the stables?"

He didn't *let* her win, but Mary Fran's mount was carrying considerably less weight, and Mary Fran knew the terrain. They called it a draw, and as Matthew escorted her up to the house, Mary Fran let herself wonder: If mincing about as a courting strategy would not impress her, then what would?

⤝⥱⤞

"Pretend you don't see me."

The Balfour estate was home to many children. Matthew had observed them weeding the vegetable plots, herding sheep, spreading chicken manure on the pastures, mucking stalls, and otherwise taking on the tasks appropriate to youth. This was the first child he'd seen in Balfour House itself, and he knew in an instant the girl dismounting nimbly from the banister was the dear and dread Fiona.

"Are you asking me to lie, child?"

She studied him with the trademark MacGregor green eyes, twirling the end of a coppery braid between her fingers. "Not lie, *pretend*. This is the ladies' wing, so I will *pretend* I didn't see you here either."

"I'm fetching my aunt, my sisters, and my cousin, to escort them to dinner. My name is Matthew Daniels."

"Fiona Ursula MacGregor Flynn." She gave a sprightly curtsy that looked more like a Highland dance maneuver. "I know who you are. You are Miss Augusta's cousin, Miss Daniels's brother, and Miss Hester's brother too. The baron is your father, and Miss Julia is your auntie by marriage, which is why she's so young."

"I'm impressed." He was also charmed by this miniature version of Mary Fran. "Lady Mary Frances is your mother, and the earl and his brothers are your uncles."

"Yes." She twirled around, smiling gleefully. "And you are our guests. I had an adventure today."

Matthew took up a seat on the bottom stair. "I expect you have adventures most days. Lots of them."

"Not like this. A gentleman should ask a lady's permission before he takes a seat, you know." In her thick, piping burr, she was reminding him of his manners as a kindness.

"A lady stays off the banisters. What was your adventure?" Because, of course, she was dying to be asked, and Matthew did not like disappointing even so young a lady.

She plopped down on the stair beside him and tucked her pinny over her knees. "Romeo came after us."

"Romeos generally do give chase where pretty ladies are concerned." And this one was going to be gorgeous, right down to the freckles she shared with her mother.

"Romeo is our bull, our *breeding* bull, though the uncles won't let him step out with Highland heifers, only with the Angus. Miss Augusta and I went for a picnic, and Romeo came calling. Uncle Ian saved us, and I was very brave."

"You've had a busy morning. How is Miss Augusta?" Visions of Augusta Merrick scrambling over a stone wall brought back childhood memories of similar escapades with her and his sisters.

"She said she'll tell Ma for me, tonight, after the ladies have had their tea. Ma won't skelp m' bum if the ladies are present. I think I should get a medal from the Queen for being so brave."

This last was bravado, the kind of bravado a child produces when she knows her opinion will not be shared by her parent.

"She won't skelp your backside. She might weep all over you, though."

Fiona grimaced and resumed twirling her braid. "That would be awful. Ma hardly ever cries. I hate it when she cries, and so do the uncs. Uncle Con makes her mad so she won't cry, and Uncle Gil makes her laugh."

"What does Uncle Ian do?"

"Uncle Ian neg-o-ti-ates. He explained it to me. It's a bit like playing pretend."

Before Matthew could fashion a reply to this revelation—Ian would be negotiating the marriage settlements before too much longer—he caught an acrid whiff of cigar smoke.

Fiona sprang to her feet. "G'day, sir. I'll just be going now." She shot off up the stairs as Altsax sauntered into the corridor.

"Taken to lurking in the ladies' wing, Matthew?"

Matthew rose and resisted the urge to dust off his backside. "I've come to fetch the women for dinner."

"You won't find that Valkyrie sister of Balfour's here in the women's wing. She bides in the family wing, where her brothers can do a better job of protecting her virtue than they did in the past. Sound strategy cozying up to the brat, though."

"Her name is Fiona." Fiona Ursula MacGregor Flynn, which did not explain why the mother was still using her maiden name.

Altsax fiddled with an ornate gold sleeve button so it winked in the evening sun slanting through the nearby window. "Getting protective already? You can take the boy out of the army, but not the army out of the boy? How very quaint, given the manner in which you and the military parted company. If you're going to bed the Valkyrie, I suggest you be about it—though that is not a woman in whose presence I'd let my guard down one bit. She'll likely steal the rings from your fingers while you lie sated and spent in her arms."

"Your opinion regarding our hostess is ill-bred in the extreme."

Matthew had managed to speak quietly—Hester or Genie could come tripping along any moment—and he had not balled up his fists or clenched his teeth. Even so, the comment was a tactical error, one that would inspire Altsax to further crudeness if nothing else.

"My, my, my!" Altsax smiled broadly, revealing tobacco-stained teeth. "Ill-bred, am I? It pains me to point out to you that I sit in the Lords and have more wealth than these kilted heathen will see in ten lifetimes. I can be ill-bred when I please, where I please, in any manner I please."

"Which freedom you feel compelled to demonstrate on far too many occasions," Matthew responded as pleasantly as he could.

The humor died from Altsax's rheumy eyes. "Mark me on this, young man: you are a good part of the reason I had to drag your sister into the wilds of Scotland in search of a title for her. Had you not left a trail of scandal clear back to the Crimea, she could have had her pick of the London bachelors. Instead, I'm put to the expense and ignominy of treating with a damned Scot for her hand, and a reluctant damned Scot at that. Cross me at your peril, *Colonel*. I can leave my wealth to your sisters and wish you the joy of a lowly barony."

A door opened a few yards down the corridor. Julia Redmond stood there, attired for dinner, a forced smile on her pretty features. "We'll be ready in just a moment, gentlemen."

"Matthew will escort you to dinner," Altsax said. "Though once the earl and I start parlaying family secrets between us, I doubt even a liberal-minded Scot would want the likes of my son at his table."

The baron stalked off as Julia slipped her fingers around Matthew's arm. "He's full of nonsense, you know. Genie has had three Seasons to pick out a swain, and she's waiting for some lightning bolt from on high to smite her and her one and only simultaneously. As an approach to matrimony, it hasn't much to recommend it."

Julia was a petite, pretty woman only two years Matthew's junior. Her marriage to Altsax's younger brother hadn't been a love match, and widowhood had left Julia comfortably well-off.

"You are kind, Julia. Altsax was speaking nothing more than truth. Association with me will not aid either of my sisters in their marital aspirations."

Julia kissed his cheek, bringing him a hint of roses and solace. "I've heard very little talk, Matthew, at least among the ladies of Polite Society. Whispers and hints at the edges of the ballrooms, but nobody seems to know exactly what went on. By this time next year, everybody will have forgotten. Let's fetch your sisters and Augusta, and go to dinner."

Amid a gaggle of pretty, merry women, Matthew traveled the earl's house to the formal parlor, where they'd enjoy whisky and conversation in anticipation of another fine meal. He'd enjoy feasting his eyes on Lady Mary Frances in her finery, too, and he'd tell himself that old army scandals would not matter here in the Highlands.

Except they likely would. Perhaps not to Balfour, or to his brothers, but if Altsax was the one relaying the tale, then at least to Lady Mary Frances, an army scandal that had Matthew Daniels compromising the honor of a young lady would matter a great deal.

❧

"I was hoping I might find you out here." Matthew Daniels sauntered up from the direction of the gardens, and the guilt roiling in Mary Fran's gut threatened to choke her.

"I'm in need of a little solitude, Mr. Daniels." She pulled her shawl more tightly around her shoulders, though it was a beautiful, soft night.

"No, you're not." He picked up her hand and tucked it over his arm. "Something has you overset. Are you feeling guilty for having spent the morning with me? All we did was talk, my lady, and admire your family's holdings."

Without her consent, he escorted her off the terrace and down into the gardens. And damn him and all his people unto the nineteenth generation, he was *right*.

"I talked. You talked, though you said precious little."

"I said enough. I don't usually burden anyone with remembrances of military life." He sounded a touch put out with himself, or maybe perplexed, but Mary Fran had been fascinated to hear his recounting of a colonel's responsibilities in the political cauldron that was the Crimea. She gathered he'd been mustered out through his father's machinations, which had left the baronial heir guilty and frustrated as war loomed ever closer.

Imagine that. An Englishman feeling guilty the same as a negligent mother might feel guilty.

"I won't be riding out with you again, Mr. Daniels."

"I was Matthew earlier today. I rather liked being Matthew to you, and I liked spending my morning with Mary Fran."

His voice held no accusation, more a sort of wistfulness she could understand all too well.

"Matthew, then." And she couldn't leave it at that. She prattled on with no more poise than Fee might show on market day, saying things a grown woman ought not to burden a guest with. "Fiona was nearly trampled by a bull today while I was out larking around with you. She might have been k-killed."

She paused in their progress to take a steadying breath. Thank God for the darkness. Thank God for the distance from the house.

He was a man blessed with fluid movement, like a big cat. He didn't spook her. He just eased around to stand directly before her, put both hands on her shoulders, and pulled her gently into his embrace. "Tell me, Mary Fran. I assume she came to no harm, or you wouldn't be out here in the darkness, flagellating yourself over a simple childhood misadventure."

She went into his arms, more grateful for the refuge he provided than she could say. Her brothers treated her to their offhand version of affection, and from time to time Mary Fran allowed herself a discreet flirtation with a passing fellow.

But to be held...

"Talk to me, Mary Fran. You don't need solitude. You have too damned much solitude even as you thunder around amid your family. Talk to me..." He went on, a low, soothing patter accompanied by equally soothing strokes of his hands over her back, her shoulders, her hair. She would not mistake him for a gentle man, not ever. His ability to *be* gentle had the tears spilling from her eyes.

"I love her," she got out. "I love her *so much*, but I'm no good at being a mother. I'm no good at it at all... I never know where she is. I never know what to say to her. I never know what she needs except that I provide it too little and too late. My brothers help, but they're only men..."

She just damn cried for long, wearying minutes. Cried until she realized Matthew had settled her on a bench and kept an arm around her shoulders. He let her wet the front of his shirt and his neckcloth, while she kept his handkerchief balled up in her hand.

When Mary Fran at last fell silent, his thumb traced her damp cheek—a small gesture, but so intimate. She turned her face into his palm, feeling foolish, helpless, and completely at sea.

"I have imposed," she said, trying to sit up.

"You have been imposed upon," he countered, keeping her against him. "You're supposed to run a very fancy guesthouse, take care of three grown men to save them the cost of a housekeeper, play lady of the manor with the Queen of half the known world for your neighbor, and raise a rambunctious child without benefit of a father's aid, guidance, or coin."

Put that way, it was hard to decide which hurt worse: the comment about saving her brothers the cost of a housekeeper or the bald fact that Gordie's family had no interest in Fiona.

"One gets weary," he said, suggesting he was capable of divining her thoughts. His hand—big, warm, and slightly rough—came to rest on the side of her neck. "Not just tired, but weary. Physically, emotionally, morally. At such times, one needs friends."

He sounded not English, but simply weary himself. A soldier who'd seen too much of war and not enough of peace. A son chafing under the demands of family. A man resigned to loneliness.

"One needs sleep too." Mary Fran made another effort to sit up, and he let her, but kept his hand on her nape. "I owe you an apology, Mr. D—Matthew."

"You owe me nothing." His thumb stroked over the pulse in her throat, which should have been relaxing but was in truth more of a distraction.

"Earlier today…" Mary Fran steeled herself for the cost of being honest. "I had plans for you. Plans that might have involved the gamekeeper's cottage, had you cast me even a single curious glance. It's our informal trysting place, because my brothers won't bring their passing fancies into the house."

His thumb paused; Mary Fran's breath stopped moving in her chest. His thumb resumed its slow progress over her skin; she resumed breathing.

"If all you'd wanted was a tumble, Mary Fran, I'd likely have obliged and acquitted myself as enthusiastically as the situation allowed. You are an exceptionally desirable woman, but I think you want something else more than you want a few minutes of oblivion and desire."

Oblivion and desire? Was that what she'd been after? He was so much more substantial than that, and the yawning need inside her wanted more too. She tried to see into his eyes in the gathering darkness, but there simply wasn't enough light.

"Let me hold you, Mary Fran. Please." A suggestion, not a command. He understood her that much, which was better than she understood herself at the moment. She leaned against him and nuzzled his shoulder until she found a comfortable place to rest.

His arms settled around her. His lips brushed against her forehead, and something eased in her aching chest. She fell asleep in his embrace, there on the hard bench under the stars.

Three

Activity was the army's typical prescription for sexual restlessness, and Matthew found it served in most cases, though after tramping through the Balfour woods for an hour, he still couldn't get the scent and feel of Mary Frances MacGregor out of his mind, or set aside the conundrum of how honest to be with her. When a man wanted something more than a flirtation but deserved less than an attachment the usual rules were no help.

"Good day. A fine morning for a ramble, is it not?"

A man sat in dappled sunshine on a rough bench a few yards up the path. He rose to a substantial height and came toward Matthew. The fowling piece over his shoulder was exquisite, the stock and handle chased with silver. The fellow's attire was as fashionable as country turnout could be.

"Good day…" Matthew's heart gave a lurch as he placed that tall figure and the slight German inflection lacing the man's greeting. "Your Highness."

Francis Albert Augustus Charles Emmanuel, Prince Consort to the Queen, father to a growing brood of princes and princesses, and devoted sportsman, stood in the Balfour woods, frowning at Matthew.

"It's Colonel Daniels, isn't it?"

"Just plain Matthew Daniels, sir."

The frown cleared. "I recall your situation now. Her Majesty has fretted over you, *Mister* Daniels. May I assure her all goes well with you?"

Matthew hesitated an instant too long, proving to himself how distracted he'd become with his hostess at Balfour. "All goes well enough. My family is visiting at Balfour in hopes of securing a match between my sister and the earl."

"A delicate business, the advantageous marriage." The prince's eyes danced while he made this observation. "Walk with me, Mr. Daniels, because my wife will want a full report on you and on the matchmaking at Balfour. I would not disappoint her for anything."

One did not refuse a royal invitation, particularly not when one had nothing better to do but brood over whether a temporary liaison with Lady Mary

Frances was worth the unpleasantness bound to ensue if she learned of the scandal hanging over Matthew's head.

"How fares Her Majesty, sir?"

"She loves it here, and the children enjoy it as well. I struggle along too, of course, between the fishing, the grouse moors, the deer-stalking. One must bear up under the press of duty." More German humor lurked in his words, both broad and subtle. His Royal Highness produced a flask and held it out to Matthew. "All is not so very well with you, though, is it? Your papa is not an easy man to spend time with."

The Queen was not the most political monarch to take the throne, but she kept her hand among the peerage socially, as Matthew well knew. "My father is a randy old jackass."

"So why not sport about at the summer house parties or among the fashionable beauties in Edinburgh? The company there is delightful for an unattached fellow."

What to say? The Prince was a devoted husband and father, a well-educated man who did much to improve the situation of the same working-class people who treated him with such disdain. He was also one of very few who knew the truth of Matthew's past.

Matthew took a nip of lovely whisky and passed the flask back. "For the present, at least, I am not suitable company for fashionable beauties, and with one possible exception, there are no beauties who interest me."

His Highness tucked the flask into an inner pocket of his shooting jacket, shouldered his piece, and sighted down the barrel as they walked along. "Do you know, Mr. Daniels, that though there is war brewing here and there about the realm, and the condition of our cities is a daily disgrace, and the nonsense that goes on at Westminster is without end, the only thing that truly can disturb me is difficulty between me and my wife? She is my exception, and I flatter myself that I am hers. One does well to pay attention to the exceptions."

"My past—" Matthew fell silent. He wasn't going to complain, for God's sake, not to the Prince Consort.

"If she's truly exceptional, that will not matter—if it even comes up. Would you like to give this gun a try? It's heavy, but flatters my vanity, and the aim is excellent. It was a gift from my wife."

Matthew accepted the fowling piece and spent another hour tramping about the woods, shooting twigs and branches of His Royal Highness's choosing, and telling himself his past really ought not to matter to Mary Frances.

Provided all she wanted from him was oblivion and desire.

❧

"The hell of it is, Gordie really had asked me to marry him." Mary Fran made this disclosure to Matthew—he was no longer Mr. Daniels, even when they were in company—while they strolled the gardens after dinner. The men had abandoned their port and cigars by mutual agreement, leaving a surprised Mary Fran to accept an invitation to enjoy the flowers.

"Were you going to take him up on his proposal?"

She peered over at her escort. The night was warm enough that he'd shed his jacket and carried it over one arm as he walked beside her. He wasn't touching her, and she... missed him. Missed the touch of him, missed the greater proximity necessitated by walking with arms entwined.

"I don't know if I was going to accept. I've puzzled over it. Gordie was the marquess's spare, and an earl's daughter would be considered acceptable in his family, even a Highland earl's daughter. I'm fairly certain I chose him because he was not acceptable to mine."

"Because he was English."

Matthew spoke the words softly, though in the dying light, Mary Fran felt the frustration in him.

"Any Englishman would have annoyed my family, but we did marry, didn't we? Gordie was as much a Lowlander by breeding as English, though English alone does not cast a man from my family's favor."

"Then what was his besetting sin?"

His curiosity seemed genuine, and she ought to tell him, but even after all she *had* told him, the words didn't come easily.

"Let's sit a bit." She glanced around for a bench, until Matthew took her arm.

"Up the hill, we can watch the stars come out."

She was a widow, they were in full view of the house, and Matthew was damnably proper with her at all times. "To the pines, then."

They walked in silence. Even when he switched his grip and held her hand—fingers laced, no gentlemanly pretense of guiding her along involved— Mary Fran didn't comment on it.

Didn't comment on the simple, profound, and rare pleasure of merely holding his hand.

"This will do." He'd chosen a spot partway up the last slope before the woods took over the park, a place where young evergreens surrounded a shallow bowl and the sod was covered with thick grass.

He spread his coat on the ground, and when Mary Fran lowered herself to it, she realized they weren't in view of the house after all, not when they were in the grass. A soldier would have known that when he'd chosen their location. Matthew came down beside her and settled back to brace himself on his hands.

"You were going to tell me the rest of it, Mary Fran. The part about why Gordie was such an ideal choice for mischief and a bad choice as a husband."

Plain speaking, indeed. She plucked a little white clover flower from the grass, then another.

"He was a tramp, you see." She spoke lightly, so the words wouldn't stick in her throat. "I knew it, knew that's how he'd come by all his flirting and flattery. He was *experienced*, and I was eighteen and so wicked smart."

"I was eighteen once too."

"But, Matthew, were you such a calculating little baggage you essentially tossed yourself under the regimental tomcat because you thought surely, a man that naughty would know how to look after you your first time?" She couldn't keep the bitterness from her voice, from rising up the back of her throat as she spoke. "I was wrong, though."

He moved closer while she systematically plucked hapless clover flowers from the grass.

"I was so bloody, blasted wrong."

The sound of ripping grass filled a small silence.

"He hurt you."

She nodded and forced her hands to stop their pillaging. "He hurt me two ways. First, he was not considerate, and then he was not discreet. The second injury was far worse than the first."

A hand landed on her shoulder, warm and solid. The night wasn't cold, but the warmth of that hand felt divine. She forced herself to continue with her confession despite the comfort Matthew was offering. "I think Gordie was trying to make me scream. Insurance, in case I wasn't going to accept his proposal. We were at the regimental ball, a throng of people right out in the corridor."

He drew in a breath, as if the words gave him pain. "You didn't scream." His hand slid across her shoulders to wrap her in an embrace. "You didn't scream, you didn't run to your brothers, you didn't ask for mercy or quarter, but you would not allow your child to be born a bastard."

"I might have." She turned to press her face against the side of his throat. "I might have cursed my child that way, except Gordie bragged to his fellows about his latest conquest. His own officers were so disgusted with him that somebody got word to my menfolk, and then six weeks later there were documents executed and the handfasting became official. Ian and Asher promised me Gordie would be sent to Canada, and I've wondered if Asher wasn't the one who made sure I was widowed. I was so stupid."

"You were so young."

His thumb traced up the tendon in her neck, a little nothing of a touch, but it eased her soul. He did it again and again, until Mary Fran began to cry.

"I didn't come out here with you to blubber and carry on like some—"

He slid his hand gently over her open mouth and left it there, giving her a place where she could finally let the screams go. As his arm closed around her more snugly, she keened into his splayed fingers, her fists clutching his shirt in a desperate grip.

"It shouldn't still hurt like this…" She shook with the remembered indignity, with the hopelessness and pain of it. She cried for a stubborn young girl with too few options, and for a sad, tired widow who had even fewer. She wept for her daughter, for all the daughters, and even for the family whose love and respect she'd betrayed.

And when the tears finally, finally subsided and Matthew's thumb was brushing gently over her damp cheeks, still she stayed wrapped up in his embrace.

"I am so ashamed. Bad enough I must comport myself like a strumpet, even worse I should seek pity for it."

Matthew snorted at that pronouncement. "If an eighteen-year-old virgin *can* behave like a strumpet—which premise I do not concede—then you should forgive her for it. Look around at your housemaids, Mary Fran. They don't know the difference between proposition and flirtation, not unless they've been in service since childhood. You were even more protected than they, more sheltered, and your grandfather very likely was overbearing and old-fashioned. Have you ever discussed this with your brothers?"

"The shame of it..." She started to pull away, needing to use her hands to better express herself, but Matthew bundled her closer.

"Spare me your Highland drama. I don't mean you need to review all the specifics. Simply ask your brothers if they ever discussed it with your grandfather. My guess is they feel even more ashamed for letting you slip the leash than you do for taking up with a man who was likely lying in wait for you, grooming you for his own ends, did you but know it."

"*Grooming* me?" She hated the term, because it brought to mind a pony standing docilely in the cross ties, preening at the attention given to mane, tail, hooves, and tack, never noticing the fellow in the corner strapping on roweled spurs and flexing a stout whip.

"Setting you up," Matthew said, "leading you on, getting his hands on the dowry your family worked so hard to save for you, beating out all the other fellows to the prettiest young lady in the shire, the most highly titled..."

She subsided against him, considering his words. He did not have the right of it, but for the first time in eight years, Mary Fran considered that perhaps *she* didn't entirely have the right of it either. Gordie could be charming and tolerant, but when he'd pressed his body to hers, the gleam in his eye had been not merely possessive, but *smug*.

Smug, like a man whose plans have played out exactly to his liking.

"I can hear the compression building in your mental engines, Mary Fran. The night's too pretty for that."

"You've given me much to think about, Matthew Daniels."

"Let me give you a little more to think about." He shifted her so she was on her back, the fine silk lining of his coat between her and the fragrant grass.

"Matthew?" *What on earth was he about?*

"You're not eighteen. You're a lovely, desirable woman with a lot to offer the right man. You have choices now, Mary Frances. Make those choices, and I'll abide by them."

He kissed her, and after no longer hesitation than it takes for a lady to smile in the darkness, she chose to kiss him back.

❦

Lady Mary Frances MacGregor had needed kissing almost as badly as Matthew had needed to kiss her. With the moon rising like a benevolent beacon and the summer air cooling around them, Matthew felt the urge to intimately cherish a woman for the first time in a long, long time.

He desired her, of course he did, but other feelings eclipsed that desire easily. Admiration for her, protectiveness—he'd felt those things for his wife, too—but also a tenderness that hadn't found a place between spouses who'd joined in an expedient union.

He and his wife had been partners, comrades in arms and convenient sources of comfort for each other, but with Mary Fran, he wanted to be a lover. Call it a dalliance, an affair, a discreet liaison—he was not worthy of her hand in marriage, but he could share pleasure with her.

"I'll stop." He made her that promise while grazing his nose along the swell of her bosom. Her scent was luscious here, flowery and sweet. His mouth was literally watering for the taste of her.

"You'd best not stop yet, laddie." She winnowed her fingers through his hair and gripped his scalp in such a fashion as to hold him still for her plundering mouth. "Not bloody... Not if you... God, yessssss."

He eased her breast above her décolletage and ran the tip of his third finger over her nipple. She went still, as if focusing on his caress. *He* certainly focused on it, on the satiny, ruched flesh beneath his fingertip, on the pale, smooth curve of her breast in the moonlight.

"Lovely. Exquisite. Gorgeous..." He closed his lips around her nipple. "Delicious." She arched up, a soft, lovely sigh escaping her as Matthew drew on her. Her fingers stroked over his hair, traced his ears, and then cupped the back of his head.

"Matthew Daniels, you are wearing entirely too many clothes."

She was smiling as she squirmed under him. He could hear her smile; he could taste it. "You're scolding me?"

"I'll be tearing your shirt off in a moment—or skelpin' yer bum."

He liked that idea, but her brother might disapprove of a shredded garment should they meet the earl upon returning to the house. Matthew rested his forehead on her collarbone. "Undress me, my lady."

"You want me to do all the work?"

"Of course not." To make his point, he straddled her and used his teeth to pull her dress off one pale, freckled shoulder. "There will be enough work to go around."

She hugged him, with her arms and legs both, to the extent her skirts and petticoats permitted it. "You make me feel foolish, Matthew Daniels."

"I make you feel pretty and desired, which you are." He sat back and started to work on the myriad buttons fastening the front of her dress. "I make you feel entitled to a little pleasure and some companionship. I make you feel, for a time, a little less lonely."

She stroked a hand over the trousers covering Matthew's burgeoning erection. "I suppose pleasure and companionship are an improvement over oblivion and desire."

Abruptly, what he'd intended as a gift to her—a gift to them both—felt inadequate. "Are you asking me to stop?"

Her brows knitted as she shaped him through the fabric and sent pleasure shuddering through him. "Matthew, I'm asking you to hurry."

He hurried. He hurried *carefully*, as though his life depended upon it, hurried through the unbuttoning and unlacing and loosening and unfastening—and without tearing a single button or seam.

When she lay beneath him, her clothing and stays pushed aside—thank God for the old-fashioned, front-lacing country variety—the moonlight turning her breasts, ribs, and belly to so much living alabaster, Matthew took her hands and settled them on his chest. "My turn."

"Close your eyes, please."

He obeyed, which meant he felt the little tugs and twists as her fingers worked at his neckcloth, then at his waistcoat, and finally, his shirt. He could not be naked with her in the sense of revealing his past, but he could share the simple pleasure of physical nudity with her.

"You are such a braw, lovely man." Her burr had thickened—a *braw, loovly mon*—while her hand skimmed down his breastbone, spreading warmth over his chest.

"I'm a man in need of kisses." He shrugged his shirt off and shifted to prop himself on an elbow beside her. "Moonlit kisses taste the best."

They felt the best too, particularly when Mary Fran's hands roamed his person as if she'd sketch his soul with her touch. She lingered in the oddest spots—his nose, the soft skin inside his elbow, her thumbs in the vulnerable hollow of his armpit—and her hands felt as though they warmed not just his body, not just his lust, but his soul.

"Ye are no' hurryin', boyo."

"I'm pleasuring." A fine idea, one his conscience took to with the dreadful enthusiasm of a martyr. Mary Fran wasn't particularly objecting either, so Matthew stroked a hand up her long, shapely leg, baring calves and knees and muscular thighs as he did. "I have the oddest urge to worship your knees."

"Ye daft Englishman." Such affection she put into her scolds. Matthew felt an abrupt pang of pity for the departed Gordie Flynn. The man had bungled badly, irrevocably, but had probably been unable to help himself.

Matthew knew exactly how that felt. "Spread your knees a bit, love. Pleasuring takes a little trust."

She spread her knees more than bit. "And far too much time."

He'd decided to keep his pants on, which meant the feel of her nails digging into his buttock was muted, a teasing hint of the intensity he craved with her—more damned martyrdom.

"Matthew Daniels, when are you going to bestir—Oh, that is..." Her hand relaxed on his bum and smoothed over him in a languorous pat. "That is lovely."

Lovely was an understatement. To his questing fingers, the folds of her sex were dewy and hot, soft and sweet to the touch. He wanted to feast on her by moonlight, visually, orally, tactilely, but did not indulge himself beyond what would pleasure her directly.

"Shall I stop?"

She shifted to flat on her back and kissed him as his fingers dallied between her legs. When he dipped shallowly into her heat, she moaned into his mouth.

"More?"

Her grip on Matthew's hair was fierce enough to distract him from the lust racketing through him.

"Aye, more. Now, if you please."

"Always in a hurry. Don't rush me, Mary Fran. I've things to see to."

She was exquisitely responsive, and Matthew had the sense she wasn't sensitive merely from long abstinence. Despite his own period of self-enforced celibacy, he found the resolve to drive her mad with arousal, then soothe her with petting and kisses, then drive her mad again.

"Matthew, I canna... I willna... Ach, damn ye..." She trailed off into muttered Gaelic, most of which Matthew understood, thanks to Scottish grandparents on his father's side. She called him daft and damned and dear, among other things. Lest she reveal unwitting confidences, Matthew increased both the pace and the pressure of his caresses.

"You can have your pleasure, and you shall, my lady. Fly free, Mary Fran."

He infused the last admonition with a touch of command, despite himself, and though he wanted to watch her face as pleasure overcame her, he instead bent and took her nipple in his mouth.

When he drew strongly on her, she started bucking against his hand in short, sharp rolls of her hips. He thrust two fingers deep into her heat and felt her body fist around him in pleasure. The sensations were in some ways more intimate than coitus, more punishing than a shared climax would have been. Inside his breeches, he was undergoing torture, but in his heart, he flirted with something approaching absolution.

"Ye wretched, pestilential mon."

"You're welcome." He pushed her over to her side and spooned himself around her. "You'll take a chill in a moment."

"Not with your great, lovely self draped around me. You make me rethink my estimation of the English."

"Don't." He tucked his arm around her, cradling a full breast in his hand.

She kissed the back of his wrist. "Are you giving me an order, sir?"

"I'm begging you not to trivialize this shared pleasure as some exercise in international diplomacy. Are you all right?"

He was not all right. He was suffering the pangs of unsatisfied lust, which he'd suffered often enough in his life, but he was also suffering more of that need to cherish a woman—this woman.

"No, I am not all right, Mr. Daniels. A relatively harmless, well-mannered if gorgeous fellow has just sashayed out under the stars with me and plucked from my grasp not only my very dignity, but also the one thing I could keep—"

Her voice caught a little. Matthew threaded an arm under her neck and gathered her closer. "The one thing you could keep?"

"Damn and blast you, Matthew." She heaved out a sigh and shifted. For a frustrating moment, he thought she was going to sit up and start dressing, but she instead shoved him to his back and straddled him. "What just happened— inside me, between us—it has happened before."

"Frequently, I hope."

She left off nuzzling his throat to frown at him in the moonlight. "Only when I'm drowsing, ye ken. More asleep than awake. It never happened with my husband. I wouldn't allow it."

"Mary Frances MacGregor, you probably drove the poor bastard right out of his mind, which is exactly what he deserved for entrapping you."

"I drove him to Canada." This was said miserably, the words muttered against Matthew's shoulder.

He recognized guilt and recognized even more when guilt had been carried too long. "Gordie had choices too, Mary Fran. A marquess's second son has a damned lot more choices than an eighteen-year-old virgin has. He could have transferred to a ceremonial regiment, could have apologized, could have wooed you properly, could have admitted he'd been desperate to secure your hand at any price because he was smitten. You would have let him serve out a reasonable penance and then taken pity on him."

She went still in his arms, her whole body in an attitude of listening. "I might have. I have a terrible temper, but I'm not unjust, usually. Fiona would say as much."

Matthew traced the bones and muscles of her back, marveling at the texture of her skin, wishing he could count the freckles on her shoulders. Her silence suggested she was still thinking, reconsidering matters she'd long ago arranged in the optimum configuration for self-torment.

He knew how that felt too.

"When he took ship, I saw him off. The night before…"

Matthew gently squeezed her nape, and she sighed. "You forgave him. It's good that you forgave him, Mary Fran. Men are much in need of forgiveness, particularly young men who've been spoiled their entire lives, and men afraid of losing their heart's desire."

When she said nothing, Matthew groped about for his shirt and waistcoat, piling them loosely over her. His next objective involved extracting his handkerchief from his trouser pocket and stuffing it into the hand she'd curled onto his chest.

While the stars winked into view and started their slow journey across the night sky, Matthew Daniels indulged—shamelessly and without limit—in the need to cherish a woman.

❧

The season was flying by, just another summer, just another stretch of long, long days between the brisk months of spring and the brisker months of autumn, and yet Mary Fran had to admit this summer was also different.

Wonderfully different. The source of the difference walked along beside her while Fiona gamboled ahead of them.

"She has your energy," Matthew observed, "your sense of things to see to."

"My sense of recklessness. I worry for her."

He patted the hand she'd curled around his arm. "You should make a list of the matters you must fret about. Write it down and haul it out at first light every day. Spend a full minute worrying about each item on the list—no skipping and no skimping—and then forbid yourself to waste any more time worrying until the next day."

"You do not have children, Mr. Daniels. See how much good lists do you when that blessing befalls you."

A shadow crossed his features, reminding Mary Fran that anything having to do with Matthew's father, even something as oblique as an allusion to the baronial succession, invited that shadow into the discussion.

"I see one!" Fiona went scampering into the stables just as a marmalade kitten disappeared down the barn aisle ahead of her.

In the next instant, Mary Fran connected a tensing of her escort's posture with the crunch of a boot on the walk behind them and a whiff of cigar smoke on the breeze. "I don't know when I've seen a child exhibit such poor decorum," the baron drawled. "Regular beatings are your only recourse at this point, Miss MacGregor."

Matthew turned but kept his hand over Mary Fran's knuckles. "Altsax, our hostess is Lady Gordon Flynn, if you're to address her properly."

"Lady Gordon Flynn? That means she's claiming to have married the late Quinworth spare, and I would have heard of such a misalliance." Altsax swung his gaze to Mary Fran, his smile diabolically ugly. "My own son is known as the corrupt colonel. You needn't put on airs to gain the notice of the likes of him."

Beside her, Mary Fran felt Matthew petrify with rage.

"Mama, come quick!" Fee's voice, redolent with wonder, came from the stables. "I've caught one, and it's *purring!*"

Altsax rolled his eyes. "No doubt my son has purred for you too, my lady. Alas for you, he's purred for many. Pity you can't ask his late wife about that, isn't it?"

"Mama!"

Altsax offered Mary Fran a jaunty bow and spun on his heel as Matthew dropped her arm. Beneath his tan, he'd gone pale, his lips ringed with white. In his eyes, there was no emotion, no warmth.

"Lady Mary Frances, if you'll excuse—"

She grabbed his hand, which he'd balled into a fist. "You'll not let that man have the last word like this, Matthew Daniels. Do you honestly think I'd believe one word of the bile he spews? Your father is unnatural. Come."

He hesitated as Altsax went whistling up the path.

"Matthew, please. You cannot help who your father is—what he is."

Fiona emerged from the stables, cradling a ball of black and white fur against her chest. "He's purring! I think he likes me—or maybe it's a she."

Mary Fran did not turn loose of Matthew's hand, but she turned an indulgent smile on her daughter. "Of course the dratted beast likes you—they all do. Take it to the dairy, and I'm sure there will be a dish of milk about for a wee new friend."

Fiona scampered off, leaving Mary Fran to half drag Matthew in the direction of the stables. "Say something, Matthew. Clootie Itnyre knows all the herbs and potions. I've half a mind to ask him what I should serve up to your father to permanently shut the baron's foul, lying, obscene—"

They'd gained the aisle running between the loose boxes when Matthew spun her up against the wall and fused his mouth to hers.

He was enraged—Mary Fran tasted that in his kiss, though the rage wasn't directed at her—and he was in some desperate, silent frenzy that was expressing itself as passion. He'd lost a wife—that explained a few things, but exactly what it explained she could not fathom, not when she had to hang on to the man kissing her simply to keep her balance.

"I could love you," Matthew whispered, his voice hoarse in her ear. "God help me, I could have loved you."

"Hush, Matthew." She lashed her arms around him, held him tightly, held him as if she could protect him from every injury. "You're grieving. When the loss rears up, there's a temptation to find comf—"

This kiss was different. His mouth moved slowly over hers, as if the tumult and desperation of the last kiss had never happened. His body no longer pressed her back against the hard boards behind her; it sheltered and warmed.

"Come." She eased sideways and took his hand, leading him down the rows of stalls to the saddle room. Wherever this was going, she wanted a locked door between her and the prying eyes of the world.

God help me, I could have loved you.

She'd no sooner thrown the bolt on the saddle room door than Matthew had her back against a sturdy wall. He rested an arm against the wall and leaned down to run his nose along her collarbone.

"You cannot defend me against my own father, Mary Fran."

The way he hung over her conveyed both passion and something else—despair, in his voice, in his posture.

"Kiss now, talk later, laddie."

Kiss, caress, tease… a little dusty sunshine came through a small window high up on the outside wall. Time slowed, and Mary Fran let the moment seep into her bones: The good smells of horse and leather, the flutter of a small bird up in the rafters, the soft wool of Matthew's jacket, and the certain knowledge that of her own volition, she was going to make love with a man worthy of the honor.

"Mary Frances?"

He was asking permission to love her, permission to make love with her. She answered him by easing back and meeting his gaze. In the gloom, his eyes were not blue; they were simply watching her, ready for her to sigh and smile, to leave him here alone with his father's accusations wreaking their vile havoc.

She shaped him through the fabric of his riding breeches. He was wonderfully hard, ready for her. When she freed him from his clothing, his head fell back, and he hissed out a slow breath. She stroked his length, reacquainting herself with the odd wonder that was the male breeding organ in anticipation of its pleasures.

As she traced her fingers over the smooth skin of his erect cock, she saw the tension in him shift from arousal to self-restraint.

"I could love you too, Matthew Daniels." In that moment, she couldn't *not* love him. Couldn't deny herself the pleasure of his body, hard, masculine, and pressed against hers in desire.

She *hated* her clothing, simple attire though it was. Drawers and stays and chemise and petticoats—the morning was cool—came between Mary Fran and the man she sought to possess. Between kisses, sighs, and a few muttered curses, she stepped out of her drawers; with some assistance from Matthew, she got dress and chemise shoved about enough and her stays loose enough to free her breasts from their confinement, but the delay, the damned, fussy delay, had her ready to scream.

"Matthew, I want…" Mary Fran lifted her forehead from his shoulder to glance around. They were in a saddle room. The plank floor was littered with dried mud and bits of hay and straw; the only solid surface was a pair of trunks along the opposite wall. The entire space was designed for hanging bridles, stowing saddles on racks, and storing brushes and riding gear.

"We can make it to the hayloft," she said, trying to find something amusing about dashing up the ladder out in the barn aisle.

"Bugger the hayloft." Matthew shifted away, his shirt and waistcoat flapping open, his neckcloth hanging loose and wrinkled. He bent, and in one

mighty heave, stacked the two trunks one atop the other. His next move was
to grab a wool cooler—a MacGregor plaid, no less—and fold it over the top
trunk. When he turned, his clothing askew, his erection straining up along his
midline, his expression was unreadable.

"Or I can come to you tonight," he said.

Mary Fran eyed the trunks. "I'm not sure exactly…"

He hauled her across the small space and hoisted her onto the trunks. "You sit."

She shifted back a bit on the trunks. The cooler was thick, folded several
times, and the seat wasn't uncomfortable. The one shaft of sunlight fell on
Matthew's red-gold hair as he stepped between her legs.

"You sit," he said again, bending his head so Mary Fran felt the words
breezing past her ear as much as she heard them. "And we love."

The arrangement was perfect. Despite the clothing, despite the surrounds,
despite the discord Altsax had tried to sow, as Mary Fran wrapped her arms
around her lover, all she felt was pleasure and the sweet, sweet privilege of
making love at long last with the right man.

Matthew's hands traveled over her slowly, touching her face and hair, trac-
ing the line of her collarbone then easing lower to cup her breast in a caress
that could only be described as cherishing. Better than that, even, was the time
he gave Mary Fran to learn him in similar fashion.

She tasted the pale scar on the side of his jaw, used her lips and tongue to
explore the contour of his small male nipples. His scent was clean all over, like
sunshine and cool forests.

And then the feel of him, ah, the hard, warm feel of him, pushing intimately
into her body. He was careful at first, a soft nudge, a sigh, another easy little
push. The sun had never coaxed a snowy little crocus to open to its warmth as
gently as Matthew Daniels joined his body to hers.

"Matthew, you're killing me. Killing—"

"Then we'll die together."

She could not rush him, could not affect his damnably tender pace one bit.
She tried, tried to recapture their previous frenzy with hot kisses, except he
somehow turned them into lazy, hot kisses.

She dragged her nails down his muscular back, urging him faster, but by
the time her hands reached his buttocks, her harrying had turned into a caress.

He was relentless in his tenderness and patience, a one-man onslaught of
caring who would neither be dictated to nor distracted from his intention to
devastate her with pleasure.

Mary Fran was practical woman, a woman who knew when she'd met her
match, so she did something she would have never have considered doing with
any other man: she surrendered and let herself be loved.

Four

MARY FRAN WAS HEAVEN, AND MATTHEW WAS A DEVIL. HE STORED UP THE sounds of her sighs and groans, saved back the memory of her heathery-flowery scent, made a miser's hoard of the pleasure of slow, deep thrusts into her heat.

He was wrong to abuse her trust like this, wrong to let her think Altsax had been spewing lies, wrong to make love to her for the first time in a damned stable—except it would be their only time, of that, Matthew was certain.

Mary Fran locked her ankles at the small of his back—her booted ankles. The clutch of her legs felt marvelous. The strength in her, the need, made a wicked, lovely contrast to the impersonal couplings he and his wife had shared.

Damn duty anyhow.

When Mary Fran started trying to scoot into Matthew's thrusts, he wrapped his arms around her and buried his face against her neck. Her fingernails dug in low on his back, a fierce, unrelenting grip. Her breath came more harshly against his skin, and the sounds she made threatened to obliterate his control.

"Matthew—"

He kissed her to stop her from begging verbally, though her body was shameless in its demands, and even more shameless in their satisfaction. As she seized around him, hard, repeatedly, her kiss became a plundering of his reason, her pleasure his complete undoing.

He tried to pull away, but her legs were scissored around his waist, and she would not allow it. He growled her name and made another attempt to withdraw, but she held him, her arms and legs a vise, and the struggle itself only heightened his arousal.

"Surrender, damn you, Matthew."

A command. Matthew understood about taking orders, and his body understood opportunity. Pleasure flooded him body and soul, a wracking release that had him pounding into his lover until his legs threatened to give out and he had to hold on to Mary Fran for both balance and sanity.

He managed to remain standing, if only to bask in the way her hand winnowed through his hair in a slow caress. She kissed his throat, nuzzled his breastbone, and still did not drop her legs from around his waist.

"We need..." His voice was hoarse, as if he'd been shouting for too long. "My handkerchief is in my left pocket."

Thank God she obliged and dug into the breeches sagging around his hips. Matthew did not want to turn her loose from his embrace, not ever.

Though he would. Altsax had seen to that handily enough.

"The next time we do this," Mary Fran said, "we're going to have a damned bed. My bum can't—"

His cock slipped from her body, slunk away in defeat more like. "There will not be a next time, Mary Fran, not unless you agree to marry me."

She stopped dabbing at him with his handkerchief. Her head came up, and the smile disappeared from her well-kissed lips. "Are you trying to trap me, Matthew Daniels?"

Just like that, she'd emotionally come about and swung her gun ports open, which was fortunate, because for the hash he'd made of things, Matthew deserved to be sunk at sea.

❧

Gordie had done the same bloody thing—started spouting off about marriage before he'd even stuffed his pizzle back in his knickers.

His relatively unimpressive pizzle, come to that.

And Matthew did not look smug or even nervous. He looked so very, very serious, even with his shirt hanging open and his breeches not properly fastened.

"I owe you an explanation, Mary Frances. I'd rather you hear it from me, because Altsax seems all too willing to give you his version of events."

"Put yourself to rights," she said, reaching under her skirts to make use of his handkerchief. She hadn't understood why he was trying to pull out until the instant he'd given up the effort. She'd come again, unbelievably hard, when he'd spent in her body.

Marriage wasn't out of the question, if the damned man but knew it.

"I can put my clothing to rights," he said, tucking himself up, "but to untangle what's between us..."

He ran a hand through hair Mary Fran herself had put in thorough disarray. She tidied herself up as best she could and scooted to one side of the trunk. "Sit with me, Matthew, and let's have none of your English dramatics."

This earned her the smallest smile, the smallest, saddest smile, but he sat beside her. He didn't take her hand, so she took his.

"I am the corrupt colonel." He recited this like a penitent's catechism.

"And I was Gordie's Highland whore. Did you lose a shipment of the cavalry's horse blankets, then? Slip them off to some orphanage?"

"I do love you, Mary Fran."

"Must you make it sound like this dooms you to misery?" Her attempt at a light moment failed utterly, and where a rosy, even optimistic glow had tried to take root in Mary Fran's heart, dread began to form.

"I love you for your fierce heart, for your courage, for your passion," he went on. "And because I love you, you must know the truth: I publicly compromised my general's daughter, and I did so while my wife of less than two years lay dying. My disgrace took place"—he kissed her fingers and then deposited her hand back in her lap—"my disgrace took place at the regimental ball."

Cold shivered over Mary Frances, a cold even worse than when, after deflowering her, Gordie had poured himself a drink and toasted their future.

"You would not do such a thing." She wanted to reach for his hand, but his posture was so calm, so self-contained, she stifled the impulse.

"I did such a thing. The girl—she was only twenty-two—went home under a cloud of scandal. I resigned my commission and put it about that my father was demanding my return. Ask anybody billeted to the Crimea, and they'll tell you all about the corrupt colonel. They have worse names for me too, of course…"

The cold became something worse, something like panic, dread, and rage, all rolled into Mary Fran's middle and jammed against her heart. "I don't believe you."

"You must believe me. It is the truth. We were found in a shocking embrace by no less than the girl's mother. Had I been single, the girl would very likely be my wife now."

"Did you make love with her?"

Why this should matter, Mary Fran did not know. For most men, particularly aroused men, the difference between kisses, caresses, and coitus was simply a few more minutes of privacy.

"I kissed her thoroughly, had my hands where a gentleman's hands do not belong, had my tongue—"

"But not your cock."

He reared back a bit, as if he'd just walked in on a scene such as the one he was describing. "Not my cock, but you have only my word for that, and the word of a cad should never be trusted."

Except he wasn't cad. Could not be.

She'd had the same argument with herself over Gordie. Told herself he would never take advantage of her curiosity, never proceed if she decided to call a halt. Gordie had made no pretense of withdrawing, and Fiona was the result. Matthew had tried to protect them from such consequences, and Mary Fran had prevented him.

"Tell me the rest of it, Matthew. If I can put this in context…"

He rose from the trunk and straightened a bridle hanging on the opposite wall. "I compromised a decent woman. What context could possibly excuse that?"

"You were grieving." Mary Fran hunched in on herself, the very idea of making excuses for him rankling—he would never make excuses for himself.

"Maybe the girl grabbed you and threatened to scream if you didn't oblige her. Maybe you were drunk—very drunk. Maybe you were trying to distract her from a fellow who would make her miserable or give her diseases."

He shook his head and tidied another bridle, but in his very silence, another idea tried to crowd into Mary Frances's misery, more a feeling than an idea.

"You aren't telling me the whole of it, Matthew Daniels." She knew this the same way she knew when Fiona was lying or her brothers had done something they were uncomfortable with. "What do you think to spare me? I've been compromised. I've been labeled a whore. I've watched my family work themselves nigh to death just to keep up appearances. I've buried a husband I had no intention of grieving, only to find myself devastated by guilt. I've put up with groping old men and sly young ones..."

He did not look at her. He faced the whips lined up from longest to shortest on the side wall, though Mary Fran doubted he saw what was before him. "I wanted to dally with you, Mary Fran. I wanted to give you some pleasure, some relief and comfort." More catechism, which only confirmed Mary Fran's suspicion he was holding back.

"Oblivion and desire, Matthew?" She wanted to slap him, to slap the sadness off his handsome profile. "We've agreed that isn't enough. When you're ready to tell me the whole of your folly, then I'll be ready to listen."

She hopped off the trunk, her limbs protesting the sudden movement, her heart breaking to leave things thus.

"Mary Frances?" He did not touch her, but his gaze pleaded with her for—what?

"Why not Lady Mary Frances, if we're to have so little trust to go along with our oblivion and desire?"

The damned wretched man smiled, a slow, gentle curving of his lips. "If I could tell you the whole of it, I would. That's as much concession as I can make."

His admission *was* a concession. She could see that in the caution lurking behind his smiling sadness. But it wasn't concession enough.

"I'd marry a cad and a bounder—I've done it before, if you'll recall—but I cannot marry a man who won't trust me."

❧

"Break my sister's heart, and I'll kill you. Connor and Gilgallon will dig your grave, and the entire Deeside branch of the clan will dance at your funeral." Balfour offered his promise cheerfully, sporting a grin that revealed even white teeth in abundant number. "A wee dram to ward off the chill, Mr. Daniels?"

Matthew nodded. They were alone in the library, and the earl's warning was probably the Scottish equivalent of permission to court, which was ironic.

"And what if you break *my* sister's heart, Balfour? I suppose I'll have to see to both your execution and your burial myself? Dance you into the grave when I haven't even a proper kilt to my name?"

Balfour's dark brows rose, and then his expression became thoughtful. "Wearing a kilt takes a certain confidence. Try it before you mock us for it."

"I have a kilt, not the full-dress business, but a McDaniel plaid."

That had been a perfectly unnecessary admission, and it didn't seem to make any impression on the earl.

Balfour poured out two stout servings of whisky. "The McDaniel dress plaid is a pretty pattern. You could wear it to the ball next week, and we'd kit you out in company style. I was serious about you breaking Mary Fran's heart."

Ian MacGregor held forth like a general, his speech—it wasn't exactly conversation—leaping from one topic to the next without any pretension of manners. Matthew followed him easily.

"And I was serious about you breaking Genie's heart." Matthew lifted his glass slightly. "To the ladies."

Balfour saluted with his whisky and took a sip. He served it neat, the way it deserved to be consumed. "Your sister Genie wants nothing to do with me. I can't see how I'd break her heart, unless it's by marrying her. I've reason to wonder why your dear papa has his heart so set on this match when the lady isn't exactly willing."

"Are you insulting my sister, Balfour? Implying she's in some way tarnished goods?"

Balfour scrubbed a hand over his face. "And people claim the Scots have bad tempers. I would not insult your sister, Daniels. She's sweet, pretty, endearingly stubborn, and scared to death of your father. That is not a sound basis for a marriage."

Endearingly stubborn. Matthew filed that description away to apply to Mary Fran at some opportune moment. "Are you declining to court Genie because you're concerned for her happiness?"

"I *am* concerned for her happiness—also for my own. My family needs coin desperately, though we need our honor more."

Made with such casual, weary assurance, the observation stung. "Genie has a notion she'll marry only for love, Balfour. I don't know where she came by it. Altsax thinks marrying for love is vulgar, stupid, and common."

"Not common enough," Balfour muttered. "I had some questions to put to you on another matter, if you've a moment."

And now the man with the piercing green eyes who made casual death threats and summarized Matthew's sister accurately in a few words took to studying a portrait of some crusty old Highlander over the fireplace.

"Balfour, I do not share my father's opinion on the matter of marriage. I married once for duty, for Queen and Country, and while it was not a horror, it was not what either I or my wife deserved. Ask me your questions. If I know the answers, I'll gladly share them, though I have to warn you—the press of business means I must travel south in the morning." The press of business and the dictates of sanity.

The emotions flitting through the earl's gaze weren't hard to name: relief, wariness, and bewilderment. "Travel on if you must, but my questions are about your cousin."

The words were parted with carefully, with a studied neutrality that fooled Matthew not one whit. "Break Augusta's heart, and the same promise applies, Balfour. She's been through enough. Too much, in fact, and all she wants is to be left in peace."

"No, that is not all she wants." Balfour spoke softly, humor and sadness both in his tone. "Neither is it what she deserves, but that's a discussion for another time. I was wondering if you could tell me the other things." He ran a hand through thick dark hair, took another sip of his drink, and commenced staring out the mullioned window at gardens he'd had years to study.

"What other things?"

"The small things… What is Augusta's favorite flower? How did she come by her love of drawing? Is she partial to sweets? Does she prefer chess or cribbage or backgammon?"

The personal things. Abruptly, Matthew recognized a fellow suffering swain, particularly in the earl's mention of the difference between what a lady wants and what she deserves.

"I could use a game of cribbage myself, my lord, and perhaps we'd best keep that decanter handy."

"Never a bad idea." Balfour crossed the room to rummage in a desk drawer. "Turnabout is fair play, too, you know." He slapped a deck of cards on the desk, then a carved cribbage board.

"Turnabout?"

"You have questions, Daniels. About Mary Fran. As long as you don't ask me to violate a confidence—the woman has a wicked temper and very accurate aim with a riding crop—I'll answer them."

Matthew fetched the decanter and prepared to lose at least one game of cribbage. He'd lost two—only one intentionally—before Balfour asked Matthew to fetch some sensitive documents back to him here in the Highlands posthaste.

Perhaps that was fitting, that Matthew be given a chance to torment himself with another glimpse of Mary Frances, and to contribute to the happiness of others—his own being a lost cause.

❦

"Where are you going?" Fiona asked the question as she tried to descend from the hayloft while holding her kitten, Spats. Mr. Daniels's horse didn't take exception to the company, but then, the horse had likely known Fee was above.

"Have you started sleeping in haylofts, Fee?"

"The sun comes up early, and I wanted to play with my kitten. Are you out for a ride?"

He smiled at her. Mr. Daniels had nice eyes—he smiled with his eyes more than he smiled with his mouth. "I'm leaving for the South, Fee. Business, you know."

This was not good. Mama had disappeared into the saddle room the other day with Mr. Daniels, and she'd been smiling radiantly at the time—also holding Mr. Daniels's hand. "Send a wire for your business. That's what Her Majesty does."

Mr. Daniels slipped off the horse's headstall and looped the reins of a bridle over the gelding's neck. "Her Majesty explains her business practices to you, does she?"

"She comes to our tea parties in the nursery at Balmoral sometimes, and so does His Royal Highness. They speak German to help us learn. If you're leaving, you ought to pay a call on her."

And he ought *not* to leave. Fiona would bet her favorite doll on that—if she could find it.

"Her Majesty is the last person I want to spend time with, Fiona."

Mr. Daniels had been in the cavalry. He put a bridle on his horse in a precise order, and he checked each strap and buckle in order too.

"I like the Queen. Why are you leaving?"

"I told you." He blew out a breath and stared over the horse's neck. "The press of business calls me away, and even if I were having second thoughts, and leaving was the *last* thing I wanted to do, your uncles need me to see to some things for them rather urgently. It's best if I go."

Things to see to must be half of what adulthood was about. Fiona didn't think such a life was going to be much fun. Uncle Ian's face wore the same expression when he talked about Marrying Won't Be So Bad. "You should not lie. Ma will skelp your bum."

"Would that it were so simple." He stared at his empty saddle, his eyes bleak. Uncle Gil looked like that when he stared at Miss Genie.

"I am forbidden to tell the truth by my own honor and by vows explicitly made to one whose requests I could not refuse." He muttered the last as he checked the horse's girth, which meant soon he'd lead the horse out to the mounting block.

"That is silly. Nobody is forbidden to tell the truth. It says to tell the truth in the Bible."

"It also says 'let the women keep silent in the church,' but I doubt you do. Put my stirrup down on that side, if you please."

Fiona put Spats on her shoulder and pulled the stirrup down, then ran the buckle up under the saddle flap. "If you are forbidden to tell the truth, and you *want* to tell the truth, then you must simply get permission first. Uncle Ian says you have to neg-o-ti-ate."

On the other side of the horse, Mr. Daniels peered over at her. "Get permission?"

"To tell the truth. You ask nicely, and give at least three reasons, and it doesn't hurt if everybody's in a good mood when you ask."

"I should get permission…" He came around the horse and scooped Fiona up against his hip, like Uncle Ian used to before she got so big. Spats hopped down, and the horse twitched an ear.

"You are a brilliant child. You're going to grow up to be as lovely as your mother, and I'm going to be there to see it—I hope." He didn't look nearly so bleak now. He looked fierce.

"I hope so too. May I have a pony if you are?"

"Not unless your mother says it's acceptable to her. I have to leave now, Fiona, but I will be back in time for the ball."

He hugged her, good and tight, and while he led his horse out to the mounting block, Fiona ensconced Spats on her shoulder again. She waved Mr. Daniels on his way in the predawn light, and watched as he cantered off. At the bottom of the drive, he turned the horse not toward the train station in Ballater, but to the west, toward Balmoral.

Which was odd.

⤝⤞

Mary Fran hated the summer ball. Not the planning and organizing of it, not seeing her brothers in all their Highland finery, not seeing how excited Fee got as the day drew closer.

She hated the ball itself—had taken all balls, dances, and assemblies into dislike the night Fee was conceived, and saw no reason to change her opinion at this late date.

"You are glowering, my lady. Have I done something to offend?" Augusta Merrick posed the question in the soft, polite voice Mary Fran would never be able to imitate.

"All this nonsense offends," Mary Fran said, glancing around the ballroom. "We won't have a flower left in the garden, and the ice alone will beggar us."

"He'll come back, Mary Fran." The same soft voice, but with a hint of something under it. "Matthew is honorable. If he told Ian and Fee he'd be back, he will be."

"I'm that obvious?"

"You're that in love."

Mary Fran peered over at the Englishwoman who was arranging flowers for a small centerpiece. Augusta had suggested keeping most of the centerpieces low, and therefore simple and inexpensive. She'd also suggested including heather here and there to keep the air fresh and the tenor of the gathering Scottish.

"You wouldn't begrudge me your cousin's affections?" Mary Fran could not have asked that question of Matthew's sisters. For some reason, they took less notice of him than Miss Augusta did.

"Let's take a break," Augusta said. "And no, we will not ring for tea."

She linked her arm through Mary Fran's and led the way out to the terraces, where footmen were setting up torches and tables while maids scurried in all directions. Mary Fran drew out her pocket flask when she and Augusta got to the first bench behind the privet hedge.

"A medicinal nip is in order." Mary Fran passed the little leather-covered flask to her guest, who did not even pause to wipe the lip before taking a sip.

"Powerful medicine."

"Each time we put on one of these fancy-dress affairs, I hate it a little more."

"Matthew will lead you out, and then you won't hate it so much ever again."

"You don't mind that we've become... involved? Nobody else seems to have noticed, not even your aunt Julia, whom I would think had some things in common with Matthew."

"Grief?" Augusta passed the flask back, but Mary Fran studied it rather than take a drink.

"He loved that wife of his. He simply didn't realize it until it was too late." Mary Fran deduced that some of what afflicted Matthew was guilt, and one had to feel some love if guilt found a way to take root.

August Merrick didn't seem at all discomfited by the topic. "I met Lydia only at the wedding. She was a plain little sparrow trying to make us think she was besotted with her dashing husband. The Queen had a hand in the matchmaking, from what Genie said, but I worried for the couple."

"He said..." Was it violating confidences to repeat words spoken in private? "He said she saved his life, ordering him moved from the hospital, fetching an Arab doctor to tend him, selling her jewelry to see him properly fed and cared for."

"And then she fell ill, and there was nothing Matthew could do. Hester has told me a little of it, but Matthew doesn't speak of the past."

He does too. To me he speaks of it, though not honestly enough.

"What gave us away?" Mary Fran took a sip, but a small one.

Augusta's smile was a little smug and a little sad. "You look at Matthew the way I look at Ian."

Mary Fran absorbed that truth, nodded, and passed her the flask. "Will you come with me to Balmoral after the shoot? Her Majesty won't be joining us for the dress ball, but she's summoned me to relay all the details afterward. His Highness might pop over for the shoot on Saturday."

"You visit back and forth as if they were any other neighbors?"

Mary Fran accepted the flask back. "We do. Fee visits the princesses often, and Ian and the Prince Consort are quite friendly. This time, though, Her Majesty has sent a formal summons."

"I suppose you'd best heed it, then."

❧

The bloody damned trains and the bloody damned coaches and the bloody damned lame livery horses conspired to make Matthew bloody damned late to the ball. The idea that he might disappoint Mary Fran made him positively frantic, so frantic he barged in on the dinner gathering in all his riding attire and dirt.

And not a moment too soon. Balfour announced Genie's engagement, and good wishes were offered all around. By virtue of careful orchestration on the earl's part, Altsax was hustled off to the library with the MacGregor family surrounding him, while the guests called toasts from all sides to the prospective bride and groom.

Amid all the toasting and familial machinations following Balfour's announcement, Matthew had not one moment with Mary Fran, not even as they joined the family for the celebratory dram in the library.

"We'll return to the ballroom," Matthew said, taking Mary Fran's hand at an opportune moment. "Somebody needs to get the dancing started, and Mary Fran is the hostess."

Balfour sent them on their way with a grateful smile, while Mary Fran remained ominously silent.

"You got word from Her Majesty?" Matthew asked.

Mary Fran, elegantly turned out in MacGregor plaid with all the Highland trimmings, looked bemused and not... not unfriendly.

Also not quite kissable. "I cannot refuse an official summons, Matthew, and you cannot go back to the ballroom dressed like that and reeking of horse."

He stopped dead in the corridor. "I stink." Which likely explained why an audience with the Queen hadn't resulted in Mary Fran plastering herself to him in welcome.

Her lips quirked. "The smell of horse has never offended me, but Ian said he'd seen to your fancy kit."

The earl was not a man to be underestimated. "I'll change then." But damn and blast, he'd wanted to waltz with her. Now he'd have to wait until the good-night waltz, but at least that was typically a slower tune.

A more romantic dance. And some romance was apparently in order. Her Majesty had looked with favor on Matthew's plight, and had apparently seen matters set to rights, but Mary Fran was still regarding him with some... speculation.

"Come with me," Matthew said, tugging her down the corridor. "A man needs an extra hand if he's to get into his evening finery posthaste."

She came along, not reluctantly, but not enthusiastically either. As it turned out, Matthew did need her assistance, because Balfour's idea of evening finery was a McDaniel dress plaid and all the trimmings, save a bonnet. Mary Fran's assistance was more than appreciated; it was necessary if Matthew was to don his clothing properly.

"Some fellows will wear their underlinen if they're in mixed company, but my brothers do not." Mary Fran stepped back and surveyed him in the confines of his bedroom. "The sporran helps protect your modesty, if that's a concern."

"Stop fussing over the clothing, Mary Fran, and tell me if you'll marry me."

Graceless, tactless, and the only question that mattered to him. She'd spoken with the Queen, gotten as much explanation as anybody could give her, and all that remained was to break Matthew's heart or crown his future with resplendent happiness.

"I wasn't sure you'd ask again, Matthew." She regarded his riding attire, heaped on a plaid-upholstered chair. "My past is no better than yours, in theory. I'm glad you told me of the scandal, but when I had time to think, to consider if something long ago and far away should control both our futures, I decided it should not."

She wasn't making sense, entirely, but her day had no doubt been long, and scandal, even scandal with a royal explanation, was a difficult topic.

He took her hand in his, relief and joy soaring around in his chest like so many shooting stars. "You'll marry me. That's all that matters. I'm sorry I could not be more forthcoming, but promises made to protect a lady's honor are not easily broken."

She gave him a puzzled look as he stepped closer. "We'll need to say something to Fiona."

"I think we have her permission." He took the lady of his heart into his arms. "Your brother approves too, of that I'm certain. Now, will you get me pinned into my sash, or will we be late to the dance, Mary Frances?"

She did get him into the sash, eventually, and they were late to the dance, too.

※

"I will bloody damned kill you, Matthew Daniels." Mary Fran did not shout, but she spoke the utter, sincere truth as she stalked along the barn aisle.

Matthew looked up from petting Fiona's kitten outside Hannibal's stall, the wee beast's purr audible at several paces. "You go calling on the neighbors with my cousin and come back in a tear?"

His expression was the cautious, teasing countenance of a man who wasn't certain what he'd done wrong.

"Don't you *cajole* me, you wretched mon." She scooped the kitten from his grasp and set the thing on the ground. "You and that scheming woman, you led me such a dance, and all along, you were a *spy*."

His expression shuttered, and he glanced around, tugging Mary Frances into the saddle room. "I thought you knew. You said you'd had your tête-à-tête with Her Majesty when we spoke of it the night of the ball."

"She'd simply sent me a note. We didn't speak of anything, not until today." Mary Fran wrenched from his grasp, ready to howl, to shout, to do murder at what her neighbor had so genteelly explained. "I was so damned glad to see you, so glad you hadn't turned your back on me over some silly scandal, except *you could have been killed*."

Her brothers might have told her to calm down; Matthew was smarter than that.

"I was an officer, Mary Fran. Of course I could have been killed. I take it Victoria only now apprised you of the details."

"I'm marrying a very quick study. She said—" Mary Fran stopped her pacing long enough to draw in a steady breath. "Her Majesty said you were charged with handling delicate matters, you and your wife, and that the two of you agreed to marry so you might be better situated to handle those matters."

That had been the Queen's term: delicate matters. Matthew, the most honest and forthright man Mary Fran knew, and the Crown had set him to sneaking and skulking.

He crossed his arms and widened his stance, a warning that he was about to be forthright again. "We were spies, Mary Frances. I was a spy, and so was my wife. She was much better at it than I was, but I'd learned Russian from some school chums as a boy and studied it further at university. There was much to be gleaned in diplomatic circles, and we were useful, even if many would not consider our activities honorable."

"Useful." She spat the word. "Honorable. Victoria said your wife came up with the notion you should compromise the general's daughter, made it a dying request to you. I hate this wife of yours, Matthew. I always will."

His expression was bleak, but again, he did not argue. "She was better at the game than I was. Her plan was brilliant."

Mary Fran marched up to him, so angry she could have shouted. "What was brilliant about a plan that compromised your honor and left your future a bloody shambles? When Victoria told me of this, I could barely keep my temper, Matthew."

He uncrossed his arms. "The general's daughter was passing secrets—perhaps unwittingly—to the Russian pretending to court her, and compromising her was a way to get her back to England without letting anybody know she'd been caught. This scheme also kept the girl safe, in that the other side would not have spared her once they realized we'd used her to pass false information."

"*What in the bloody hell does that matter?!* You spared your Queen embarrassment, kept a dying promise to your wife, saw a foolish young woman safely home to England, but *I could have lost you.*"

She turned her back on him, because the upset of it was still too raw. "I could have lost you over a stinking little military scandal, except you were clever enough to get around your vows and promises and see the truth laid at my feet. I love you, you dratted man, but I hate the truth."

A white handkerchief scented with cedar dangled over her shoulder.

"When you thought it a stinking little military scandal—just another randy officer misbehaving with a foolish young lady—you were willing to marry me, Mary Fran. If I didn't love you before, I will always love you for that."

She snatched the handkerchief from him and blotted her eyes. "I want to wallop you, and you talk of love. What if Her Majesty hadn't been willing to trust me with the truth?"

A hand slipped around her waist, and a muscular male chest warmed Mary Fran's back. "Then I would have told you, somehow, in some version that skirted all those vows and all that honor. I'd made that decision while I was traveling from here to London and back in less than a week. I could not let you go on thinking I'd play false with a woman's honor out of something as cavalier as drunkenness or carelessness. Doubt me all you like, Mary Fran, but never again doubt your own judgment. The rest of the world, even my own father, can think what they please, but you deserved the truth."

A second hand slid around Mary Fran's waist and tugged her gently back against Matthew's taller frame. "What am I to do with you, Matthew? The thought of your sacrificing your good name when I know how much it means to you... I'd like to skelp your bum but good, but I love you—heaven help me."

"You can do both, you know. Love me and skelp my bum."

His chin came to rest on her temple, and Mary Fran stood in his embrace for long moments, absorbing the calm of him. She turned and wrapped her arms around him when it became apparent he'd said all he felt needed to be said.

"Is there more, Matthew?"

"More I cannot tell you?"

She nodded against his chest, dreading his answer.

"There's more I have to say to you, but nothing more about my time in the Crimea. I did a lot of translating, a lot of lurking and overhearing, and not much flirting. Russians are a jealous lot, with good aim and loads of determination. War with them will be a difficult undertaking."

"Marriage with me will be a difficult undertaking."

"Life without you would be impossible. Then, too, I'm sure as a husband, I will be far from perfect—you might have to skelp my bum regularly." He sounded so certain, no shadows, no doubts. "I want a family, Mary Fran. Not for the succession—we don't have to use the title if you don't care to—but for us, and for Fiona. Your brothers will make sure she has cousins, but she'll be a marvelous big sister."

Still Mary Fran remained in his embrace. "Leaving my brothers will be difficult, Matthew. Difficult for me and for Fiona."

"We won't go far. His Royal Highness said there's a fine property a little farther along the river, which has just come up for sale. I've plenty of investments and rental properties, so we can bring up the children right here in Aberdeenshire."

He kissed her cheek, and Mary Fran felt her heart melt. "We need a bed, Matthew. Right now, we need a bed and a door with a stout lock on it."

"I have something better, Mary Frances."

He kissed her other cheek, and she rocked into him more tightly. "What could be better than a bedroom with a locked door and you and me on the mischief side of it?"

"Not much, almost nothing, in fact."

This time he kissed her mouth, a luscious, lingering kiss that had Mary Fran wondering if the two trunks were still stacked along the wall. She eased back, prepared to drag him bodily to her bedchamber.

He resisted long enough to reach into his vest pocket and withdraw a piece of paper.

"What's that?"

"The only thing better than that locked bedroom, my love. This is a special license, and it has our names on it."

As it turned out, they made use of the special license fairly quickly, with all of Mary Fran's family in attendance, including Fiona and one black-and-white cat. Thereafter, they made use of the bedroom with the locked door with great frequency, until Fiona was a big sister many times over, and the MacGregor brothers uncles many times over as well.

About the Author

New York Times and USA Today bestselling author Grace Burrowes's bestsellers include *The Heir*, *The Soldier*, *Lady Maggie's Secret Scandal*, *Lady Sophie's Christmas Wish*, and *Lady Eve's Indiscretion*. Her Regency romances and Scotland-set Victorian romances have received extensive praise, including starred reviews from *Publishers Weekly* and *Booklist*. *The Heir* was a *Publishers Weekly* Best Book of 2010, *The Soldier* was a *Publishers Weekly* Best Spring Romance of 2011, *Lady Sophie's Christmas Wish* and *Once Upon a Tartan* have both won *RT* Reviewers' Choice Awards, *Lady Louisa's Christmas Knight* was a *Library Journal* Best Book of 2012, *The Bridegroom Wore Plaid* was a *Publishers Weekly* Best Book of 2012. Two of her MacGregor heroes have won KISS awards. Grace is a practicing family law attorney and lives in rural Maryland.